Saddam's Spies

Saddam's Spies

By DALIYAH HANIN

Southern Hills Press

Published by Southern Hills Press, Pittsburgh, PA, USA.

Printed in the United States of America.

Hanin, Daliyah
Saddam's Spies / Daliyah Hanin. – 1st ed.

Summary: Having grown up in a protected home under the watchful eye of the Iraqi dictator, Fatima Atik is taken away from her family to become a spy for her country. After learning the dreadful ways of the Iraqi empire, she is drawn in many directions, and must make difficult and quick decisions that will determine her fate and the future of her country.

[1. Fiction/Mystery   2. Suspense   3. Iraq]

ISBN 1-933882-04-2

*In memory of all those who died at the hand of
the dictators of oppressive regimes worldwide*

*In honor of the men and women who try to
save them*

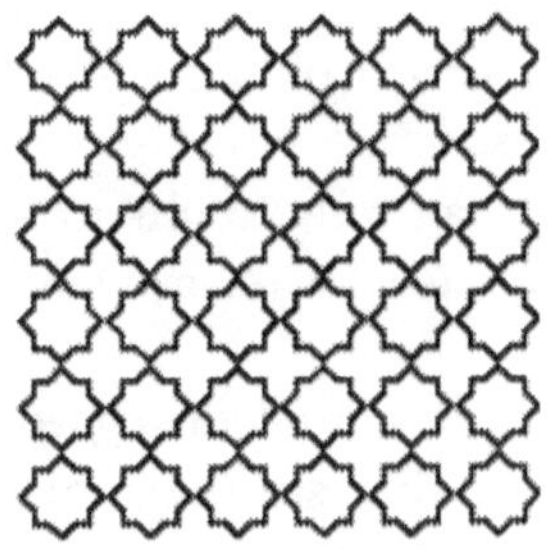

Chapter 1

When the lights blinked for a fraction of a second longer than usual, General Ayad Atik sensed a problem. In an effort to focus more clearly on his suspicions, he purposely ignored the words of Lieutenant General Ali Hassan al-Majid, who was busy glorifying himself as the leader of the Anfal Operation. As Ali droned on about how he poisoned the traitorous Kurds who supported Iran during the eight years of the war against Iraq, Atik stood up and circled the room. He heard a slight scratching noise behind the wall, but he couldn't identify where it was coming from. He scanned the ceiling for movements or flaws, but the stonework appeared intact. Gently rubbing his fingertips along the wall as he strolled around the perimeter, he realized he had caught the ire of Ali.

Ali, the President's cousin, was almost as egotistical as the President himself and he despised anyone who insulted his honor. Ali's pulse quickened and his face sweated more than usual as Atik, also a relative of the Iraqi leader, snubbed his presentation. Raising his voice slightly, Ali explained how his low-flying helicopters successfully obliterated whole towns in a matter of minutes.

Atik's fingernail got caught in a small crack in the wall, but he casually released it and moved on slowly.

Furious at Atik's total disregard for his words, Ali banged on the table, stood up, and shouted at the general, "Not even a single plant survived our magnificent attack on Halabja! And what have *you* done to defend the honor of our country, Ayad?"

The general turned to Ali, raised one eyebrow, lifted his rock-hard fist, and then, swinging viciously around, punched a hole in the wall where he had spotted a gap moments earlier. Everyone in the room, except the President, shuddered at the loud sound of the bang. Rather than remove his hand, though, the general struggled inside the broken wall. Someone was on the other side, and Atik's powerful grip held him tightly.

"Guards," he called to the two sentries by the door. "This spy must have come in through the electric closet in the hallway. Go get him." He clutched his prisoner's arm and then answered Ali's question by mocking him with an Arabic proverb, "*Example is better than precept.*"

When the guards ordered their prey to raise his hands slowly, Atik extracted his arm from the fissure. "Please go on with your report, Lieutenant General," Atik said, returning to his seat.

The muffled conversation in the hallway delayed the meeting. "Turn around slowly," one guard ordered. "Now!" he shouted. An instant after the last word, the guards heard a clink on the ground, a popping sound, and then silence. "Where is he?"

The spy had released a small smoke bomb, briefly clouding the area. He darted away, chased by his captors. Following the sounds of the guards' footsteps, the military men from the meeting joined the pursuit. Ali made sure his cousin saw him race out in front of everyone to show his brave dedication, and to save face for his rash display earlier. In a gentlemanly fashion, Atik said, "Excuse me, your Excellency," and exited the room after receiving the President's nod of approval.

Atik presumed the guards would radio ahead to the watchman by the main doors, and they would set up a blockade. Moreover, a spy that could have infiltrated so far into the building would know that as well. He therefore calculated that even though the man had gone in that direction, he would probably run up the fire escape to the second floor and head back the opposite way.

Atik rushed down the hall, knocked open the door to the gym, spotted his protégé, and summoned him. "Gamal, I need you for a few minutes." The well-built man, drenched from a long workout, ran quickly, and the two hurried upstairs. Ostentatious paintings of Arab war successes adorned each side of the broad hallway. Though golden chandeliers swayed slowly from the high, arched ceilings, no structures on the ground lent themselves to Atik's ambush. "Turn this way," Atik said to his partner, as they stood near one wall facing away from the direction from which they expected the spy, "so he won't know we're waiting for him."

Atik closed his left eye and pretended to scratch his forehead above his right. Placing his palm on the lens of his glasses, he converted them into a mirror. He watched behind him as a lone man approached cautiously. Walking normally to avoid attracting any unwelcome attention, the spy stepped right by his opponents, thinking his escape was only moments away.

When Atik whispered to Gamal, "Take him down," the intruder never had a chance. Like an Olympic gymnast, Gamal dropped both of his hands to the ground, flipped over them and wrapped his legs around his opponent's neck. He pulled back, yanking the man down backwards to the floor. The spy shot his hands out a moment before his head smashed into the ground and tried to struggle, but Gamal tightened his legs around the man's neck and grabbed hold of his calves. Even though Gamal was below his adversary, he controlled him.

"I'm surprised at you, Faraydoun. You would never have tried this on your own. Whom do you work for?" Atik questioned the man whom he finally recognized.

Faraydoun Assi Mustafa's head felt very warm as he lost the oxygen supply to his brain. He closed his mouth tightly to show he could not be intimidated.

"My dear boy, you should tell me now. Otherwise *they* will ask you the same question, and I suspect it will be a rather unpleasant conversation," Atik threatened gently, motioning towards the mob of security men racing in their direction.

The lights began to spin, and Faraydoun's world went black. Gamal held on for another moment, and then dropped the spy's head from the choking hold.

"Did he tell you anything?" Ali demanded of Atik as he arrived on the scene.

Atik shook his head.

"We will get the information from him," Ali asserted.

"I'm sure you will," Atik responded.

★ الاكبر ★ الله ★

One week later, around my sixteenth birthday, as my father finished telling me the spy-capture story yet again, the doorbell rang. I raced to open it. Two of the President's guards appeared, already sweaty from the early morning sun. "Is General Atik in?" they asked.

"One moment. I will fetch my father."

Dressed in his pressed uniform, my father appeared. I stood far behind him to watch. They handed him an envelope and shook his hand. "The President would like to thank you for your excellent work."

When they left, my father peeked inside the envelope, and then looked outside as the sound of the guards' car hummed away. He smiled at me and said he'd drive me to school.

"Thank you, father," I said, surprised at his unusual offer. I raced outside to his car, but found it missing. Instead, there was a brand-new black Mercedes in the driveway. He walked outside after me, opened the envelope, and pulled out a set of keys. He winked at me, waved the keys, and said, "Your uncle is quite generous ... sometimes."

That afternoon, I was met by one of my uncle's limousines on a quiet street as I came home from school. I was told that I had been summoned to the palace. Though I was surprised, I assumed that my father was receiving some special honor for his bravery. I had visited the presidential palace before, but had only seen the foyer and dining rooms. This time, however, I was brought into a private lounge. In regal style, the colors in the room coordinated handsomely, with cranberry fabric on all the chairs sitting atop the royal blue rugs. The seams of all the upholstery, embroidered with golden thread, reminded me of the intricately designed covers of my grandfather's holy books.

Two polished silver swords hung crossed on the wall above a firmly cushioned seat. Alone in the room, I wandered closer to see them. I looked at my reflection. When I blinked quickly, a game I used to play as a child, there was a strobe-like effect that made the moment move in slow motion. Stupidly, I stroked one of the blades just as my uncle's secretary walked in. Although I dropped my hand quickly to hide my action, he had already noticed. "You insult your uncle's honor with your weak hands? Those blades have cut the throats of over 400 of the President's enemies and you reach out to touch them! Your hands should be cut off, child!"

"Yes, your Excellency. Pardon my stupidity. I am just a girl and have much to learn from you," I bowed as I recited the formula that I knew would save me. After many beatings in my childhood, I had learned the words to quell the anger of Iraqi men. *Who uses swords anyway?* I thought. *These days, there's no shortage of bullets.*

"Next time, child, you will not earn forgiveness so quickly. Allah is helping you now." He paused, and then began to explain. "You have been chosen for a different path from that which your classmates will follow. You will be educated in the palace from now on."

I had been attending a diplomatic school in Baghdad, and was being groomed to marry a member of the presidential family. Eventually I would have the honor of bearing him sons. Few girls were ever chosen to be a primary wife to one of these cousins, but the ones who attended the diplomatic schools usually had a better chance of attaining a higher connubial rank. I never thought much about whether it would be a good life, since it seemed the only choice I had.

"Stand tall, child," he commanded. I was embarrassed because I was more physically mature than most of my friends, and I tried to maintain my modesty by slouching. He pushed my lower back forward and angled me towards the door. I followed his lead and planted myself firmly on my feet. A bodyguard walked quickly into the room, looked around, and then held open the door for my uncle, the President. The secretary saluted elegantly, and I bowed.

Unfairly criticized for his harshness, my uncle spoke kindly and briefly. "I am pleased you will be joining us in the palace, Fatima. Your father has served the kingdom well, and I believe you will follow in his footsteps." He focused his dark eyes directly towards my face, looked up and down my whole body, and then smiled slightly under his coalblack mustache. I nodded my head slightly, unsure of what to say, and he left. For the next two years,

President Saddam Hussein never said a word to me, nor saw me for that matter.

I was pleased that he compared me to my father, since he was both a hero to me and to many in Iraq. If I could live the same exciting life that he led, always traveling, meeting high-ranking people, and catching spies, I would have a chance to escape my virtually predestined motherhood/wife/servant future.

It did not take long before all my dreams of life in the palace were rudely shattered. I was introduced to my instructor, Madame Moreau, a former French nurse who had married an Iraqi ambassador. I'm not too sure, but I think when he could no longer stand having her around, he had her assigned to her post as resident mother in the President's special school. In a brown dress and blue head covering, she stomped into the room and ordered me to follow her. She moved quickly down the side of the corridor, and I followed, always avoiding any contact with the men who passed.

Feeling a little too bold at first, I requested permission to contact my parents. She didn't acknowledge that I had spoken, so I assumed she had not heard. "If you please, Madame Teacher," I began.

"Shut up, you obstinate rat!" she interrupted me, grinding the words out between her front teeth. "Your parents are not your concern." That was all she said. I had hoped that as a woman in the palace, she might have wanted to be friendly to another woman, albeit a young one. We walked through a maze of hallways. I realized that if I wasn't careful, I'd get lost, and I didn't see any friendly faces to ask for directions. I paid close attention to the artwork on the walls, trying to follow the progression of the paintings in order to learn my way. "In!" she barked as we stood by a small doorway next to a Koranic painting of Ibrahim bringing Ishmael to the sacrificial rock. A musty room with a single light bulb would be my quarters until I was eighteen.

On the floor of the room was an old suitcase with a broken handle that I recognized from my parents' home. I opened it to find a few personal items, a Koran, a spare pair of glasses, two pads of paper and a letter from my father saying only, *Serve your people bravely, my angel,* I saw a single, small water stain on the note that I imagined was one of my mother's teardrops. In the room, there was a wind-up alarm clock on a three-legged nightstand. The closet held four sets of clothes, all the same, all used. There were head coverings and white, loose-fitting outfits. I had a sink and a toilet behind a curtain. The sink dripped, and later that night I discovered how easily nightmares can develop from the sound of trickling faucets and the ticking of twenty-year-old clocks.

After Madame Moreau left and I had explored my room, I wondered what to do next. Slowly turning the door handle to see if she had locked me in, I was relieved to feel the bolt release. Inspecting the area, I did not see any guards around. The long hall was defined by evenly spaced doors every couple of meters, with oil paintings of holy scenes between them. Each one had a spotlight illuminating it, so the colors stood out. The rest of the hall, however, was poorly lit. The light patches stood out like tombstones in a graveyard on a moonlit night. Closing the door carefully, I re-entered my room. There was nowhere else to go.

I sat on my cot for an hour or two looking out of the small window to a parking lot until it got dark outside. My parents had sent a new toothbrush but no pajamas. In fact, I had no underwear at all. Changing into one of the outfits that had been left for me, I washed my undergarments by hand and prayed they would be dry by the morning. Listening to the water drops and the clock, I eventually fell asleep.

My first night's sleep in this new reality was haunted by a vivid dream. I was on a throne with my uncles' swords swinging above my head like a pendulum. I tried not to move, but unlike the sword of Damocles, one of them slipped, diving straight for my heart. I leaped out of the way, waking myself up by pushing the blade away from my chest. Hearing a tearing sound, I felt my shirt loosen before I fell back to sleep. When the sun woke me at 5:30 the next morning, I discovered my shirt was split right at the seam and my shoulder was exposed.

On the solid floors of the palace, I could hear the sound of approaching footsteps. Not Madame's, thank God, but a man's. I pulled off my torn shirt and stretched towards the closet. He knocked on the door twice. I stuck my arms into the new shirt as he opened the door, and then I pulled down my shirt completely. *Did he see me naked?* I wondered as he said, "Good morning. It is time to go." Still blushing from embarrassment, and feeling very tired, I had the gall to ask him for one more minute to get ready. "As you like, Fatima," he said, "I will wait right outside."

His answer was the first reasonable comment I had heard since entering the palace. I prepared myself quickly. He wasn't dressed like the other men around. He wore exercise clothes, and on his arm there was a patch indicating that he had participated on the Iraqi karate team in an international competition. He walked much more slowly than Madame, which made me like him right away, and he brought me to the gymnasium.

"I am a trainer," he said. "You will focus on your strength and speed here." He briefly explained his position in the palace. "I was sent to Japan six years ago, where I studied for four years. I have a black belt in three different martial arts. My name is Al-Hasan bin Ibrahim Gamal, but you may refer to me as *Sensei*, which is the Japanese word for teacher. If you have no questions, we will begin." I couldn't believe it – he was open to questions.

"If you please, Sensei, why am I here?" I asked.

"We must all serve according to our abilities, Fatima. And the Kingdom feels that you have extraordinary skills."

"I don't understand."

"Your uncle, President Hussein, has great vision, dear child. He doesn't see what you can offer today, but what you can offer in ten or twenty years. He has recognized you as a seed that must be cultivated. When you blossom, you will know what you must do."

"And what will you teach me, Sensei?" I inquired.

"I will teach you to use your body. You will learn to breathe, walk, see, feel. You will learn to protect yourself from your enemies, and you will learn to kill." He said the last two words very slowly, and I felt myself shiver.

"But why, Sensei?"

"Your uncle teaches that for a man to achieve greatness, he must have the heart of a warrior. A warrior can fight and kill. I believe the same is true for a woman. You, too, are destined for greatness."

"How do you know?"

"Because your uncle has so decreed. Come child, we will begin. You may ask more questions later." He sent me to the changing room where I found an exercise suit like his, though without any patches. The fabric was cool and cottony, but felt sturdy. The exercise uniforms I had worn in the past were basically old clothes. This outfit, on the other hand, looked like a professional athlete's and made me feel strong. He told me to hurry since we only had two hours before my next class. It was much more time than I needed. He started by making me run around a track that, after fifteen minutes, nearly killed me. He let me stop early that day and said I would find a shower and a towel in the dressing room.

After I cleaned up, I returned to find the gym empty. I wasn't sure I could find my way back to my room, but I was afraid of being late for my next session. Outside the doors, I recognized some of the pictures. At one corner, there was a tall portrait of my uncle with his red beret, and that was the reminder I needed to get me back to my room.

The swift pace of Madame's gait announced her imminent arrival. She didn't bother to knock. "Come, child!" she commanded. She still wore her brown outfit and blue wrap. I glanced at her shoes. They were black, with square toes. She handed me a large book in English called *Chemistry – The Building Blocks*. In the library, she told me to review chapters one through five by lunch. *Review*, I thought, *I never learned this the first time.*

The English posed a bit of a problem, but having learned it at the diplomatic school, I had some idea how to read it. "Complete the problem sets at the back of each chapter," she said, "and I will collect them at noon."

By 11:00 a.m, I had hardly finished the first chapter. The material was so foreign to me that I had to read each paragraph twice. Thinking about all the recent events also affected my concentration, and I realized I would never finish the assignment. Turning the pages was like lifting an ancient stone tablet filled with hieroglyphics. I couldn't stop myself from checking the clock every few minutes, dreading Madame's return. Sure enough, at 11:58 a.m., I heard the approach of her solid shoes. I closed the book and neatly laid the blank pad of paper nearby. She looked at the two neat blocks in front of me.

"You are here to learn, child. You will stay until you have finished this assignment," Madame commanded. I loosened the muscles I had been clenching in my shoulders and they lowered down comfortably. Until that point, I hadn't realized how much physical tension this work caused me. Relieved that she didn't punish me, I tried to redirect myself to the text. The room was quiet, so I leveraged the sense of solitude to compose my frame of mind. The occasional far-off footsteps or, worse, the groaning of my stomach, distracted me. When I got to the first set of questions at the back of chapter one, I saw that someone had made faint marks in the margins with answers, but the thin gray lines were mostly erased. Nonetheless, I used these marks to guide me towards completion. Eventually I finished one problem set after the next, and just before sundown, I had completed all the assignments.

On the way back to my room, I passed one of the palace kitchens. The maids were cleaning up, but they seemed to recognize me. I stopped and looked at a short girl who must have been my age. She had a brown scar from the outer corner of her right eye diagonally across her face towards her nose. Someone had obviously hit her there once, very hard. She was bringing some almost empty serving plates to wash, but spotted me examining her. "I am sorry, Lady, I should have closed the kitchen door," she apologized for no reason.

"It's quite all right," I responded. "May I try some of this rice?" She lowered her gaze and offered me the plate. With the oversized serving spoon I stuffed a few large bites into my mouth. She scurried away, and then returned promptly with a bottle of water. I recognized it as the type that my teachers at the diplomatic school would drink. "Thank you," I said.

"It is my honor to serve you, your Highness," she said. I smiled and told her I was not a "Highness."

"I am here as a student to learn in the palace," I told her.

"I see," she responded, though I believe she knew my relationship to my uncle. "May your studies bring Allah's blessing on the people of this palace, and may your learning be a source of greatness for the destiny of our people."

No one had ever made me feel so important. "What's your name?" I asked.

"Aisha, your Highness," she said.

"You are a kind girl, Aisha. Here is one of my pencils from my studies. Perhaps you can find a good use for it, too." She accepted the freshly sharpened gift cautiously, stuck it in her apron, and smiled. "Good night and blessings," I concluded, and walked to my quarters, only twelve paintings away.

I closed the door of my room behind me, felt the musty air fill my nose, and drank the bottle of water that my new friend had given me. I placed my shoes and my books on the floor of my closet and, as I stood up, I heard a brief scream from outside the room. It stopped with the sound of a thud. I cracked open my door and peered out. Stifled struggling sounds came from the direction of the kitchen. I walked barefoot on the cold stone floor in that direction and heard a man's intimidating voice, "You are a dog! A bitch whose sole purpose is to serve her master."

I reached the corner and looked around it to see the chief cook holding Aisha's arms behind the back of the chair into which she was pinned. With one hand wrapped around both her small wrists, he crushed the other over her face and mouth. The man talking was one of my uncle's sons. He held the pencil that I had given her in his hand and continued, "You do not speak to the royal family. You do not look at them. You should be grateful for the chance to wash their clothes and bring them food."

He bent down to look straight into her eyes, placing his gorilla-like hand on her shoulder. He pressed his thumb deep into the pressure point by the bone and continued, "Do you think that Allah cares about your blessing? That He would listen to a dog? You think that you can bring a blessing to a princess? You are a curse on this house!" I could see the pain in her upper body was unbearable. Her eyes started to roll back. He let go of her, and she inhaled deeply through her nose, making a grunting sound with her muffled cry. "You sound like a pig!" he barked, moving the pencil around in his hand, "and pigs do not write!" With that, he jammed the dagger-like writing implement into her leg. He tipped her over backwards and then pushed her solidly onto the floor. Her head made a dull thump as it hit the marble surface.

With a slight rise of his mustache, the man smiled from the side of his mouth and walked away. I heard him laugh a bit. The chef walked into the kitchen and ordered, "Clean up the dog!" Two other young maids came out to help. I saw Aisha's limbs move, and I think I saw her breathe. With no men in sight, I silently approached her body. The two maids spotted me. With tears in her eyes, one of them whispered, "Please, Your Highness, please do not help us." I stopped, wanting to care for Aisha. But realizing the dangers, I slipped back to my room.

Plagued by a sleepless night filled with images of Aisha's skull cracking against the floor, I sat up in bed at 5:15 a.m. I washed and dressed before waiting for my gym instructor. I heard every tick of the clock until his footsteps echoed in the quiet hall outside. As I greeted him, he smiled. "Good morning, Fatima," he said, warmly. His deep tone of voice made my muscles relax. Just seeing him made me forget the cold solitude of the stone walls.

After some vigorous running around the gym, Sensei laid two thin mats on the floor in the center of the room. He directed me to lie down, and he reclined on the adjacent cushion. "Breathe in deeply," he told me, "and then exhale slowly. Count to two as you inhale, and count to eight as you exhale." Again and again. We just breathed, counting in our heads, for about a half hour. "If you can control your breathing, you can lower your heart rate and your blood pressure. You'll be able to think more clearly and understand more of what's going on around you. Close your eyes, Fatima, and focus."

He had a small stereo with a cassette player, and he played some music with a rhythm that helped me count "two in, eight out." He watched my breathing closely, and said I was doing well. "Beautiful," he commented. I know he was evaluating my technique, but I also imagined that he was complimenting me. *Beautiful.* Maybe I was.

Madame was late. At 8:10 a.m, she marched into the library, clutching my assignment. "Do you understand the chemistry lessons from yesterday?" she asked as she sat down opposite me at the table.

"I have tried, Madame Teacher."

"Was the assignment difficult?" Madame continued. I was concerned that I had not done very well, and I nodded shyly. At the same time, I began my newly learned breathing technique to prepare myself for her reprimand.

"You got everything right," she said to my surprise. Relieved, I smiled a bit. Abruptly, she stood up. Leaning over to me, Madame lifted her right hand high in the air and smacked it down on my ear and cheek. The strike was harder than I had ever received from any man, and I felt her ring cutting my face. "But you cheated like a thief. You copied the answers that had been erased in the textbook. You have ruined your life here and disgraced your father's name." I was still dizzy from the shock of the blow, and the ringing in my ear almost deafened me. Madame Moreau pushed the papers in her hand towards me along with the books, and walked out.

My jaw started to shudder, the way it does just before crying. My eyes pricked with tears that were ready to fall. But I refused to give into the almost involuntary response of crying. Instead, I started counting to myself, "two inhale, eight exhale." Moments later, I felt in control, hearing Sensei's comforting voice inside me, instructing me to direct my emotions by controlling my breathing.

Madame did not return to the library that morning. I sat at the table for around an hour, skimming over the pictures in the chemistry books. I probably should have redone the assignment, but due to the stinging sensation in my face I was in no mood to do so. Still holding the papers, I headed out. I stopped by the kitchen and saw one of Aisha's friends. "May I please have some ice?" I requested, to stop the swelling. In a certain way, I was proud of the mark on my face. That way the girls in the kitchen would realize that I was a person, too, not like the animals who abused them. One of the girls bagged some ice cubes for me, and handed me some dates along with them. "May Allah bless you with a quick recovery, your Highness," she whispered, sure that no one could hear, and then she hurried back into the kitchen.

At that point, I replayed Madame's words in my mind: *You have ruined your life here.* Was I going to be sent away? I decided to go to see Sensei, at the very least to say goodbye. As I got closer to the gym, I heard shouts and grunts. Bracing myself for another torture scene similar to Aisha's punishment, I opened the gym door and slid in. No one could see me as I quietly worked myself towards the main floor of the gym. There I saw Sensei and another man engaged in a gruesome but thrilling fight.

★ اﻟﻠﻪ ★ اﻟﻠﻪ ★

Two floors beneath the palace lobby, dozens of men and women spent their final days suffering as their own broken bodies, drained of food and water, absorbed the final hammering of their interrogators. General Ayad Atik had personally witnessed 19-year-old torturers slamming olivewood clubs into the faces of elderly victims who were too weak to beg for their lives; two or three hateful blows finally separated their souls from their bodies. Lying on the floor in pools of blood and urine, these enemies of the state were dragged off by other inmates to have their bodies reduced to ash in a garbage incinerator.

In complete contrast to the dazzling architecture above, the palace's basement mirrored London's infamous dungeons. General Atik could hardly see in the darkness of the long, gray hallways, since his eyes were used to the bright sunlight. He laughed at the miniature palm trees and rose gardens that Saddam had scattered throughout his powerful dwelling. The general pictured the arched gates, majestic stairways, and vaulted ceilings above. He silently mouthed the words of the inscription that he had seen written on the more than sixty-million sand-colored bricks that had been used to rebuild the fallen 600-room castle of King Nebuchadnezzar II: *In the era of Saddam Hussein, protector of Iraq, who rebuilt civilization and rebuilt Babylon.*

Interrogation room '6' had a chalkboard hanging on the door with the name of Faraydoun Assi Mustafa lightly scratched in the middle. The general dismissed the two guards and then entered. The room stank, and four glaring spotlights illuminated the bloodstains all around. The grossly disfigured inmate was hanging naked on the back wall, crucifix style. General Atik studied the wretched figure for a minute, unsure of his identity. "Faraydoun Mustafa?" he asked.

The jailed man's head jerked to the side, as if he were getting ready for an assault after hearing his name.

"I won't hurt you, son," the general continued, as he began to unshackle him. "I have spoken to your father and told him you were all right. I guess I spoke too presumptuously. I apologize." When Mustafa's broken arm fell out of the cuff, Atik saw the extent of the damage the inexperienced interrogators had inflicted. *And they still couldn't extract any useful information. Idiots!* Atik thought. "Can you walk?"The semi-lame prisoner tried to summon his inner strength, inspired by General Atik's brief display of kindness. He walked a few steps, but then collapsed on the floor by the chair in the center of the room. Leaving the paralyzed heap, Atik fetched a cup of water from the office down the hall, and then spent fifteen minutes nursing it into Mustafa. Supporting the badly beaten man, Atik then walked him to one of the guards' resting rooms. "Excuse us," he said, ordering the guard out. "Wash your face, Faraydoun, and lie down here."

When Mustafa slumped on the thin mattress, Atik shut the door and lights. It was the first time in three days that the sleep-deprived man enjoyed the peacefulness of darkness. He had been kept under strobe-bright bulbs since being brought downstairs. Every time he nodded off to sleep, someone would come and beat him. During the evenings, the guards would sometimes throw a bucket of water at his head to block him from dreams. One handy watchman connected a timed sprinkler system to the sink so that every few minutes, a splash of water would cut across his face – a modern derivation of the ancient Chinese water torture.

The real goal of the original Chinese torture was psychological – not so much pain, but mental agony, eventually leading to insanity. While restrained, victims would get hit by a few drops of water every twenty or thirty seconds. The drops would begin to feel harder and harder, and hurt more and more, even leading to bruising. The victim would eventually come to dread each impending drop. And since he couldn't drink the water, he suffered from being constantly reminded of his thirst – unable to reach satisfaction only inches away. The Iraqi approach lacked all subtlety, and wasn't successful. The sprinkler bursts simply stung the prisoner so much that he couldn't fall asleep.

Lying in the dark, rehydrated, with no one touching him, Mustafa fell asleep. *He probably doesn't even remember who he's working for,* Atik thought as he pulled out his copy of Albert Camus' *The Myth of Sisyphus* and waited for his prisoner to wake up.

★ اكبر ★ الله ★

Each man was a like a powerful engine, with arms and legs rotating like carefully timed propellers. The difference, though, was that Sensei's opponent had a desperate and angry look in his eyes. He made violent noises that frightened me as he kicked and punched. Sensei kept looking into his enemy's eyes, absolutely unaffected by the fierce growling.

The speed of the attacker's punches suddenly increased, putting Sensei on the defensive. Double punches screamed towards his face and throat, forcing Sensei to hasten his moves. I was scared, and I imagined myself handling such an assault. While finishing an incredibly fast left jab straight towards Sensei's neck, the assailant prepared a powerful right punch by pulling his elbow back and releasing it like a cannon shot. As the blow approached his chest, Sensei dropped to the ground and split his legs like scissors. The enemy missed his target. Sensei used the force of the failed blow against him. He snapped his legs closed, pushing the knees of the enemy forward while kicking his feet back. That tripping motion, magnified by the energy of the missed punch, caused the enemy to drop weakly to the floor, right onto his chest and chin.

"Oh," I sighed a little too loudly, relieved that my teacher had won. Sensei glanced over his shoulder to identify the source of the sound and I smiled, embarrassed. He winked at me to let me know it was okay. When he gave a little nod, I came out of my hiding place to greet him, and then heard *"ki-yai"* as the adversary swung his leg high into Sensei's shoulder, knocking him over on to the floor. I ran down to the mats and grabbed my teacher's hand. He was quiet. I looked at the enemy, whose eyes gleamed with glory, and I said, "My uncle will have you killed for this."

The opponent laughed, and then Sensei looked at me said, "Not so fast, Fatima." He turned to his foe and said, "You see, my son, you must never let yourself get distracted by a woman." My heart fluttered when Sensei admitted that I was a woman who could distract him. "You are dismissed, Da'uud," he said to his son. After bowing to both of us, Da'uud put on his jacket. It was decorated with a patch from the Iraqi boxing team. "Peace to you," he said.

Sensei indicated a spot next to him on the floor where I could sit. "Why have you come now, Fatima?" Holding back my tears, I explained how the chemistry assignment had been painfully difficult, and how I made use of the answers in the back of the book. "I thought someone would teach me, Sensei, like you teach. But instead," two breaths in — eight out, "instead she just beat me like a slave." I couldn't keep my strength any longer, and I cried.

"Breathe slowly, Fatima," my teacher said as he placed his warm hand on my shoulder. I slid closer to him and allowed him to put his arms around me. "I will take care of it for you."

My tears kept falling. Embarrassed, I buried my face in his neck. I wasn't sure if he would push me away since the religious Muslims in the palace were very strict about men and women touching. He seemed happy to hold me, and I wanted his touch. He was sweaty from his bout with his son, and my cheek got wet. His muscles were firm, and he held me tightly. "Shh," he whispered quietly. His warm breath tickled my ear as he stroked my hair. He took hold of my wrists and led me on to the training mat. "Lie down." He moved his grasp from my wrists gently towards my fingers and held my hands. He was leaning over me, squeezing my fingers with a rhythm that was supposed to help me time each breath. I no longer needed the breathing technique to calm my emotions, however. I had the protection of my teacher, whom I believed had so much more to offer me than Madame Moreau.

Nothing more was ever mentioned about the chemistry issue. When Madame picked me up the next morning, she escorted me to a very modern conference room. On an oblong table were seven laptop computers – one at the head, and three on either side. The black leather chairs had wheels, and were adjustable to ensure maximum comfort. A large portrait of my uncle hung in the center of the wall. The painting was the most original that I had seen so far in the palace, melding the image of the flag into the body of the President. Madame instructed me to sit in the place right next to the head of the table. "Wait here," she ordered. She handed me a folder and then left me alone in the room.

After she went out, I took time to inspect the surroundings. First, I peeked out of the door to make sure no one was there. Since there were no windows and only one entranceway, I took a tissue from my pocket and jammed it under the door to pry it open a bit. That way, I was sure to hear if anyone came down the hall. Each of the computers asked for a user name and password, but having hardly used a computer before I wasn't sure what to do. I rubbed my hand over the wall to try to figure out what it was made of, and then I touched the other items in the room. Everything seemed very strange. The room looked like a businessman's office from America or England rather than a classroom in the palace. It was clear, in fact, that the table was made of some very hard, imported wood.

There was a wire coming out of the back of each computer that ran through a hole in the table. Curious to see where it went, I bent down to examine the underside of the broad work surface. Suddenly, I heard footsteps outside the room. Getting up, I looked towards the door. Above the opening I noticed a small black, glass hemisphere on the ceiling. It must have been a security camera. Everything I had done had been recorded, including my placing the door wedge and my thorough inspection of the room. I stood by my chair and waited.

A very tall man opened the door. He looked at me, and then looked down and picked up the tissue. "You are a c-clever girl, Fatima," he said with a stutter. "I hope you will put your ss-s-skills to good w-w-work." After he spoke, I recognized him. He was a cousin of mine, considerably older, who had been working in the palace for many years.

"I am honored, my cousin, Yousef bin Fahad bin Khalifa." I greeted him with his full name as a sign of respect. I inquired about his family and we spoke for a few minutes.

"As you know, Fatima, you have been selected by our uncle to serve the palace. M-M-M-Madame Moreau has asked me to oversee your education here. You are very lucky, my cousin. The education you will receive in this room will be tailor-made to your pace and skills. Our uncle has spared no expense in getting the f-f-finest educational equipment and trainers in the whole world. Your laptop will guide you through each of your c-c-courses, and I will be available to help."

Yousef led me through the folder that I had received. The opening page included my user name, *Fatima*, and the password, *Al-Khansa*. He suggested that I change the password, but I rather liked it since Al-Khansa, a contemporary of the prophet Mohammed, was both a poetess and a warrior. The syllabus included a broad series of courses, many of which were uncommon in Iraqi schools. Along with traditional Islamic texts, the mainstay of my education until that point, I would learn math, English, German, Spanish, Hebrew, chemistry, history, international literature, and computer programming, as well as other science and liberal arts topics. "This seems beyond my abilities, my cousin," I said.

"You have b-b-been chosen for this education, Fatima, because you will succeed. You will be here for two more years until you m-m-move on, so you shall have a great deal of time to complete all the courses." It didn't occur to me to ask him what "move on" meant, but the time passed quickly, and I was soon to leave the protection of the palace. Yousef spent many hours training me to use the computer, and I found that I enjoyed using it every day to explore the world far beyond my small life.

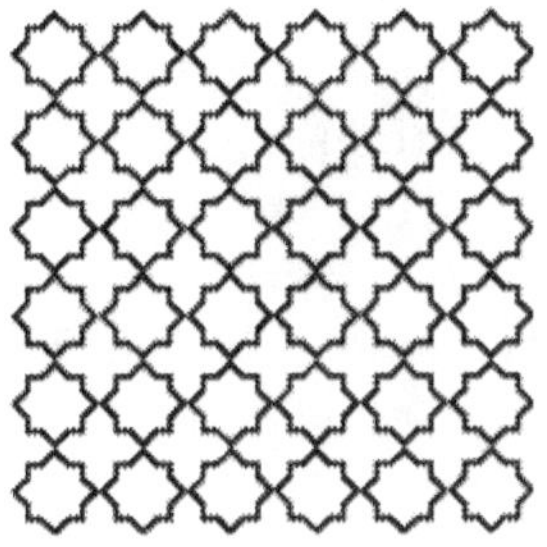

Chapter 2

About a week later, after I was awakened by the sound of honking in the parking lot outside my window, I went to wash up behind the curtain in my room. When I came out, wearing only my white pants and holding a small towel, I was surprised to see Sensei standing in my room. I was sure that he knew he would catch me off-guard, and I quickly covered my front with my hand towel. "You have come very early, my teacher," I commented, but I didn't move.

He looked at me closely. "We will learn something new today, Fatima. It is a chilly day, and I came early to tell you that you should dress warmly. Perhaps you would like to wear a training jacket like this." He handed me a jacket like he wore. I reached out with one hand and the corner of my towel dropped a little. Seeing his eyes look over my body made me feel warm; hot, in fact, and I thought I wouldn't need the jacket. I wanted to put my towel down and try on the garment he had brought so he could see me in it, but instead I turned around, letting him see only my back. I folded my towel, put on a t-shirt and then slipped into the jacket.

"Thank you. I think this will keep me comfortable."

We went outside the palace to his car. He had one of the special all-terrain vehicles that my uncle bought for his elite soldiers. All of the windows were darkened. As we drove towards the exit of the large parking lot, he told me to climb into the back seat and hide on the floor. He then opened the window and spoke with the guard at the gate. "You are leaving very early this morning, Captain Gamal," the soldier noted. Sensei laughed, "Oh yes. I think I left the coffee on the stove, and I'd hate to come home tonight and find my house burned down by accident."

"Good luck, Sir," the attendant replied to Sensei's smooth lie, and then I heard the large steel gate slide open.

"They get a little carried away with perimeter security around here, Fatima. A couple of months ago, in fact, a sculptor who was making a bust of your uncle got confused at this checkpoint. He didn't stop quickly enough, and one of the snipers up there took him out." He pointed to a building across the street. "That afternoon, Saddam hired a new artist to finish the project, and gave a Mercedes to the guard as a reward for his marksmanship. You can come back up front now."

He put music on the radio by the American pop artist Billy Joel. "Isn't this banned in the kingdom?" I asked.

"For those in your uncle's domain who travel, it is important that they have exposure to the different cultures that they will encounter. That is why you should learn the music, dances, art, and theater of many countries. You will be given books to read on all these topics. I will try to bring you many of these tools for your education." The music was loud, but I liked Billy Joel's sweet voice.

We drove off the main road on to a desert path and came to an area of low mountains and hills. "Grab one of the bags in the back, Fatima, and bring it here." In the trunk I found two small backpacks. I took both to my teacher. In each bag was a long rope, as well as a few harnesses for rappelling. He told me that we would learn to go down quickly and then practice climbing up using only a rope. He took off his jacket and demonstrated how to attach the straps. He wrapped them around his solid shoulders and legs. He then helped me adjust the lengths and put my belts on. "It needs to be firm, Fatima, but not too tight," he told me as he felt my arms and legs to confirm everything was in place. I could feel how all alone we were and I wanted him to keep touching my body, but he stopped and asked if I was ready.

He showed me how to control the speed of descent and how to lean back and trust the rope. We practiced on a five-meter drop so I could get the feel of the new techniques, and I found it rather easy. It was a windy day, so he gave me a helmet and told me to be careful not to get blown into the mountain. The arms of my eyeglasses pressed into the sides of my face under the pressure of the helmet's hard plastic straps. Close by, we arrived at a tougher drop, about 40 meters. I tried to peer over to see the bottom, but the ledge blocked visibility. "Don't worry, Fatima," he told me, "it's just like the practice run. You're not scared, are you?" I winked at him.

Hitched to my rope, I walked slowly backwards over the side of the cliff. It was hard to push away from the rock, but Sensei said to jump and release some rope. That allowed me to drop below the ledge and slide down more easily. I immediately lost sight of my teacher. Determined to prove my bravery, I slid down the rope swiftly, not looking down in case I frightened myself.

The ride down was gusty, but the wind was not strong enough to push me off track. I heard some voices as I neared towards the bottom, and then looked down. Some shepherds were relaxing near my landing point and I was afraid I might land on one of them. "Watch out," I called. They just looked at me and laughed. One of them joked, "Our prayers have been answered. Allah has sent us a beautiful virgin."

When I got to the bottom, I lost my balance and fell on my back. The sharp rocks hurt and I banged my head, too, but the helmet protected me. None of the three men came to help, but as I stood up they approached. I took off my helmet to see them better and shook my hair loose. Perhaps they would recognize me and leave me alone. I glanced up to see when Sensei would arrive, but he hadn't started coming yet. "Who are you, and what are you doing here?" I asked firmly. They laughed.

"Who are you, an angel from on high?" one of them inquired as he started examining my rope.

I yanked the rope out of his hand. "I am from the President's palace and you are trespassing on the President's land."

He turned to his comrades and mocked me, "We seem to have taken a wrong turn, my friends. We have stumbled onto Saddam Hussein's land, and this must be his queen." He bowed very deeply, overdoing his show of humility and, while he was prostrate, he grabbed my rope again and pulled it backwards, making me once again tumble on my back. I tried to unfasten the clips, but being too unfamiliar with my gear I found myself tied down by my own equipment. Again I looked up, hopeful that my teacher would slide down to my rescue, but nothing.

"Well, your Majesty, let us see what kind of a queen you truly are." Two of the three attackers grabbed my arms, while the apparent leader stood over me. I struggled to roll away, but with my harness being used against me, it was hopeless. To distract him for a moment, I smiled seductively.

"Let me show you our special technique in the palace," I invited, hoping to buy a few moments until help arrived. The sidekicks tried to take off my harness, but it was too difficult. They didn't waste the chance to fondle me, though, which made my stomach feel sick. I stopped fighting, and the leader bent down on top of me. He untied his wrap, and then asked me my name. "I am Queen Hussein," I said.

From his belly he laughed, and moved his face towards mine. His vile breath and broken teeth made me question my strategy, but I figured that Sensei would get there at any moment. The men on my sides seemed more interested in touching me than holding me, so as the leader got his face close to mine, presumably to kiss me, I yanked my hands away from the assailant's, grabbed his head and pulled it straight towards my forehead, smacking his upper lip and nose into the hardest part of my head. He curled back in pain, and as he stood up to get off me, I cocked my knee close to my chest and released all the power in my leg directly into his groin. He grabbed himself and laid on the ground, unsure whether to nurse his bleeding face or crushed testicles.

I then rolled over to one side and lifted my harness off over my head, like taking off my shirt. One of the clips fell off and I grabbed it to use like brass knuckles. One of the shepherds grabbed my other hand before I could stand up and, pulling it towards him, looked at me directly and said, "There is no Queen Hussein. Do you think you're Queen Zenobia?" His reference to the ancient monarch of 2000 years ago surprised me. Her husband had been king of Palmyra, now part of Syria, and when he died, she took his place and fought courageously against the Romans. She won many battles before being captured by the aggressors. "Why don't you come home with me?" he said. Comparing me to Queen Zenobia, who ended up living as a matron in the Roman Empire, seemed to go too far.

"You don't have golden chains to take me away," I replied, alluding to the way she was led off by the Romans. "But I've got this," I said, swinging the rappelling clip towards his head. He blocked my advance and I only scratched his face slightly. I pulled both my hands towards my chest and rolled away.

As I turned upwards, I saw Sensei's rope dropping into place over the side of the ledge. In a minute he would arrive to save me, so I knew the fight wouldn't last long. I called his name, but the wind made it impossible for him to hear my cry. My opponent jumped on top of me and put his weight squarely on my hips, stopping me from getting up. He put his filthy hand over my mouth and kept me pinned in place.

The third man took his walking staff and positioned himself near Sensei's landing point. My teacher, unaware of what was below, continued his backward descent. Near the bottom, he slowed down and looked between his legs. His attacker stayed behind him, out of view, and prepared his swing. Unable to break free, I couldn't call out a warning. I heard a loud cracking sound as the wooden weapon hit Sensei's helmet, and then a brief grunt of pain when his legs took the next impact. With great might in his arms, he pulled himself up the rope, one hand over the other, until he was about five or six meters in the air, well out of reach of the stick.

The man on top of me rolled me over onto my stomach and pulled my hands behind me. I felt him start to wrap my rope around them, and though I couldn't release myself from his strong grip, I intertwined my fingers and pushed my wrists apart a few centimeters. Forcefully he completed the knot. "Stay here, Queen," he commanded, and then grabbed his staff and headed to the mêlée. As soon as he had taken a few steps, I escaped from the ropes. Having left a little space between my wrists, I was able to wriggle out of the bindings rapidly. Without any weapon, however, I was of little use in the battle.

The two aggressors started batting wildly at Sensei. He was too high for them to reach, but their strikes shook the rope so much that he couldn't climb any higher. Sensei began rocking back and forth, causing his tether to sway from side to side. The motion made the two men separate from each other, each one trying to hit him on one end of his arc or the other. He then pulled up the length of rope that was below him, wrapped some of it around one of his arms, and looped another part of it around one of his feet. That gave him a stepping area to support himself and enabled him to lessen the strain.

As Sensei's swings grew larger, I grabbed my climbing harness in one hand and an attached clip in the other and moved behind one of the attackers. Presumably Sensei intended to attack one of them while I hit the other. With an animal-like shout, he propelled himself up in the air and came crashing down on his target. The enemy swung his staff at Sensei, who used the excess rope that he had gathered around his arm to catch the solid weapon.

At the same time, I came from behind, threw my choker around the face of the other one and yanked backwards. I lifted my leg high, putting it in the small of his back, and caused him to lose his balance and drop backwards on the jagged rocks. I fell, too, but having been prepared for the drop, I wasn't hurt. My harness was caught under his chin, so I placed my feet on his shoulders and pulled as hard as I could.

Having grabbed the weapon of his assailant, Sensei jabbed him in the groin, causing him to keel over in pain. He then held the stick at both ends and rammed it into the back of his neck. His opponent's face took the total brunt of the fall on the rocks.

As I struggled to keep the harness over my enemy's face, he tried to pull it off from around his neck. Having conquered the first attacker, Sensei spun around and saw the two of us on the ground. He lifted up his newly acquired weapon and then drove it right into the center of his target. I heard the gasp of pain the enemy made as he grabbed his stomach, unable to breathe. Since he was limp beneath me, I released my hold on the harness and stood up. He was unable to move, using all his strength to gasp in a little air.

Before looking at my teacher, I glanced at all three of our attackers to make sure they weren't able to start again. Two were bleeding profusely from their faces, and the third was still struggling to breathe. I looked towards Sensei for approval. He looked at my victims, shook his head in disbelief, and then smiled at me. "You are a smart girl, Fatima."

"Thank you, Sensei. But why do you say I am smart?" I said, thinking his compliment was unusual.

"If you were strong, you would have broken them with your strength. However, your muscles are not powerful – yet – so you have outsmarted them."

"Well, my teacher, you are both smart and strong. Thank you for coming to save me."

He corrected me, "It is you who saved me. I shall repay you. In the meantime," he said loud enough for them to hear, "What shall we do with them? Shall we kill them?"

At that moment, after their vicious attack, the offer seemed reasonable, but I believed he was kidding. "Let us find out who they are," I suggested.

Sensei walked over to my first victim, who was lying on his side in a fetal position, laid a foot on his ear, and placed the staff on his neck. "The lady has asked a question," he said. "Would you care to answer it?"

His face was quite a mess. It was impossible to tell if the blood was coming from his nose or mouth. He spit out and then answered, "We are shepherds. We have done nothing wrong, so leave us alone."

His impudence annoyed me, and his accent revealed his background. I kicked some sand into his face and told him not to speak that way to royalty. "A Kurdish pig should not defile the lands of the President." He winced when the sharp, gritty cloud hit him. "It's time for you to leave before I ask the Captain to make good on his offer to execute you."

Sensei released his prisoner. The man scurried away, narrowly missing Sensei's staff aimed at his backside. The two others slithered and limped quickly after him.

"If they are shepherds, Sensei, then where are their sheep?" I asked as I watched them get a safe distance from us.

"They're not shepherds, Fatima. They're petty thieves. I've seen them around before, but they never got in my way. Had we killed them, we would have served the kingdom well."

"So why didn't we kill them?" I followed up.

"I offered, my dear, but you appeared to decline. Please take my offers seriously in the future."

"I shall, Sensei."

For several hours that morning we practiced climbing up the side of the mountain and then rappelling down. As I hung onto my rope, I kept thinking, *was he serious, and what offers will he make in the future?*

After I cleaned up from our simple picnic lunch, Sensei called, "Here," as he tossed me the car keys. I used them to open the back door and pack up all of the equipment, and then went to hand them back to him. "You drive," he said.

"I cannot drive, Sensei," I smiled.

"It's time to learn," he responded, and seated himself on the passenger side. The previous summer, my father had taught me some of the basics of running a car, so I knew how to start it up. Sensei told me to switch into drive and get going. For about an hour, we bumped along to unfamiliar places. Eventually, we switched seats and he drove me back to the palace. He had me conceal myself in the back again, and then he dropped me off near my room. As I got out of the car, he handed me a large envelope that had been concealed between the front seats. "Take some time to review this," he said.

My muscles ached from the strenuous exercise and the tension from learning to drive. But as soon as I entered my room, I opened the envelope. There was a driving manual and a magazine called *Cosmopolitan*, which had a picture of a beautiful woman on the cover. I desperately wanted to read how to drive well, but I found the headlines on the cover of the magazine more appealing. The advertisements were as interesting as the articles, teaching me about the forces that drove the actions of American women.

Knocking my shoes under my bed, I lay down to start reading. "What men really want to hear" was the feature article. The piece extended over several different sections, so I had to keep turning many pages to reach the next part.

As I flipped my way through, I studied advances in makeup, the lifestyles of important people, better ways to have shiny hair, and how to interact with men.

There was a knock at the door. I was wearing a light t-shirt and loose pants, and I decided to try one of the new lines that I had learned from this journal of womanhood. Cracking open the door, I saw my teacher's back and the karate patch on his arm. "I was hoping it would be you," I whispered, and opened the door for him to enter.

"My Queen, I am surprised to hear you say that." It wasn't Sensei, but my assailant from the morning. "But I, too, was hoping to find you." He forced a terrible smile, showing me his brownish teeth. I couldn't scream for help, though, because I was afraid that the guards would find out that Sensei had taken me off the palace grounds in the morning and we would both get into trouble. That could ruin our special relationship.

"How did you get in here? And where is the Captain? How did you get his jacket?" I spoke firmly, but quietly.

He dropped his view from my eyes down to his own hand to show me the bloody knife that he was holding. "The Captain," he began, "will not be climbing down any more ropes." He snorted. "Inside, please." He held his blade straight up in front of his face, walked in, and closed the door behind him.

I decided to try to enchant him with words. "A man who could succeed in beating the mighty Captain Gamal must surely be a lion among cats." He took a step closer. His breath smelled like rotten coffee, and his breathing was getting deeper. I wanted to lure him to sit on the bed in order to have a chance to break away towards the door. He kept himself between the door and me, forcing me to back up towards my bed. His tired eyes had deep lines, and he hadn't cleaned the blood off his face from his earlier defeat. I quoted an old Arab proverb, "Dwell not upon thy weariness, thy strength shall be according to the measure of thy desire."

"My weariness does not concern me, my Queen. And I think you know what it is that I desire." He loosened his collar with one hand while he adjusted his knife with the other.

Since he had already killed Sensei, there was no secret to protect anymore. "Get ..." I started to scream, but he wrapped one hand around me, pressing the side of his knife into my back, and he stifled me by hugging my face into his hairy chest.

"The whisper of a pretty girl can be heard further than the roar of a lion," he began, also quoting from our tradition. "If you call out like that again, I shall slit your throat. And if you even whisper, I shall consider that a roar as well." He held me tightly for a moment, and then loosened his grip slightly as a test. Without fighting, I bowed my head to demonstrate my submission.

He held his knife vertically in front of him. I was mesmerized by its power. "Take off your clothes, my Queen," he said quietly. I held the bottom of my shirt and slid it up my body. The knife appeared to extend, becoming more of a dangerous blade. When I removed my top, I let it drop on to the floor below my pillow. I crossed my arms to cover my chest. The knife had grown into a broad sword, and the blood had completely vanished.

He held it firmly at the base with both hands and let it sway towards my face. I stood motionless until he commanded me to remove my pants as well. I followed his order and stood naked, this time letting my arms hang by my sides so he could examine me. He bowed his head low, using it to point to the bed, "If you please, your Highness."

I lay down on my bed in full view of my enemy. He stared at me, and I studied his magnificent sword. I readied myself to feel his weight on top of me. He placed his knee between my legs and then laid his sword upon my chest. His hands pressed down my shoulders and he descended on my body like a funeral shroud. The steamy air from his mouth warmed my neck. His immense size began to compress my lungs, making it hard to get enough oxygen. He remained still. I expected him to start moving, but for a few moments he didn't stir. There was more wetness on my shoulder, and I realized he had drooled on me. "Are you ready for your king?" he asked.

"My king!" I thought. His words jolted me back to reality. I had wanted to know what the sword would feel like on my skin, but he was a thief, not a king. I slid my hands up his sides, rubbing him firmly, until I got to the sword. With my left hand on the flat side of the blade and my right hand on the handle, I pushed him away from me and slid the sword towards his throat. He made a short gasp, and then collapsed on top of me. Warm blood started gushing all over my neck and chest. Spurts of red shot up towards my mouth. "Get up," I said to him, afraid there would be no response.

The pouring blood was leaking around my chest onto my mattress and I could feel it in my back. Please, I thought, get off me. The wetness was everywhere, covering my whole body. Finally, I used the sword as a lever and rolled him off me onto the floor. His body hit the solid ground with a drum-like thud. I started to wipe his face with my shirt. I wanted to see his lifeless expression, to see the damage I had inflicted on this animal. The pool of blood was beginning to roll towards the door. I was worried it would leak underneath, through the too-big crack between the floor and the door, and someone outside would see it.

As my shirt cleaned off the top part of his face, I realized that the eyes were not those of my enemy. The open eyes staring at the single light bulb above were Sensei's. I continued to clean off the blood to make sure, but it was true. I had cut my teacher's throat. He had come to make me his, but I had killed him. I bent down to press my body against his wound. The blood flowed quicker from his neck, covering the floor, racing to the door.

There was a knock at the door. Startled, I sat up in bed. My magazine fell to the floor, and I found that my pants were stained from my period. "Who is it?" I called out

"It's Sensei, Fatima. Are you alright?"

"Oh, yes, my teacher," I said, grateful to hear his voice, "I was hoping it would be you. Please wait a moment."

I looked around for evidence of my nightmare, but my room was clean. I changed my pants but left my slightly damp shirt on. I opened the door, saw my teacher wearing his training jacket, and invited him in.

He looked over me briefly and asked if I was feeling well. "You appear rather flushed."

To avoid telling him the truth, I told him I had probably overexerted myself that morning. He instructed me to see the doctor, and said he would arrange it.

★ اكبر ★ الله ★

The pillow slowly reddened as Faraydoun Mustafa's open cuts bled through the thin cloth. Hours later, he tried to elevate his head, but the sheets had begun to attach to the clotting wounds. He peeled them off, groaning from the pain of reopening his mending skin. "Lay still, son. I'll come back in the morning," said the General.

In the hall, Atik took the chalkboard that had been hanging on the door and wrote, "No one may enter this room. – General Ayad Atik." He turned to the guard, noted his nametag, and told him, "I hold you personally responsible to enforce this command." Turning the key firmly, Atik removed it and took it with him.

At 5:30 a.m. the next morning, he found the same guard sitting on the floor, leaning against the door, asleep. The man jumped to attention when the General arrived. "Per your command, Sir, I have not moved from this position."

Atik smiled warmly, reached into the paper bag he had brought, and handed the man a pack of cigarettes. "Well done. You may go now." As the guard was ready to protest his dismissal, the General raised his hand, letting him know it was fine to leave him unguarded.

Mustafa was sitting up in bed. He had washed himself and taken some of the clothes that he found in the closet. "Here's a fresh outfit, son. Why don't you change, and then we can talk while you eat," said the General.

The confused prisoner agreed. After days of extreme torture, he was suspicious, but grateful for any compassion. General Atik was known as a firm leader, but not a cruel one. The bare room had a desk, a phone, a picture of the President, and an alcove meant for a bathroom. Mustafa changed while Atik pushed aside the guards' paperwork and laid out a simple breakfast for him.

"You could have gotten yourself killed in there," Atik began. "Those goons don't know when to stop. Were you trying to kill yourself?"

Mustafa kept quiet.

"Don't worry. I told you yesterday that I won't hurt you, and I meant it. Suicide is like this," he began, quoting Camus' philosophy. *"Killing yourself amounts to confessing. It is confessing that life is too much trouble for you or that you do not understand it.* Albert Camus wrote that. Do you know who Camus is?" Mustafa kept eating. "If you let them kill you, that's the same as suicide. You could have just told them what they wanted, and then they wouldn't have been killing you – and you wouldn't have been killing yourself. If you were spying on the President, I think you must have known what you were doing. I don't think that you were killing yourself because you don't understand life. For all its absurdity, I bet you do understand a lot more about life than most of the people around here. Rather, son," Atik placed a hand on Mustafa's shoulder and could feel the muscle tremors, "I think that life is just too much for you. Like Camus said, suicide *is merely confessing that life is not worth the trouble.*"

With his damaged arm lying almost lifeless in his lap, Mustafa looked up at the General, "Thank you for rescuing me," he said, finally.

"I'm sorry I couldn't get a doctor down here to look at your arm. Eat, Faraydoun, I shouldn't distract you with my talk of old philosophers."

General Atik did not object to the use of torture in principle, but he disapproved of it in practice. Unimaginative officers and brutish soldiers enjoyed the application of pain far too much. Atik had studied the work of the famous Nazi interrogator Hans-Joachim Scharff, who questioned fighter pilots at Dulag Luft. He was legendary for his ability to extract critical data from his targets. His unusual technique was to treat prisoners with respect and dignity. After the war, he moved to the United States and worked as a mosaic artist, eventually having his works displayed in Cinderella's castle at Disney World.

Atik had no interest in befriending the spy, who he felt deserved jail time, but he needed to find out his ultimate mission. Moreover, Ali Hassan al-Majid was scheduled to see the prisoner later in the morning and if Atik did not have any information by then, Ali would use considerably more force and might kill the man without obtaining any information. "His death will be an example to others," Ali would say. *Yes, but we won't know who the others are,* Atik imagined himself responding.

"Camus pretty much felt that life was crazy. It's like we spend all of our days pushing a giant rock up a mountain, and then, just when we get to the top, it tumbles back down. You must know that feeling," Atik continued.

Looking at him, Mustafa couldn't contain a small laugh. "You're talking about the absurdity of life to a man who has just had several bones broken by a group of morons."

"Oh, that's rich," Atik laughed strongly. "You should write a philosophy text now, too. Although Camus did a good job already. He said, *Suicide is a solution to the absurd.* Tell me, son, do you think that's true? If life is just a series of absurd events with no real meaning, shouldn't we all just kill ourselves? Camus said that if you really believe there's no meaning, then that fact alone should dictate your actions. Let's make a pact now, my friend, just you and me." Atik drew his gun, "Since this whole business here is just insanity, let's kill ourselves together." He pointed the gun directly at his own temple. "I'll just pull the trigger now," he said, slowly cocking the gun, and then when I'm done, you do the same. We'll simply write the name Camus on the table and see if any of those morons even understand the reference. Shall we make the pact, Faraydoun?"

Confusion filled the young man's eyes.

"You were going to kill yourself in room six, weren't you? And that probably hurt a hell of a lot. This suicide will be painless. Although after you see my brains blown out, you might get scared. So you go first." The General handed his prisoner the cocked gun. The young man carefully wrapped his fingers around the wide grip of the Browning Hi-Power.

Gun in hand, Faraydoun realized he could attempt an escape. The 9-mm pistol felt heavy, probably fully loaded with thirteen or fourteen rounds. This model gun was one of the first to utilize a double-stack magazine, which meant that the bullets did not sit directly on top of each other, but rather were housed staggered, so that more could fit inside the handle of the weapon. Would that suffice? He looked straight into the eyes of his opponent, or was it his friend? Backing up quickly would give him the chance to take aim and disable the General without killing him. But could he even get past all the guards? Was the General telling him the truth that he wasn't going to hurt him? After all those days of torture, did he really want to die?

"Camus must be wrong, Sir," the spy said as he returned the firearm. "Just because we do not understand all the complexities of life, it does not mean that life has no value. I cannot tell you what it is, but I believe there is some reason for us to be here, and we each have a job that we must do. I don't believe in the absurdity, and therefore I do not believe in the need for suicide. So I am not going to kill myself, and nor am I going to try to kill you."

While accepting his handgun, Atik asked, "So what do you believe in?"

"I want you to know that I do believe that Saddam Hussein is the rightful president, and should be the president of our glorious country. However, I think that we need help from the outside. I think a fair and impartial organization like the United Nations can play an important role helping our government fit in better with the Western powers while still being an important leader in the Arab world. And you know, General, that is who I was helping. I was sent by the U.N. to gather some information. I'm not a spy who goes around killing people. I was a university student at Cambridge when I met some great people who taught me about the possibility of a gentler world. They suggested that I study math and literature, not bomb-making and chemical warfare."

Atik nodded, "Go on."

"And over the years, I've helped them to understand the ways that our leaders think in order to help them help us. They really are dedicated people whom I'm sure you'd like."

"This world, and especially this country, could certainly afford to be more gentle. I would like to meet them. Where should I go?" replied Atik.

The young spy, pleased with his explanation to a reasonable colleague, took a long drink from his water bottle and breathed a refreshing sigh.

"What is a 'do not enter' sign doing on this door?" a strong voice came from outside.

"Who is that?" Mustafa asked.

"It sounds like Ali Hassan al-Majid."

"Oh my God, he'll kill me. Please tell my father I am not a traitor."

The door burst open and Ali shouted at Atik. "What have you done with this prisoner? I was told he did not cooperate and you're treating him like a prince!" Spotting the injured arm, Ali grabbed the young man's sensitive limb. He caused a dagger-like pain to go shooting up the whole side of his body. "Enough of your belligerence," he barked. Drawing his gun, Ali jammed it into his victim's ear, tearing the skin and breaking the delicate cartilage. "Who sent you here?"

Moments from death, Mustafa's face looked boyish. "I believe you did not betray me," he said looking at the General.

"Who?" yelled Ali, twisting the broken arm more.

"Take it easy, Ali," the General interjected. "There's no need for that."

"I know what we need, Atik," Ali growled back. "Who? Who sent you, Mustafa?"

"I think it is true," the young man continued to Atik, trying to contain his pain, "that suicide is a solution to the absurd. I'm beginning to get the feeling that this is absurd." He turned to Ali and yelled back, "And I believe that you are a moron!"

"Don't do it," the General ordered as he tried to stop Ali.

As Ali cocked his gun and began to squeeze the trigger, Mustafa began to say to Atik, "Please remember to tell my fath...."

Atik didn't move. Covered with the splatterings of the young spy's blood, he told Ali, "He was about to give me names when you walked in."

"He wasn't going to tell you anything," Ali tersely replied and stormed out of the room.

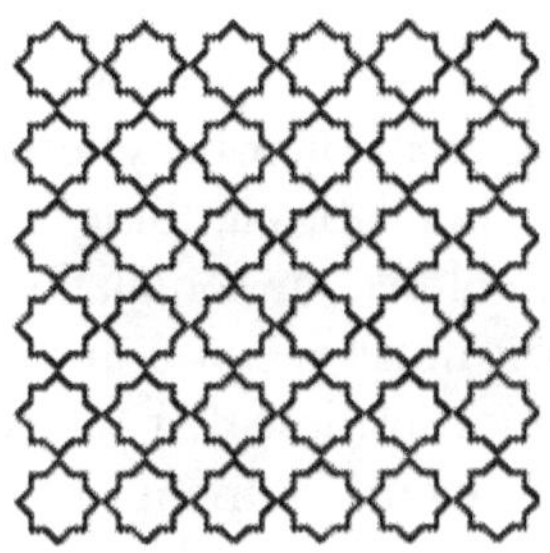

Chapter 3

"You learned very well this morning, Fatima," Sensei began. "And you fought as bravely as a true warrior. You seemed to enjoy the training, too. Right?"

I nodded.

"As you progress through your years in the service of our President, you must remember that most battles are not won with the sword. Too often, soldiers believe that they can kill a few people and then declare victory in their battles. That, however, doesn't always work. It's better if you can control people through love or fear. If you choose to lead through love, you must understand what they want to hear, and you must lead with wisdom. If you try to control them through fear, you must keep them frightened of you every moment of the day. The moment they stop fearing you, they will revolt."

"I see, my teacher. But why have you studied how to fight and kill?"

"My karate encompasses much more than hitting hard and fast. When I spar, I spend just as much energy studying my opponent as I do on the physical contact. You must develop your ability to focus on every aspect of your life, to see clearer and to absorb the knowledge in front of you. Whether you're studying in the computer lab, climbing a mountain, battling a Kurdish soldier, or tantalizing a general at a dinner party, you must see and analyze every detail. The skills of concentration that you will learn in karate must be used every moment of the day."

Adopting his wisdom, I listened to every word and considered how it applied to all the aspects of my life. "I am trying very hard, Sensei, to succeed here. Is there something more that you are trying to tell me?"

He placed his hand on my shoulder. "You've got excellent intuition, Fatima. You sensed that perhaps I was avoiding the central point. And you were right." He slid his hand down my arm slowly. "While you live in the palace, I hope to teach you a great deal. That will mean that you and I will spend much time together. However, it is imperative that you excel in your academic studies as well." He gave me a penetrating stare as he held my hand. The hairs on his mustache spread apart a bit as he smiled. I wanted to touch them, to kiss him. "You can control the intelligence in your mind," he said moving my hand up to my head, "with the strength in your heart." He gently pulled my hand back down to my heart, with his knuckles touching my breast. He slid it away slowly, stimulating me, and then pressed my own hand on my chest.

"I see, my master," I choked a little. "I will focus on my studies as well as on you." His hand covered mine, which I kept on my chest.

"I will see you in the morning, Fatima," he said as his fingers glided across then down and away from me. *What would happen if I grasped his hand and pulled it back towards me, if I invited him to touch me?* I wondered, and then bid him a good day.

After Sensei's lecture, I wanted to succeed in all aspects of my education, both physical and academic. I wanted to impress him with my abilities. From that day on, I began to spend long hours in the computer lab. When there was a portion of the studies that troubled me, I called upon my cousin Yousef to help. He was brilliant, especially in the sciences. He would sketch the molecular structure of different chemicals on my notebooks so I could review them while walking to and from my room.

Yousef told me one day that there was a way of using the computer to connect with other computers, to see what other people were looking at. "Some computers," he explained, "are networked with each other. Eh-eh-especially big companies and governments. Would you like to see?" He was very excited as he unplugged the phone wire from the phone on the table and stuck it into the modem of my laptop. "Watch this." He typed in a phone number and after a painful whistling sound came from the computer, an entry screen appeared: "Welcome to the Baghdad Diplomatic Girls Training Academy. Today's date is October 22, 1989. Please enter your password."

Yousef inserted a floppy disk into the drive and copied a program on to the hard drive called "pdanl-sys." He ran the program, which instantly began to crunch through various codes. "Let's have a coffee," he suggested while the computer worked. I prepared the thick, over-sweetened *kawa* that most of the men drank. For myself, I sweetened a lighter cup and added milk. I had read an article in *Cosmo* that mentioned some actress who drank many cups a day that way. After about twenty minutes, the program flashed, "Password acquired." It was a series of numbers and letters, which he copied into the proper place on the screen.

The monitor turned black, looking like the computer crashed. A few seconds later, though, a new image appeared, "Welcome Dr. Rahim." I laughed out loud when I realized that we had broken into the computer at my old school, and the computer thought that we were the principal. "Shall we check out your grades?" Yousef suggested.

We navigated through various menus until a list of students appeared. My name was missing. "It must be because they took me out of the class. Let's try this search function here." I pointed to the screen and he filled in my name. A record slowly appeared on the screen listing my name, address, and my parents' names along with my date of birth and next to it was my date of death – the same day that I was summoned to the palace. "Look at that," I commented, "they think that because I'm no longer in the school, I must be dead."

Yousef did not laugh as I would have expected. Computers were always doing funny things, so a mistake like this made sense. "Perhaps we should log off now, Fatima," he suggested.

"I'd like to call my parents to see what they know." I unplugged the phone cable from the computer and replaced it in the phone to call home. I hadn't spoken to my parents since arriving here because Madame Moreau seemed opposed. When I dialed home, though, all I could get was a busy signal, as if the line had been disconnected.

"Perhaps I'll call my father in his office. Do you think he'll be there?"

Yousef said he didn't think it was a good idea to call him, but I called my father's direct line at work and he picked up after a few rings, saying our family name as his greeting.

"Father, it's me, Fatima," I said happily.

He was quiet for a moment, and then said, "Who is this? My daughter is dead. You should not call me."

"But father," I protested, sure he would recognize my voice.

"Whoever you are, do not speak to me!" I heard the phone on the other side slam once against the table, missing its target, and then disconnecting.

My cheeks shook, preparing to cry, but I forced myself to breathe properly. "Why do you think he hung up, my cousin?"

"Perhaps we should not have explored your school's computer," Yousef replied, changing the subject. "Please continue your chemistry lesson." He popped his code-breaking diskette out of my computer and then left me alone to study.

A few minutes later, I decided to try calling my mother again. Surely there was some terrible mistake. After all, my father had sent me a note wishing me well. Why would he think I was dead? When I lifted the receiver, there was no dial tone. The security regiment clearly didn't want me making any more phone calls.

Since Sensei had asked me to focus on the academic side of my palace experience, I resolved to complete the day's work before going to investigate my own death. Everyone faces the fear of his own death, but it seems like my death had already happened, leaving only confusion, and no fear in its wake.

As I was finishing up, I reached into my bag and withdrew a large folder that I had used for my papers. Inside the folder was a blank diskette. I placed the folder neatly beside my laptop computer and, while hiding the motion of my fingers with the papers, I slipped the disk into the computer's drive. With the cameras in the room watching, I didn't want anyone to see me copy Yousef's computer code breaker onto my disk. Once the file transfer was complete, I manipulated my papers once again, making it look like I was just straightening up. With the disk buried in my school supplies, I pushed in my chair and headed out.

"I have a meeting to go to this morning, Fatima," Sensei told me when he came by the next day. "I am not sure how long it will take, so do some stretching yourself and then go to see the doctor. I scheduled you for a complete exam at 7:30."

"But Sensei, I have something I must discuss with you."

"I know, Fatima, but it'll have to wait until later."

I didn't bother asking him how he knew since I figured out that the only way a person can keep a secret is if he's dead. "But listen, my dear," he said handing me a bag, "I think you'll like this."

Another gift! I gratefully accepted his present and started imagining what he meant by his "dear." He left with a friendly salute and I checked out the contents of the bag. Beneath a few music CDs was a new portable CD player. I had a friend who had one, but they were so expensive that I never imagined owning one myself. I played the Madonna album since I had heard her before. While I did warm-up exercises, I danced to the beat of "Material Girl."

The doctor's visit took almost an hour. He asked me in-depth questions about my medical history, and then started talking to me about what I thought about life in the palace. He wanted to know about my dreams and my interactions with others. He asked if there were things that I was afraid of, and if I had ever tried drugs or sex. It became clear that the exam was not only physical, but more of a psychological exam, as well.

A nurse came in and told me to get undressed. She had a tape rule and took measurements of every part of my body. Afterwards, she gave me a small gown to wear and told me to sit on the examining table. The doctor returned and put my legs in stirrups for an embarrassing gynecological exam. Luckily, the whole thing took just a few minutes and he said I looked fine. He started scribbling on a clipboard and walked out of the room. The nurse returned and looked me over as she handed me my clothes. "You know," she said, "at your age it's time for you to focus on some hygiene issues. Here are some razors. Have you ever shaved before?"

"I tried when I was younger," I admitted, "but I ended up getting all cut up." She was quite professional as she told me where and how to shave.

"I see that your acne is also getting to be a bit of a problem," she said. I was surprised because I thought that had mostly cleared up. "I will ask the doctor to give you a prescription for that."

When I saw him next, he handed me a few boxes of pills that he said would help. "The important thing," he said, "is to take one pill every day before you go to bed. The dispensers are special because the day of the week is written by each pill so you'll not forget. It can be dangerous if you skip even one day." I didn't know what the danger could be, but I was glad that my face would look even cleaner for my teacher.

Sensei met me outside the doctor's office. "How are you feeling?" he asked.

"Thank you, my teacher, I am fine."

"You had an unusual experience yesterday, Fatima. You surprised everyone by calling your family. That was not something you should have done, nor something you may do again." He escorted me to one of the quiet, empty palace libraries and pulled a local newspaper off a shelf. It was a recent edition, dated the day after I came to the palace. My picture was on the front page under a headline that read, *Tragedy Strikes the Atik Family*. Sensei told me to read the article.

"While in a taxi on the way home from school yesterday, 16-year-old Fatima bint-Jamal Atik was tragically killed when the driver of the vehicle lost control and swerved off the N'amaniya bridge. The car exploded on impact, instantly killing both driver and passenger." I turned to the next page to see photographs of my family and friends crying beside a casket. Seeing their tears, I started to cry, too.

"Oh, Sensei. Something is very wrong. What has happened? Why is this story in the newspaper?"

"This was done for your own protection, Fatima, and your family's."

"Why? We were in no danger. My father is an important aide to my uncle. Everything was fine." I started getting angry, feeling deceived.

"Please, Fatima, let me explain. Your father has done some very important work for the country. And you, too, will be able to serve as very few can do."

"I want to serve, Sensei. But now I am ready to have my family back. Please take me home." I spoke firmly.

"I'm so sorry, Fatima, but I just can't do that. In the future, it will be better that no one knows that you're connected to your family. It could put them and you in grave danger. Right now, in fact, only a few key people know your true identity. As far as the rest of the world goes, my dear, you died two weeks ago."

It seemed a bit like a joke. "You're not kidding, are you?" I asked.

"Look, Fatima, you're getting a chance that others would only dream of. You're going to live a privileged life without the weight associated with your past. You must remember, though, that a great deal is going to be expected from you. You'll have a new identity, maybe several in fact. You'll have training and access to top-secret information. The resources of the palace will always be available to you. And you must realize, the strength of the palace goes far beyond these walls. It penetrates not only the Arab world, but everywhere in the world. While you live here, Fatima, you must learn to master both the physical and academic challenges. Once you leave, you will need all of your education to succeed and survive."

"Do you really think I can be a spy?" I asked, finally recognizing what this whole episode was about.

"You're a natural. You've consistently been the most successful student in your class. You're extraordinarily creative. You have a predisposition to languages, having been brought up speaking Arabic, English, and German with your parents and grandparents. And you're beautiful. You know that, don't you?"

I didn't know what to say, so I smiled and tried to play down his compliment. "Oh my, Sensei, you do not need to say such nice things."

"Shyness isn't your strength, Fatima. Modesty maybe, but that's just a learned trait. I knew you were the best candidate for this position as soon as I saw you. You have eyes like your mother, blue like the sky. Your hair flows gently on your shoulder, and when you move your head it covers different parts of your face. Every man would desperately want to see and touch your dark complexion. Your lips seem ready to kiss at any moment. And you have a beautiful body. You are a perfect woman; you have hips that rock side-to-side when you walk, and your shape is like a movie star." Sensei was sitting opposite me at the table. I felt his foot under the table touch my toe as he shared his feelings. I, too, wanted to tell him how I admired his personal power. Instead, I kicked my sandal off and let him glide his foot briefly over mine.

"I selected you for this program, Fatima, and I will take care of you. I can only hope that you will forgive me for having arranged it this way. It's just that no one must ever know about what you really do here, and if we had just asked your mother if we could take you away for this responsibility, I'm afraid the answer would have been no. And then you and I would not have been able to be together like this."

"I want to be with you, too, my teacher. I am glad you chose me."

"There is much to do, Fatima. Continue with your studies, and we will exercise tonight after dinner." He moved his foot up slightly below my knee, and then slowly tickled my skin as he brought it to the floor. He held on to the sides of the wooden table and pushed himself up. "I will be by at seven tonight."

"Good day, Sensei," I replied, standing up for him.

He left, and I remained to re-read my obituary. Each word was important because it spoke of my life, my family, and friends. I studied the photographs, too. My mother was unable to maintain her composure, and they took the picture as she lay over the casket. My father was further back, maintaining a stern look on his squarish face. After checking for security cameras and finding none, I folded the newspaper and stuck it in my bag.

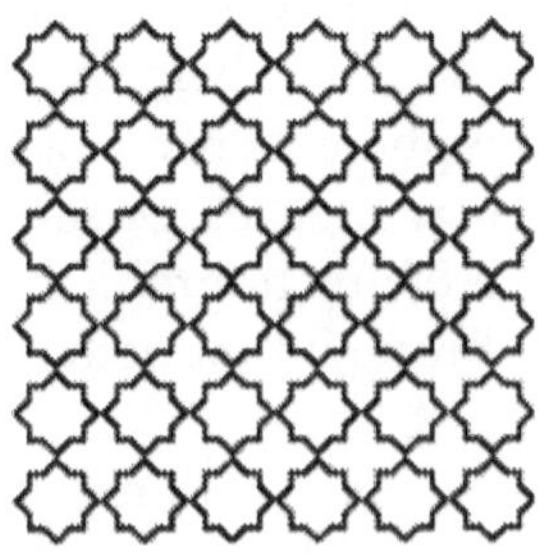

Chapter 4

I arrived in the computer room before Yousef. I settled in and then logged on to my workstation. I looked for the code-breaking program but, as I had suspected, someone had come in before and deleted it from my hard drive. No surprise, I thought, since they wouldn't want me to have the ability to hack into other computers. Nonetheless, I had made my own copy.

"You knew I was dead, my cousin. I saw you at the funeral," I confronted Yousef when he arrived. With the newspaper on the table to prove my point, he stuttered, "Of c-c-course I knew, Fatima. However, I was under orders not to tell you."

"Not to tell me I'm dead! Listen, Yousef, I thought we got along well and liked each other." He nodded. "It's hard enough in this place with no friends, so can we at least agree to help each other out?"

He held my chair for me to sit down and then rolled me into place. "I will help you, Fatima. I hope you forgive me."

Had I really made him feel so guilty that he felt he needed my forgiveness? With my warmest smile I forgave him, and perhaps even won a bit of his heart. He spent all day with me, helping me complete assignment after assignment. My language skills were sharpening, and I was feeling comfortable using the computer to solve my math problem sets. At around 4:30 p.m., I left to rest and eat before my evening exercise.

Instead of sleeping, I read my magazine and listened to a Joe Jackson CD from Sensei's gift bag. At 6:20 p.m., I went to Aisha's kitchen to grab a bite. The girls there liked me and always saved special meals for me from the President's banquets. When I returned to my room a half hour later, there was a black canvas bag on my bed. Excited to get another gift from Sensei, I opened it quickly. The bag was packed and very heavy. I pulled some black clothes off the top —a sweatshirt with zippered pockets and black pants, also with zippered pockets. There was a thin black rope that was clearly very strong, and some rappelling gear. I found an interesting pair of electronic goggles, and near the bottom there was a walkie-talkie. A note was taped onto it, "Get dressed now and call me on channel 12 when you're ready."

I quickly changed into the outfit and was amazed that it fit perfectly. It was as though the clothes, including the leather gloves and black ski-hat, were designed and made just for me. When I was all set, I turned on the two-way radio and, pressing the button, said only, "Okay."

"Shut the light in your room and put the scopes on."

I obeyed, and finding a switch on the top of the night-vision goggles, I turned them on. The rubber eye cups fit tightly, and the weight pulled my head down a bit. The rubber straps were the right size for my head, allowing me to turn from side to side without the device slipping. With the lights off in my room, it took a moment, but then I could see almost everything in a green hue. "Okay," I reported.

"Turn on the infrared illuminator on the left side of the goggles."

When I flicked the switch, everything lit up even more. I later learned that the scopes had a flashlight attached that filtered almost all visible light, leaving only infrared. This area of the spectrum was invisible to the normal eye, but helped light up the area for people with the right equipment.

"Come out through the window, and we'll rendezvous below. No more radios."

I hooked the radio to my belt and then looked around my room for a place to attach the rope. I was very excited to be using the real military equipment that Sensei had been teaching me about. A wide pipe below the window was made of steel and served as a solid anchor for my rope. With a fishing knot that I had learned on a camping trip years earlier, I tied the rope two times around the pipe. As a backup, I also tied it around the metal foot of my bed. The latch on the window squeaked when I turned it, so I moved it slowly to avoid making too loud a noise. I dropped the coiled rope out the window, and it unraveled into a neat line down the side of the building.

With my harness on tightly, I hooked my clips onto the rope and began to lower myself the three stories to the parking lot. As I hovered at the level of the first floor, I glanced down. I had learned from Sensei's mistake that you must always check your landing spot. His car was around a hundred meters away, but between he and I was a security guard sitting on the roof of a Mercedes limousine. Even though this was just a training exercise, if the guard saw me, he wouldn't know what to do, and would probably shoot.

I could see the side of the guard's face, since his gaze was focused on the gate to the main street. He took a puff from his cigarette and just sat with bad posture on the car. I had watched the parking lot guards many times before, and I knew they were supposed to walk around. But he just seemed tired. I considered climbing back up to my room, but Sensei's orders were to come down to him, and I was determined not to fail.

Rather than pushing myself far away from the wall and sliding down in one quick rush, I inched myself down. Walking down the side of the building, I was able to keep a quiet profile and I didn't attract the attention of the guard. When I got to the ground, I lowered myself completely so I was lying on my back. I disconnected the rope and my harness and then rolled onto my stomach.

Trying to copy a cat whose soft paws make no noise, I crawled towards my teacher's car. The paved surface was still warm from baking in the sun all day. The gloves protected my hands from the sharp edges of the rocks as I slid along the ground. At one point, I slithered under a car. Wearing the goggles presented an obstacle because the scope protruded about six inches from the front of my face and I nearly banged it into the exhaust pipe. For a moment, I took them off and saw that in fact, the guard had no way to see me since the whole area was virtually pitch black. I replaced them and moved more quickly toward Sensei's car. I went around to the passenger side and while still on the ground, I tapped gently on the door.

The window opened all the way. I checked out the area to be sure no one could see, and then quickly climbed in through the car window. Once I was halfway in, my teacher helped me by grabbing me under the arms and pulling me. I was amazed at how strong he was to lift me from such an awkward angle. I straightened myself in my seat and he closed the window. I removed my headpiece and ski-hat and then let my hair shake down.

"You did very well, Fatima," he congratulated me. "Those guards had no idea you were there."

"Guards?" I asked, shocked since I had only seen one.

"There are three guard stations in this parking lot. One by the back wall over there," he pointed. "One by the entrance to the building where you normally go in and out. And then the third station where the guard is assigned to patrol the area. But he's got a bit of a hangover and has perched himself on one of the limos. You did a great job avoiding them. Didn't you see them?"

I laughed. "Well, I only saw one, the one drinking. I guess I had beginner's luck."

"This was good practice anyway, Fatima. These guys are some of the dumber guards around here. And you had a great advantage over them with these night-vision goggles. These are the best ones on the market. I chose them personally from a company called Electro-Optics, and only our very elite troops get to use them."

"They were excellent, especially with the infra-red light boost," I complimented.

"Did you bring the other equipment in the bag?" he asked.

"I wasn't sure how it would all work or if I should, so I left it upstairs. I hope that's okay." There had been some other cases and heavier items on the bottom of the bag he had left for me. Sensei explained that they were different tools that could be used for spying and moving around surreptitiously. He told me how they worked and said that next time, I should take them all. "After all," he said, "even though they're heavy, it's better to have them and not need them than to need them and not have them."

"What we're going to work on now is moving around at night undetected." He continued, "Like what you did here, but we'll do it in less familiar terrain. We'll go to buildings that you've never visited before, and you'll have to memorize the blueprints. Going out your own window to the same parking lot you've seen every day isn't much of a test."

"Where will we go?" I asked.

"We'll use other palaces and office buildings to get started. Then we'll work on going inside the buildings. It's a lot of map work and memorization. Frankly, climbing ropes is the easy part. It's knowing which side of the building to drop from that's hard. Tonight we'll go to one of the mobile chemical labs. Our goal will be to start from the car, go to the door of the lab and..." His car phone rang and cut him off. "Hang on, Fatima, I'm expecting an important call."

He answered and then listened intently for a few minutes, saying only "hmm," from time to time. At the end of the call he affirmed, "I understand. I'll be there soon." Then he turned to me and said, "Something has come up, Fatima. We'll have to do this later."

"Can you tell me what it is, Sensei? Is it something to do with Kuwait?" I had overheard a mention of the neighboring state when he was on the phone.

"You don't quite have the security clearance to know, but I trust you. Please don't let this out."

I swore on my honor.

"We've been having a lot more trouble with the Kuwaitis recently. Since the war with Iran, they have been stealing our oil from the Rumeila oil fields. It's cost us billions at a time when we are financially strapped. The President is being backed into a corner on this point since we need the revenues from the oil, and our supposed 'friends' have been letting the price drop well below fifteen dollars a barrel." He paused and I saw his lips tighten as he thought about the situation.

I was familiar with the problem of stolen oil because it had been going on for years. I knew my father had worked on the problem during the war, but it never seemed to go away. During the war with Iran, we had to stop drilling in the fields along the border with Kuwait. They kept going, though, even siphoning off oil from our side. Most of my knowledge of the topic was from reading newspapers, so I was thrilled to hear first-hand accounts of the details.

"To make it worse, Fatima, they not only steal from us, but we can't seem to engage them in any diplomatic resolutions. They are trying to kick us when we're still recovering from the last war. This call I just got was because one of our senior negotiators was refused a meeting with the Emirate when we asked to discuss our claims on the Warbah and Bubiyan islands. How are we supposed to handle our deep-water shipping needs without more control? How can we stay at peace with those arrogant puppets when they won't even talk to us?"

"Why do you call them puppets?"

"They just kowtow to the Western oil buyers. They have no sense of independence, no pride, no real history. Their true background is really Iraqi. When the Ottoman Empire fell, all of the Al-Basrah province was supposed to be Iraq - and that included what is now called Kuwait. But the British decided to keep Kuwait as their own protectorate. They wanted to make sure they could control passage to India, the 'jewel in their crown.' Talk about arrogant! When the Brits decided they no longer needed Kuwait in the early '60's, they set it up as its own little state. That's when we really should have made a stand and taken back what they had been using for decades. Why do we have to negotiate with them about our own land? We should just take what's rightfully ours. Talking with a Kuwaiti prince is like talking to a spoiled child. They're only rich because they don't let anyone in the country have any rights except the families of the oil sheiks. And, since the beginning of the century, they relied on the protection of England instead of defending themselves."

I was familiar with this view of history, so I added, "The British have their paws in everything, along with the Americans and Zionists."

"Don't be so quick to point fingers. The British never understood our true traditions. The Americans like watching Arab infighting. And I don't think the

Israelis care one way or the other. They're a useful satellite of the Americans. When we need to hit the U.S., we can hit Tel Aviv instead."

"So where do you have to go now?" I asked.

"There's a strategy meeting that I must attend. It'll be held down south, Fatima, so I'll probably have to be away for a while. While I'm gone, you should keep training on your own. I thought of asking my son to train you in boxing, which is his specialty. But right now he's away, participating in some competition. In any case, you can practice with these things." He pointed to my night-vision and climbing equipment. "Always remember to keep your eyes wide open and listen carefully to all the noises around you. If you had done that, you would have known about all three of the guards that might have arrested or shot you tonight. Please, Fatima," he placed his hand on my left knee, "please don't get shot." He laughed at his own joke, and then told me to go back to my room.

"May Allah keep you safe on your mission, my teacher." I worded my phrase to suggest he was going to do something rather than just attend a meeting. I wanted to see his reaction to let me know if he, too, was some kind of spy. But he just thanked me, and then told me to open my door slowly and not to slam it as I left.

I got down on the ground right away, slid under his car, and headed back towards my room. With the night-glasses, I checked out the three sentries and felt secure cloaked in the darkness. Sensei started his car and drove away. None of them paid attention.

The harness wouldn't help me ascend, so I stuffed it into my bag before climbing the rope. Without great strength in my arms, I couldn't climb as smoothly as Sensei. But hand over hand, I eventually got to the ledge by my window. I pulled up the rope and tossed it inside on the floor. Feeling like a ghost who could go anywhere without being seen, I surveyed the different areas of the parking lot and then checked out how my room looked in green.

It was amazing how the lines of the bed and sink showed up in bright jade-like shades. Though the room was almost pitch black, the fifty thousand times light gain from the goggles, amplified by the infrared illuminator attached to them, allowed me to see many details. I looked at the door and saw a mouse squeeze its way underneath. Though I wasn't afraid of rodents, I was never the one to kill them in my house. I watched as it sniffed around the corners of my room until it got to my bed. It scurried up the sheets and then started heading towards the window. It must have smelled the fresh air and was looking for an escape. Not wanting it to crawl over me, I reached in, took hold of the window, and gently pulled the frame towards me. It clicked slightly and the mouse ran across the inside ledge of the windowsill. Then I realized my mistake.

I was stuck outside with no rope and Sensei had already driven out of range of the walkie-talkie, so I had no one to help me.

Jiggling the window only made noise and set the lock more firmly in place. The crash of breaking glass would surely attract the attention of the guards, and without a rope, I couldn't safely drop the three flights to the ground. Moreover, even if I got down, how would I get back into the building without being noticed? I would certainly look suspicious trying to enter a Hussein palace dressed in tight black clothes and carrying climbing equipment and night-vision goggles.

With no way either down or up, I stood on the narrow ledge with my back to the wall. The fabulous view afforded by the scopes allowed me to keep an eye on the guards as I inched cautiously around the side of the building looking for an opening. Before rounding the corner, I peeked to the side and everything went dark for an instant. The momentary loss of my sight made me lose my balance, and I grabbed hold of a small nick in the wall to steady myself. The goggles had picked up on a light and shut down to avoid blinding me. Otherwise, they would have magnified the incoming signal the same amount they magnify the light from a dim star.

When they automatically recalibrated a second later, I realized that the headlight of a car entering the main gate had caused my trouble. As cars stood at the entrance so the sentries could check the drivers' papers, their headlights beamed directly on the wall of the palace. They illuminated my private darkness. The cars came in every few minutes, and there was no way to know when they would show up next. The next window was about twenty meters away. From my perspective, I could not tell if it was open. In fact, I suspected it was the kitchen, but having never gone all the way inside the cooking area, I didn't know if it had any windows. The guard waved at another car to stop for questioning. While they spoke, the wall became like a drive-in movie. I certainly did not want to act the part of the shadow puppeteer. As soon as the vehicle was permitted entry, I sidestepped towards the next window. After getting around the corner, though, a truck pulled up, making me return to my hiding spot for another few minutes.

I adjusted my scopes and discovered that there was a magnification switch. When I flicked it, I could see an object at about two or three times the normal size. I looked outside the palace at the highway to see if more traffic was coming. A few minutes later, my chance came again. I paced myself as quickly as I could, and got about halfway to the window when I spotted a delivery truck slowing down on the highway with its blinker on. I heard the sound of my clothes rubbing against the wall behind me as I sped up. The truck began to turn and his lights started sweeping across my wall. I got to the window as the beams were almost on me. With a light push, it wiggled, but didn't open. Peeking in, I saw that I was right and it was the kitchen. I gave a harder push and the hinge squeaked open. Just before the headlights exposed me, I hopped through the opening and landed silently on the floor. I crouched down and rolled under a table to survey the room.

On the other side of the kitchen, I saw the chef who had tortured Aisha standing over an industrial-sized mixing bowl. The motor growled, but not too loudly. Though his back was towards me, he was facing the direction of the door. If he turned around, I'd be caught, and there was no way for me to get to the only exit without him spotting me.

A series of knives were held magnetically on a cabinet behind him. I could grab the sharp cleaver and ram it across the back of his neck. That would sever the spinal cord and probably kill him instantly. God knows, he deserved it for what he had done to that young maid. Practically, though, I would still have to get back to my room and the hallway could be teeming with people. Moreover, when they found his dead body, they would probably assume it was one of the girls from the kitchen and then they would all be executed.

A microwave sat on the next table and its plug was hanging over the side. Someone had been cutting fruits next to it and left a small paring knife alongside the machine. Staying low to avoid making any shadows, I hurried under the table, grabbing the knife as I slid into my new hiding spot. The power cord for the microwave required many slices because the blade of the knife was dull.

Once I had the plug and about twenty centimeters of wire dangling from it, I twisted the copper wires together and pressed the plug into the outlet. It made a loud popping noise from the short circuit I created, and there was a flash from the wall. Instantly, everything turned green. The electric fuse had shut the power to the room, and to the whole wing, I hoped. With my goggles, I could see fine. I stood up, walked right past the cook, who was cursing, and opened the door. Several people were in the corridor, but they were all holding onto the wall as they continued to their destinations. I walked right down the center of the passageway to my room. I opened the door, scaring the mouse out into the hall, and got ready for bed. Reaching under my mattress, I slipped out my favorite bedtime reading material, *Cosmo*, and read myself to sleep.

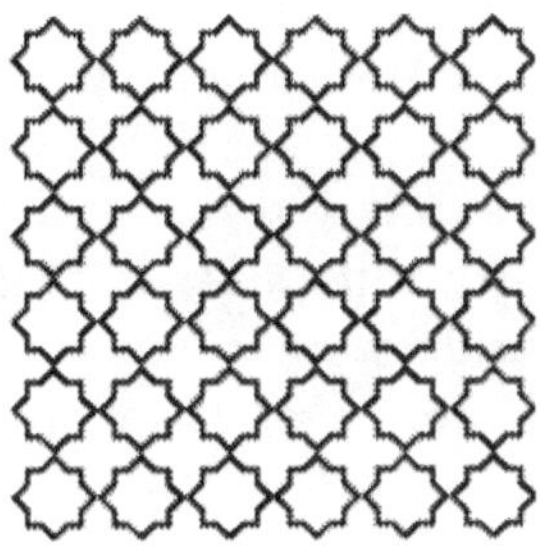

Chapter 5

Without the enjoyable distraction of Sensei, I focused on my studies. There was no way to contact him, and I was afraid to arouse suspicions by asking about him. Yousef told me that Sensei's son, Da'uud, had embarrassed the palace by losing the international boxing match that he was supposed to win.

Yousef spent hours in the computer lab with me, sometimes teaching me and always answering my questions. He told me that my memorization techniques were too basic. He taught me ways to have instant recall of numbers, names, faces, and any other information using mnemonics. As I mastered this new approach to learning, I tested myself by memorizing decks of cards, learning thousands of new words in foreign languages, and studying newspapers and magazines to remember the identities of all the people in the pictures. I impressed Yousef by memorizing the periodic table one evening.

"The student has surpassed the t-t-teacher," he commented. "Now let us apply your knowledge in real-life applications." He escorted me to an underground lab on the other side of the palace. Entrance required a five-digit code on the pad outside the door. "0-1-3-0-2," Yousef told me. "Its mnemonic equivalent is 'Saddam Hussein,' so it's easy t-t-to remember."

The large room had to remain sterile, so everyone wore special outfits and shoe and hair covers. The scientists inside were working with all sorts of chemicals, and in the back was a special glass partition behind which a team of three people wearing gas masks was working.

Yousef introduced me to a few of the people, and then began to explain about the effects of different chemical combinations on humans. The section we started with contained the tools to make a variety of different poisons, all with different levels of toxicity. He told me to memorize several potions made from more commonly found ingredients.

"What are they doing?" I asked, indicating the protected glass chamber.

"I'm not sure, Fatima."

"Come on, dear cousin, I thought we had an agreement to help each other," I cajoled him.

He bent down over one of the bottles so no one would see him talking, and he whispered, "They study biochemical reactions in order to create more p-p-potent weapons." Subtlety was not his strong point, so I stopped questioning him. I didn't want him to get too nervous answering questions when we were in public.

For over a week, I got private lessons in practical chemistry from my cousin. Now that I had the combination to the door, I could use the lab to run my own experiments. I gathered my own collection of different drugs and chemicals, filling small vials that would eventually find their way into my pockets. I stored them with the walkie-talkie that Sensei had left for me.

Eventually, Yousef gave me more details of my uncle's chemical weapons program. Since the other countries had their own stores, we needed to keep one step ahead. "Do you really think the Russians and Americans actually destroyed all of their small-pox and bubonic plague supplies?" Yousef explained. "Why would they eliminate one of their most power-ful d-d-deterrents?"

Within the palace compound were many differ-ent laboratories, some duplicating the efforts of oth-ers and some doing independent work. I got to visit them, and became friends with a few of the scien-tists. The head of one of the labs had been born and trained in England, but preferred to do his work in Iraq. One of the other divisions was run by Dr. Areebah Bari, a woman who got her PhD in the United States. She was a distant relative of the Saudi royal family, but was sent away to Iraq as a child when they realized that she was extraordinarily clever. During one visit she told me, "They had to choose to kill me or deport me because I was smarter than all the men in the family. Luckily my father had a cousin in Iraq that he sent me to allegedly for mar-riage, but really just to save my life."

For over a month, I spent at least ten hours a day involved in my academic studies. Apart from morning stretching, which I did while listening to CDs, I didn't do any physical training, and rarely had the chance to explore the area at night using my night-vision tools. I wanted to investigate a certain area near one of the labs, but Yousef told me that it was off limits. Since no one else seemed to care that it was about to be my seventeenth birthday, I decided to present myself a gift of satisfying my curiosity.

The evening was cold and dark, with only a sliver of the moon showing. Humid air threatened to turn to rain, minimizing visibility. It was a perfect night to investigate unnoticed. At around 10:00 p.m., I changed into my black body suit and harnessed up. I prepared a minute quantity of dilute cantharidin in a vial, and placed it in the small pocket in the shoulder of my outfit next to the walkie-talkie. My wide belt had metal rings that I used to hook on some of the other tools that Sensei had left for me, even though I had no experience using them. Fastening the rope to the wide pipe, I shut my light, turned on my night scopes, and slid quickly down to the parking lot below.

Crawling under cars, I first headed towards the guard leaning on the limo. I had watched him for many evenings, and as usual, he was drinking a small cup of coffee into which he had poured some liquor from his hip flask. The sounds of cars passing on the highway camouflaged the occasional noise that I made on the ground. I rolled to the car, opposite where he stood, and opened the vial that I had prepared. I waited for him to walk around, but his feet never moved. To get him going, I turned on my walkie-talkie tuned to channel eight, the frequency I knew the guards used since I sometimes eavesdropped on their conversations from my room. I pushed the button that created a brief static sound and caught his attention. He stepped towards the nearby car on which his radio sat. Looking under the car, I could see his feet were pointing away from me. I stood up, emptied my vial into his drink, and dropped back to my hiding place. He fumbled with the radio and then replaced it. Back to the post, he reclined on the car and sipped his spiked coffee. I maneuvered my way through the parking lot, staying low between the cars, and staying alert to where different guards stood.

As no one was standing by the entrance to my target building, I simply walked inside. There was a box of bottled water that was to be brought into the lab the next day. Someone had already taken a bottle or two, so I also helped myself. At night, the hall lights were all off, allowing me to move freely, hidden by the darkness. By the private offices, I could hear some people inside. The old door was locked. I took a sip from my water, dumped the rest into a nearby cactus, and then sliced the bottle with my penknife. With the flattened out piece of firm plastic, I slipped it in the crack between the door and frame, just above the doorknob. Pulling it gently down and back towards me, this effective tool pushed the latch of the lock into the door, releasing it. With a gentle push, the door opened.

The lights in the corridor were off as well, but now inside, with the door closed behind me, I could hear the voices more clearly. "I am the sports authority for this country. When you embarrass our team, you embarrass me. When your father represented us, we could walk with pride. When you go out there, it's like we're sending a girl into the ring." The familiar tone got louder. "What kind of punches were you throwing? This," he paused, "this is a punch." There was a firm clapping sound and a short scream. Then

I heard several other punches with no further responses. "Wake him up. I'm not done."

The sound of water splashing, followed by moaning, echoed down the hall. "Bring me a razor," the commander ordered. Though I was petrified in case they would find me, I hurried towards the fight. As the door was slightly ajar, I was able to see in. Tied to a chair, a bloodied, naked man sat crying. I could not identify him clearly, but I was almost certain it was Da'uud, Sensei's son. The same monster that nearly killed Aisha was battering this poor soul.

With his short beard and nearly shaved head, I recognized the torturer as Uday, my uncle's notorious son. He stood behind the victim, placed one hand on his forehead and pulled it back. He laid the razor on the unfortunate man's vulnerable neck and pressed the blade a little bit. The man begged for his life. I tried to think of a distraction to avert the murder, but anything I would do would surely lead to my own death as well.

Uday then lifted the blade and laughed. "If I cut your throat, you stupid girl, you'll bleed all over my office." Still holding his forehead, he shaved off the eyebrows of the wounded man. Along with the pain of the beating, this humiliation would bruise his pride. Uday washed his hands in a sink in his office and sat back down at his desk as if he were just going to continue with his regular routine. "Take him downstairs," he commanded his aides, "and make him swim."

One of the henchmen, wearing a white keffiyeh, bent over and picked up the leg of the chair, toppling it sideways. As his skull hit the floor, the man was knocked unconscious. Two men then dragged the body and chair, which were still tied together, towards the door. I tried to figure out which way they would go, so that I could run in the opposite direction. Presumably, they would take him to the stairs near the entrance to the building, so I darted down the hallway. I rounded the corner just as I heard them leave the room. Weighed down by their load, they moved very slowly. I lay down on the ground and peered back around the corner from where I came to confirm their direction. My intuition was wrong, and they started heading my way. I looked for a hiding place, but all the doors were closed and I didn't think I could pick a lock fast enough with my plastic trick. "Turn on the lights," one of them said to the other. "You want me to trip?"

"Where's the switch?" the other asked.

"Near the end of the hall."

If he got to that control before I got out of the hall, they would spot me instantly. One of the offices looked slightly open, but when I turned the doorknob, it was locked. As I heard them approaching the turnoff, I decided to try with the torn-open plastic water bottle again. I slipped it above the lock and tried to slide it down. It got caught on something inside. Rather than yanking it out and trying again, which might have made a noise, I abandoned the tool and ran to the end of the hallway. There I found the staircase to which the men were heading. I ducked inside the stairwell and headed up, since I had heard Uday order them to bring him down. I saw my shadow appear on the stairs in front of me as they flicked the light on in the hall.

"What's this?" one of them asked the other a moment later.

"It looks like someone didn't like his bottle of water." They had found my elementary lock opener, but luckily didn't know what it was.

As they hauled the body downstairs, I was tempted to follow them to see if I could stop the impending drowning. I knew, however, that there was nothing I could do. When I was sure that they had descended one flight, I came back to the hall and pulled my water bottle out of the door so there would be no evidence of my presence. Before running back to the stairs, I pulled the fire alarm. Maybe the distraction would stop these ghouls from murdering Da'uud, if that's who it really was. I continued up the stairs to the top and went out on the roof. The thick darkness allowed me to spy out the area without anyone spotting me. Without stairs, a ladder or a fire escape, I was almost stranded on the top of the two-story building. One of the unusual tools that Sensei had left me was a device that looked like a spring-loaded soda can. I unhooked the dense item from my belt and popped open the top. Instead of coming off completely, it remained attached with a strong wire. I wrapped the cord around the base of a satellite dish that was bolted to the roof. The small tab that hooked onto the cable created a strong loop around the pole. Pulling the thin cable out of the can required a firm tug. I attached the clip on one end of the cable to my belt and walked towards the edge of the roof. The can stayed next to the satellite dish, feeding more cable out as I moved away.

This remarkable invention allowed me to walk down the side of the building, like rappelling, but with the slow release of the cable protecting me. It was scary to bet my life on the technology of this unusual tool, but it worked perfectly. I heard a distant sound of a siren. The alarm must have automatically called the fire station. When I got to the bottom, I moved as quickly as I could to transfer the clip from my belt to a water pipe on the ground. When it was firmly in place, I grabbed the wire that was tightly strung between the roof and the ground and gave it as a strong a yank as I could. That pull caused a razor at the top to slice through the wire, allowing the winding mechanism inside the can to start spinning, spooling the wire inside itself as it came zipping down the building. It smacked the ground with a thud, made a whirring sound as it finished winding up the rest of the wire, and I grabbed it. Even through my thin leather gloves, it felt hot from the friction of the fast-moving cable inside. Staying low, I sprinted towards my home base.

On channel eight, I listened to determine if any guards would get in my way. I heard someone in charge order everyone to man his post and not come to help with the fire. I had to take a slight detour around the parking lot because two guards had popped out of the building for a smoke. As I came back around the perimeter, I had to pass the guard on the car. Though I could see him pretty well, I couldn't make out the expression on his face. I crouched behind a car about ten meters away and saw him rub his stomach. A moment later, he hopped off his perch, bent over beside the car and started to vomit. That was my cue to run right past him towards my window, and climb quickly up the black rope.

Knowing how to use poison to affect someone properly was a fantastic tool. I had dropped a minute amount of cantharidin into his cup earlier, and now I was free to walk right past him. Cantharidin is popularly known as "Spanish Fly," and it has the false reputation of an aphrodisiac. In fact, however, it was quite a deadly substance that, if used in small quantities, would just make someone sick. Yousef had told me that in England in the 1950s, a man named Arthur Kendrick Ford had heard of the loving effects that the drug could produce. He was 44, and there were two young women, aged 17 and 27, whom he was interested in. He told a colleague that he needed some cantharidin to help his neighbor's rabbits reproduce. The chemist informed Ford that the drug was, in fact, quite dangerous, but gave it to him anyway.

Ford bought some pink and white coconut ice candy and using a knife, pressed some of the deadly powder inside. He served his two targets, and ate some himself. Within an hour, all three were violently ill and had to be taken to the hospital. The women died, but he survived. On autopsy, the poisoning was quickly discovered because, according to the toxicologists, their internal organs had been burned away. Ford eventually went to jail for killing the two women.

With that history in mind, I had administered a very diluted dose to the guard. I suppose that's why it took him such a long time to get sick. The timing worked perfectly, though, and allowed me to scale the wall, reel in the rope, and close my window.

A few minutes later, I heard on the radio, "It looks like there's a problem with the switch. There's no fire here." I shut my walkie-talkie.

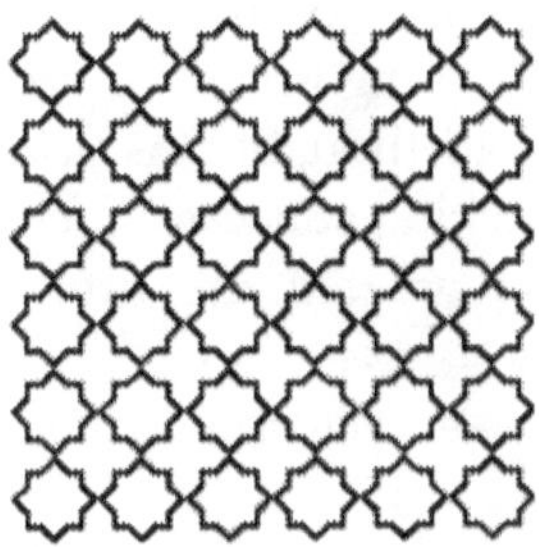

Chapter 6

For months, I continued my studies. Though I desperately wanted to see Sensei, I had grown accustomed to my routine of long hours in the computer lab. Yousef got me to focus on my English skills, memorizing thousands of vocabulary words and doing various word puzzles. At one point, he accompanied me on a visit to the U.S. embassy. After being checked by a marine, I was escorted into a quiet room where three other people were sitting at desks. Another marine walked in, gave us instructions about not cheating, and handed out a standard aptitude test. It was similar to the work that Yousef had been giving me, so I completed it in around two hours and left. The other people looked unhappy and were scratching their heads a lot.

"I t-t-trust it went well, my cousin?" Yousef asked me in the waiting room. I nodded. "Captain Gamal requested that you take this exam."

I was excited that someone had heard from him. "Really? When did he give those orders?"

"He sent a memo to the palace t-t-two weeks ago with instructions."

Back at the palace, Yousef dropped me off at the entrance near my room. As I walked down the corridor, one of my nightmares came true. The cruel villain whom I had thought was gone had returned. With several matching suitcases lined up next to her, Madame Moreau greeted me firmly. "Good afternoon, Fatima."

"*Salaam aleikum*, Madame Teacher," I responded politely.

"You have been summoned by Captain Gamal."

My heart started beating rapidly, and I had to contain my smile. I didn't want Madame to see how thrilled I was.

"We must go right away," she said. "I have taken the liberty of gathering some of your personal items, and these other bags have been packed for you."

I could not imagine what was contained in the four suitcases, but I figured I would check that out later. "May I go wash up?" I requested, curious to study her demeanor.

Reasonably, she agreed. "There is an outfit inside for you to wear. Please put it on. If you have any problems, I am here to help." What could be hard about getting dressed?

When I got inside, I closed the door and checked to see how much she had snooped around. All of my night-vision equipment was gone. She left the magazines, even though I assumed that this was not the type of reading that the palace encouraged. But if she had found the scopes, ropes, and black clothing, she could figure out what I had been doing. Feeling slightly sick, I went to the bathroom and washed up. When I came out from behind the curtain, I spotted a black outfit hanging on a hook. Next to it was a veil. The fabric was heavy, much warmer than the cottony outfits that I had worn until now. When I held it out, I realized it was a *burkha*, the traditional garb of married religious women.

After taking off my clothes, I tried to wrap myself in the new garment, but had trouble getting it right. Worse, it itched terribly. Since I knew we were in a hurry, I swallowed my pride and called through the door for Madame to help. She came in and looked at me. "Why are you undressed?" she asked. Before I could answer, she explained that women usually wore regular clothes underneath. Within a few minutes, I was covered from head to toe. She attached the thin veil in front of my face, through which everything looked fuzzy. In place of my regular sandals, she gave me black leather shoes with heels. Walking on them felt like standing on my toes. I liked feeling taller, but my calves hurt after a short time.

Three maids whom I did not recognize were standing outside my room. They wheeled the suitcase to the parking lot, walking about five meters behind us. There was a stretch limousine waiting. The driver loaded the bags, and Madame and I sat in the back. The car remained in place. It was hard to breathe through the veil, and I moved it to the side. "Fatima," Madame scolded, making me re-cover my face. She didn't continue.

A minute later, the door opened again. Yousef climbed in and handed Madame a large envelope. He had changed his normal clothes, and was now wearing a dark gray business suit. His unshaven face and new keffiyeh looked out of place on top of his expensive outfit. Madame knocked on the glass that separated us from the driver and he started the car. Examining the contents of the package that she had just received, she told me, "Your passport and papers are here."

"I thought we were going to see Captain Gamal," I commented, not knowing why I would need travel documents.

"We will rendezvous with him in Frankfurt," Yousef interceded. "At that point, he will give us further instructions." I decided not to mention that he had told me he was going to be in southern Iraq. Perhaps he had purposely not told them where he would be, and I certainly did not wish to divulge any information I had about him.

"You will be traveling as Sara bint-Muhammad Aziz, Yousef's sister. He shall be called Ahmed bin-Muhammad Aziz," Madame continued. She handed us our passports. Opening mine, I saw my picture along with my new name. There were stamps in the small book from several other Arab countries indicating where I had been recently. The forgery was brilliant. "Ahmed is a member of the Iraqi diplomatic corps. As you are traveling with him, no one should ask you any questions or search your bags. If you are stopped, you will say nothing. It is inappropriate for a religious Muslim woman of your stature to speak with any stranger. His task is to escort you to your husband, a senior diplomat, Dr. Jamal Hasim. When you see him, you shall not refer to him by the nickname you have used in the past, 'Sensei.'" I was embarrassed that she knew anything about my relationship with Sensei. However, I concentrated on the details of the names and listened intently. As was common in Muslim marriages, the wife did not adopt her husband's last name, but rather kept her family identity. Obviously, Madame Moreau was much more of a professional that I had ever imagined. "Having been born to Saudi Arabian royalty," she taught, "your marriage to Dr. Hasim created a crucial tie between President Hussein and King Aziz. You will be seen as a wealthy and powerful tool." She showed me two matching diamond and ruby bracelets, which she told me to wear. "Do be careful with them, Sara."

"Who will see me?"

She glared at me. "Sara, when your husband tells you he would like a drink, that is a fine time to ask a question – 'What can I pour for you, my husband?' But when you are portraying the wife of a senior Iraqi minister, you do not question."

I said nothing. The forty-minute car ride gave me ample time to imagine why Sensei would summon me. Perhaps he needed me to attend a meeting, or to follow someone, or maybe just to help with translation. Almost suffocating in my new outfit, I dozed off to sleep.

"Mrs. Aziz," the driver called me pleasantly, leaning into the back of the car. "We have arrived." I awoke slowly to find myself alone in the back of the car. My two companions were coordinating our luggage while I got out of the car. I did not speak to the driver. Further down the long sidewalk in front of the airport terminals, thousands of people were bustling about. The last time I was there, years earlier, was when my family flew to France for a vacation. This time, however, we went through an unmarked door far away from the crowds. Our entourage followed.

We walked from the street-side of the airport, straight through the building and down an escalator. We came out the other side, directly on to the tarmac. A clean white Lear Jet was parked about 200 meters away. The tail had the emblem of the Iraqi government; the tips on the wings were each painted with the colors of the flag. "Let's go," Madame ordered, and we hurried along. The sides of my feet were beginning to hurt from the shoes, and walking on rough asphalt exacerbated the pain.

The pilot looked back at us as we entered the craft. "Welcome aboard, Mr. Aziz, Mrs. Aziz," he said in English. He was one of the British pilots who was brought to the country to fly diplomats around. "Ahmed" returned the greeting, but I simply slowed down to show I had heard and then moved on. Madame followed us on board and watched as I sat down. She bent over to help me with my seatbelt and whispered in my ear, "Remember who you are, and do not speak to anyone." She walked to the cockpit, leaned in to say something to the men there, and left.

The plane taxied and took off. I became accustomed to the loud noise of the engines after a few minutes. Yousef and I were the only two passengers, though a stewardess came by to offer us drinks and snacks, which I refused. Next to my seat was a magazine rack. I reached down to grab a copy of *The Economist*, but Yousef whispered, "No, Sara. You are illiterate."

I stared across the plane at my cousin for a long time. No reading, no talking, obviously no movies ... Yousef's chin dropped to his chest as he fell asleep. The plane started flying higher and faster. I was pressed into my seat and could hardly life my arms because of the excessive force. A door on the floor suddenly flipped open, and the Kurdish thief from the rappelling fight climbed out. He held his sword in his right hand, crawling out of the hold towards Yousef. I tried to call out to warn him, but the veil wouldn't move from my mouth and I couldn't inhale enough to release even the smallest sound. With a quick slice, the silver blade slaughtered my teacher. His head swung to the side and then dropped back down, as if he was sleeping. His shirt began turning red.

I strained to move my hand towards my mouth. Using my fingers to crawl up the armrest and to my clothes, I inched my hand towards my face. The strong pressures of the plane had no effect on my enemy. He stood up, still wearing the same filthy clothes that had been bloodied when we fought months earlier, and he spit on the dead body. My hand was near my shoulder, almost able to uncover my mouth to call for help. "Why do you always want to fight me, my Queen? I will help you," he laughed, placing his hand atop my head.

With a determined push of strength, I fought against the gravity that was holding my hand down, and grabbed the veil that had become attached to my mouth. I tore it off, and my hand fell into my lap. "No," I screamed.

"Sara," Yousef whispered loudly. "What are you doing? Put your veil back on!"

The five-hour flight ended up being more exhausting than I had expected. Two thousand miles was more than enough for me. In the Frankfurt airport, we were escorted into a special hangar. A luggage handler unloaded the baggage compartment and a very tall man came to greet us. "*Willkommen nach Deutschland, Herrn Aziz,*" he said.

"*Vielen Dank,*" Yousef responded flawlessly.

"*Folgen Sie mir bitte,*" he said, indicating we should follow him.

The blond-haired man led us into an office just outside the hangar, where our passports were promptly viewed, stamped, and returned. As we walked out, I saw the French Minister of Education walk in. I remembered his face from having seen it in a newspaper three months earlier. He, too, had an Aryan-looking escort. Within minutes, we were outside the airport gates, getting into another limo. Our car was standing in a line of six other, similar vehicles, all presumably waiting to pick up their high-ranking passengers. The German representative closed the bulletproof door behind us and, wishing us well, said, *"Geniessen Sie Ihren Aufenthalt, meine Freunde."*

"Danke," Yousef replied, *"Salaam aleikum."*

After a silent thirty-minute drive, we arrived at the Grande Veranda Hotel. The architect had tried to emulate a royal palace, though he had probably never seen a real one. There were columns and waterfalls inside the lobby, but through the veil I could see very few details. We were escorted by our driver. Serving as a bodyguard to bring us into the hotel, he looked at all the people who came close to us. His mean expression and dark skin discouraged tourists from coming too close to view the veiled woman.

The manager greeted us by the elevator, handed Yousef a magnetic key card, and chatted with Yousef as the elevator doors opened. "Please let me know if you need anything, Mr. Aziz." A moment later, Yousef and I were in an elevator going up to the presidential suite.

He escorted me to my room and knocked on the door. While we waited for a brief moment, a security camera mounted on the ceiling further down the hall monitored our movements. Wearing a silken smoking jacket, Sensei opened the door. "Thank you for escorting my wife, Mr. Aziz," Sensei said to Yousef. He held the door for me to come in, and Yousef left. Sensei put his finger to his mouth to shush me and then handed me a handwritten piece of paper. *The room is bugged*, he had written on top. *Read the script below and don't say anything else.*

"Good day, my husband," I began.

"Welcome to Germany, Sara. I hope you had a good trip."

"It was fine, thank you. It's a beautiful hotel. I do hope we will have the chance to visit some of the sites."

"Soon we will go out. And you will join me at some of the diplomatic parties. They always serve excellent food." He laughed a little, and I followed suit. "Let us rest, Sara, and we will talk more later. Please bring me a cigarette." He pointed to a box on the table. I handed it to him along with a lighter. He took back my completed script and burned it up over the ashtray.

It was no wonder that the Germans always look so bitter, I thought later as we walked out of the hotel across the street to a nearby park. Their fall air was bitter and dry. The traditional Muslim garb kept me warm, but I could taste the chill in the air. No children used the park, even though there were swings and climbing toys. We sat on a bench and Sensei explained our reason for being there.

"Many of our connections work out of Germany," he told me. "It's important for you to meet them. And while you're here, we'll go for some advanced training. While we're in public, you'll have to wear this costume. But once we get out of the city or until things change, you can dress however you like.

The Germans usually try to follow us a little bit and snoop on our conversations. But their budgets have been cut, and they no longer have the manpower to follow us all over the place. So be careful what you say in the room. Do you like your new identity, Fatima? Or should I call you Sara?"

I smiled, but then realized that he couldn't see my expression. "It's a fine new look," I said. "Funny that they made me your wife."

"I must take credit for that. I designed this project and felt that no one would suspect anything unusual if we were always together. As my wife, you should be by my side for the duration."

He surely had no idea how much warmer he was making me feel by his talk of being husband and wife. "How long will this trip last?"

"I suspect we'll be on the road for about a month or two, depending on circumstances. Did you have any other plans?" He patted my leg lightly. "During the down time, I expect you should have many hours to work on your studies. Yousef has prepared a laptop computer with your coursework, and that will go with us wherever we are. I understand your language studies have been going well."

"Where else will we be going?" I inquired.

"After you're feeling better, we'll head off to the United States."

"I'm feeling fine now, thank you. The flight was bumpy, but it didn't make me sick."

Sensei turned to me with a slight frown. "That's not exactly what I meant, Fatima. Do you know why you have to wear this outfit?"

"It's traditional, religious garb. I assumed that the cover you're using requires a wife who takes the Koran seriously."

He shook his head. "Everyone knows that since your uncle took power over twenty years ago, Iraq has emerged from the dark ages. If you want strict religion, go to Iran or Saudi Arabia. You know that girls today get much the same treatment as boys. Consider your mother; have you ever seen her walk around with her face covered?"

I shrugged, and he continued, "You need to be covered so that no one accidentally recognizes you. When we threw that taxi over the N'amaniya Bridge almost a year ago, that marked the end of the Fatima Atik that you knew." My stomach began to churn. I had been ignoring that reality for many months, still assuming I would someday go back to my former life. "Since you can't stay bundled up like that forever, we're going to give you a new look. Some of the best plastic surgeons in the world work here in Germany."

"But Sensei," I protested, "I am fine the way I am. Why can't I just change my hairstyle? Besides, if I stay out of Baghdad, who will ever know me?"

He started to answer, but I continued to argue my point. I was quite scared at the prospect of having an operation on any part of me. "What if there's a problem and they ruin me? In any case, I could just wear a lot of makeup. I never wear makeup, so that would certainly change my look. And when I go back home eventually, what would my parents say?"

He placed his hand gently over my veiled mouth. "Fatima, there's no going back now." I knew that Sensei had gone to great lengths to establish my new identity and to train me for high-level service to the government. Nonetheless, watching the girl that I had been die in a crash made me feel disconnected not just from myself, but from my family, friends, and country. I was a tiger, sent off by its parents to make its way in the wild.

"When?" I asked.

"We'll meet the doctor tomorrow." We sat silently for ten minutes. No one else came to our park. I was an empty person, about to be filled up with a new personality, sitting in a vacant park. "Let's go back to the hotel," he said, standing up.

The stupid heels on my shoes sank into the grass as we took a shortcut to our destination. As soon as we got inside the lobby, I started to boil inside my outfit. The manager greeted us and offered any assistance we might like. "*Gibt es alles, das ich für, Sie tun kann, Sir?*"

"*Abendessen für meine Frau und Ich,*" Sensei said ordering a meal from room service. "*Und Ihr bester Wein.*"

"*Wir holen es in der halben Stunde,*" he responded, letting us know that the food would arrive in thirty minutes. I could already tell that in Germany, when someone set a time for an event, it would happen precisely at that moment.

When we were alone in the elevator, Sensei gave me a whispered reminder not to speak of anything sensitive, and to act like husband and wife when in the room. Once inside, he suggested that I unveil and remove my heavy clothes. He helped me unwind some of the fabric, like a man would help a beloved wife. The cool air was a great relief, and since the palatial suite had two bathrooms, we could both wash up at the same time. "Why don't you rest in the jacuzzi, my dear, and then afterwards we can watch a movie."

It was like being on a date without having to leave the room. I winked at him and ran off to my dressing room. Almost an hour later, after trying all the beauty products and shampoos, I came out wearing a cool, silk bathrobe with the hotel logo on the front. Also in a silk bathrobe, Sensei was reading *Der Spiegel* and sitting at the table with two covered meals in front of him. When he saw me, he put down the paper and looked me up and down. "You seem much more relaxed now," he commented. Like a British knight, he stood up for me, held my chair and invited me to join him. When I was seated, he brushed his hand down my long hair and said, "And you look very beautiful."

His warm touch penetrated my whole body. The glow from the wine that he poured made me feel soft and sexy. I stared into his handsome eyes as he told me funny stories about growing up in his family with nine brothers and sisters. Having little experience with alcohol, my subsequent walk to the couch was quite difficult. My legs wobbled, and Sensei held my hand. He put his arm on the couch above my shoulders as we sat close. I liked the way his gray silk robe touched my white one. "Have you seen *Casablanca*?" he asked.

I gave a drunken smile, "Nope."

For the next two hours, I watched both the movie and my teacher. I loved how he laughed during the film, and how his expressions changed with the progression of the story. Like the story, we came from far apart to fall in love. The slippery fabric of my robe moved around, and I knew that it was hanging loosely on me. I did not fix it, hoping that just as I could catch a glimpse of him, he could also take a closer look at me. At the end of the movie, I rested my head on his shoulder. He clicked the TV off and rested his hand on my shoulder. The weight of his arm pulled my robe back several centimeters. I was reminded of the time we first met in the palace, when my torn shirt exposed my shoulder. "As I feel the texture of your robe and then your shoulder," he said, rubbing his knuckles over my bare skin, "they both feel as smooth as silk."

Our faces started moving together. I loved how he looked deeply into my eyes. His breath reached my cheek, and as he ran his hand slowly down my arm, inside the loose sleeve of my robe, I reached for his face. His freshly shaven cheeks contrasted with the short hairs of his mustache. With the tips of my fingers, I rubbed from the smooth cheeks to the trimmed mustache and then across his lips. I held my hand in place to savor the feeling of his mouth, which I had dreamed about. He kissed my fingers.

With my robe draped half off, his hand could feel my heart pounding. He massaged my body, and then slid his arm all the way down until he got beneath my knees. In a slow and powerful move, he picked me up in his arms. Like a new groom carrying his bride over the threshold, he carried me to the king-sized bed. He laid me down with great care. With one knee up, and one leg straight, I let my body relax. Only a few parts of my skin were still wrapped by the hotel's robe.

Sensei reached to the headboard and shut the lights. Glimmering reflections from the city lights shone in the giant glass windows that surrounded the bedroom. His dark skin became a shadow. "I missed you," he said. I closed my eyes and felt every new sensation as his lips touched mine.

When I awoke early the next morning, I found myself alone in bed. I heard Sensei shaving, so I went to my private washroom to shower and dress. Once again, when I came out, he was reading the paper while he sat by the table. We only drank tea, and there was no sweetener. "Would you like me to get you some sugar?" I offered.

He started the day by winning my heart when he replied, "If you would please just touch my cup, that would make it sweet enough for me."

He gazed at me lovingly, though we did not discuss the previous night. "We're meeting the doctor soon, Sara," he told me. It took me a moment to get used to my new name.

Arriving at the medical center before it officially opened, we went straight into the doctor's office. After he greeted us, he told Sensei that he could return at around 4:30 p.m. "The anesthetic should be wearing off by then," he said.

"I thought this was just a meeting," I whispered nervously to Sensei.

"Yes, my dear. First you'll meet with him and then when you've made all your decisions, he'll get started. I have arranged for his schedule to be clear all day."

Protesting would have been futile. "But Sensei, I'll be a different person when you come back for me."

He leaned over, "No, my dear. You'll be the same person with a different look. Nothing he does, however, will make you any less beautiful. The whole process will take a few hours, so don't worry."

"Don't you want to stay with me?" I desperately wanted a companion.

"You'll be fine. You don't need me. The nurses here are wonderful, and they'll take care of all your needs. Focus on your breathing and you'll stay calm."

The pudgy nurse, Dorothee, told me I should remove my *burkha* and wear a hospital gown. She took my clothes and said, "You won't be needing these anymore. I'll get rid of them." After a blood sample was drawn and x-rays were taken, Dr. Goddard examined me closely. He asked me similar questions to the ones asked back in Iraq. When he inquired about any medications, I told him about the pill I took daily to control acne. "I am not familiar with the brand name," he said. "What is the active ingredient?"

After studying so much chemistry, I had become quite familiar with the pronouncing of the names of many medications I had seen. "It's ethnyl estradiol."

"Has it helped your skin?"

"It's hard to say," I admitted. "I think so."

When he leaned over his desk to look at me more closely, the many pens tucked inside his white medical jacket tapped the surface. "Have you been careful to self-administer this medicine at the same time every day?"

"Yes, sir."

"I assume you're aware of the other benefit of this drug?"

I shook my head.

"It's birth control, Sara. I hope you weren't trying to get pregnant."

At first I laughed, but then I felt used. Maybe Sensei had devised the original medical exam just to put me on the pill. He knew that I would let him sleep with me at some point, and he wanted to make sure there would be no surprises. On the other hand, I reasoned, he probably wanted me as long as I had desired him.

"Sara," the doctor said, taking me out of my own thoughts.

"Yes, sir. I'm sorry. What were you saying?"

"You may continue taking the pill after the surgery. Are you using any other medicines or drugs, even recreationally?"

I shook my head again as he asked about other medicines.

"Have you taken aspirin recently, or any antihistamine? How about vitamin E?" He marked my answers on his clipboard.

"Would those stop the clotting process?" I asked, having been taught that by Yousef when I learned about emergency medical care in battle.

He nodded and told me that I should start taking a lot of vitamin C since studies suggest it can aid the healing process. I also told him that I drank tea with no sugar that morning. "That's fine," he told me, "as long as you didn't eat any solid food."

The medical history took about twenty more minutes. After the x-ray came back, he showed me sketchbooks of different face-changing techniques that he could apply in my situation. "Our goal," he asserted, "is a dramatic change in appearance while still maintaining your beauty. Though you'll be okay in a couple of weeks, the final results will only be clear in about a year. In any case, you can change other attributes of your appearance, such as your hair or eye color, non-surgically."

With a basic sketch of my face, he took a pencil and started showing me how he could alter every dimension. "I would suggest," he said, "that we focus on just a few areas." He lightly drew higher cheekbones, "which will give you a chiseled, contoured look, like models have." When I asked how he could access that part of my face without leaving a scar, he explained, "We will make a small incision inside the back of your mouth, about three centimeters long."

I put up my hand to stop him. "Maybe it's better if I don't have any more details," I suggested, feeling a little sick from the details of how he would cut up my head.

We went on to choose a nose, plan a chin, and create a fuller look to my lips with a collagen injection. He called his nurse to bring me some water, which I drank along with some pills that were on the tray. "You know that we can also work on other parts of your body," the doctor told me. "We can enlarge your breasts and round out your buttocks."

The nurse was still in the room and she looked at my body. "What do you think, Dorothee?" the doctor asked.

"It won't help much. She has developed beautifully and is already quite large where the men like it."

The doctor agreed with her, but wanted to show me some before and after pictures in case I changed my mind. He lowered the lights and showed some slides of the various successes he had had. As I watched, I found it difficult to stay awake. "I'm sorry, Dr. Goddard, I think I need to lie down," I apologized. He walked around his desk and took my hand to guide me someplace.

The next thing I knew, I was asking Dorothee, "Where is my husband?" I was happy that the drugs didn't affect my ability to remember my assumed identity.

"He was here last night, but the hospital doesn't allow visitors to remain overnight. He left you these," she said, pointing to dozens of flowers against the wall.

The surgery had taken a long time, and apparently I had slept soundly. Dorothee suggested that I continue with painkillers for most of the day. She said the operation went well, but there was nothing to see yet. Sensei called later in the morning, five minutes after a large-screen TV was brought into my room. "You might get a little bored," he told me, "so this will help." Then he broke the bad news. He was calling from Jordan, where he had to go for an emergency meeting. "Don't worry," he tried to reassure me. "I should be back next week."

Later in the day, Yousef popped his head in the room. "I'm sorry, I must have the wrong room. I was looking for Sara Aziz."

"It *is* me, Ahmed, dear brother. Thank you for visiting me." I laughed at his joke, though it hurt to smile. Since my face was pale and puffy, with several dark bruises developing, I didn't mind that Sensei would miss seeing me. Yousef didn't seem to notice, and in fact was interested in the surgical practices. He watched when the doctor checked the splint on the outside of my nose, and even a few days later when he removed the nasal packs. They had served their purpose of limiting the bleeding and keeping adhesions from forming between the incisions. Yousef made sure the humidifier was kept on in my room all the time, which made breathing much more comfortable.

Even Madame Moreau stopped by. I was not only surprised that she was in Germany, but that she would care enough to visit. Yousef later explained that after I had been drugged in the doctor's office, she accompanied me every moment until I woke up. Her job was to make sure I didn't start releasing confidential information while under the influence of anesthetic. Apparently I had done quite well.

"Aren't you going to say hello to your grandmother?" Madame said in French, letting me know her identity. She bent down and kissed my forehead.

"*Bonjour, Grandmère,*" I said, "*comment ça va?*"

She patted my head and told me to rest. Though there was no reason to remain in the hospital, I had no place else to go. Madame arranged a private suite where I could relax and study. Yousef worked with me, and even arranged to have doctors and nurses come in to teach me biology and chemistry.

Though I felt fine three days after the operation, I ended up staying in my secluded suite for almost two weeks. As the swelling in my face disappeared, I began to like my new look. My favorite change was the cheeks. Just like Dr. Goddard had said, my face had sharper angles and I felt like a girl in *Cosmo*, far, far away from the Fatima Atik in the diplomatic school in Baghdad.

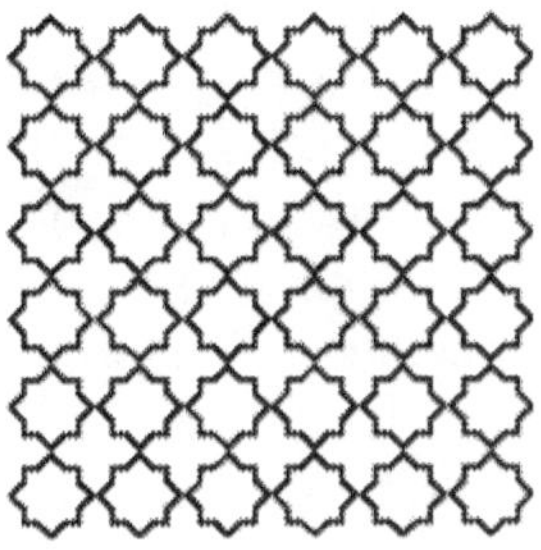

Chapter 7

Eventually, I moved back to the hotel, where I stayed by myself for around a week. Madame instructed me not to leave the room until we finalized the new look. A hairstylist from the fashion industry was brought in for a consultation. I liked him right away, probably because he kept saying how excellent my hair looked. He was strange, though, and kept referring to everyone, including himself, in the third person.

"What Simon will do is change the texture and add some color," he said, rubbing his silver comb up and down his bicep. He wore a tight black t-shirt that hugged his lanky body. "Does Sara Aziz like that idea, hmm?" He did not wait for an answer. "And Simon will make bangs that curl over your forehead. They will touch your eyebrows, which, of course, Simon will shape to perfection." He walked around me over and over, touching and primping my hair.

"Sara Aziz will have many curly locks," he decided. With a rapid clip of the scissors, he sliced off about half the length of my hair, which had lain neatly halfway down my back for years. He used gels, creams, and styling tools that I had never tried. After two hours, he explained how to maintain the look and then announced, "Simon is finished." He handed me his business card, which I memorized.

The following morning, Madame brought an optician to teach me how to use my new colored contact lenses. I hated the idea of getting close to my eyeball, but after a long struggle, I eventually got them in place. Of all the changes I had gone through, this was the most dramatic. I had never liked my glasses, and without them blocking my face, the new accented curves stood out. Placing a large, clean mirror on the table in front of me, the optician said, "You look like a new woman, Mrs. Aziz."

I could not detect even the faintest tone of the original blue in my eyes. The soft lenses had changed my color to hazel green, a slightly unusual color, but very pretty. I assumed Simon had known what color I would have, because it complemented the highlights in my hair.

Madame brought a makeup specialist a few hours later. "We'll use some base to lighten your skin tone," she said, "but not too much, or else it'll look fake." Using an easy touch, she made a number of changes using just eyeliner, blush and lipstick. "If you make the outer part of your lips a little darker, it'll make them look even more kissable," she told me. She suggested that the process remain simple, so I could do it everyday. A French manicure to top off the new look made me feel ready to step off a catwalk with the latest fashion.

After the beautician left, Madame asked me if I could keep up the appearance. "No problem," I told her. She called Yousef and asked him to meet us upstairs. "Your brother will take you out now," she informed me. "I'll take care of the packing." A minute later there was a firm knock followed by three light ones on the door. Madame handed me a stylish raincoat. She opened the door, and holding my arm, she walked me quickly to the elevator. The sand-filled ashtray that normally sat by the side of the elevator had been moved to block the door. I glanced back and saw Yousef holding an open, oversized umbrella underneath the hall camera. He had blocked its scope as I moved out. Standing next to me, Madame pulled a veil over her head, moved the ashtray out of the way, and then walked back towards the room. Out of the line of site of the monitor, I waited in the elevator for Yousef to join me. Disguised as me, Madame was filmed looking perfectly reasonable. No one would know that Dr. Hasim had had a different woman in his room.

"When the doors open," Yousef said, "Walk straight out the front of the hotel. Turn right and go to the first intersection. Turn right again and continue straight until you hit a traffic circle. Follow it counter-clockwise until Bettinaplatz Street. Go right, and about halfway down the block you'll see a McDonalds. Go there now. I'll go a different way." He placed two hundred deutschmarks in my hand just before the doors opened, and I hurried out, slipping the money into the pocket of my London Fog overcoat.

I walked down the street like a normal person. No one knew me and, in fact, I didn't know myself. I felt an eerie sense of freedom, as if I could say or do anything I wanted. A few men looked at me invitingly, but I hurried along. What if I had spoken to one, met a wealthy businessman, and disappeared from the whole Iraqi intelligence network?

A few minutes later, I waited on a very straight line at McDonalds. With a burger and Coke in hand, I walked up to the next floor, from where I could monitor the entrance. Wearing a handsome business suit and sunglasses, Sensei walked in. His "one week" had turned into many more, and I was excited to see him. For fun, I decided to see if he would recognize me. I turned around and started speaking to an old lady behind me. If it looked like she and I were together, maybe he wouldn't spot me so easily. Acting like a tourist, I asked her in English if she knew the weather forecast. She seemed very interested in the topic, and started telling me much more than I wanted to hear about the weatherman's predictions. Meanwhile, Sensei wandered around the whole restaurant, and even walked by me. Assuming I hadn't yet arrived, he sat at a nearby table, also positioning himself with a view towards the entrance.

Excusing myself from the boring woman, I stood next to Sensei and offered to take his order. He looked up, said "no thanks," and then stared a moment longer into my face. "Oh my," he said, "aren't you a dream come true!"

"Welcome back, stranger," I said, "What a surprise to see you. I thought you had bought a house in Jordan."

"I am sorry it took so long, Sara. Things are getting very tense now." He glanced around and asked if I had been followed from the hotel.

"I doubt it."

"Let's be sure. You go downstairs and out through the kitchen. We'll meet in an hour in the park that we sat in on our special night." He handed me an unwrapped watch, a gold Omega with diamonds marking the hours. "As the clock has ticked, I have thought about our evening many times." He let his fingers roll over my hand after giving me the gift. After he touched my hand, and my heart, I decided not to mention the deception regarding the pill. I was glad that he had had the doctor prescribe it, and wanted to benefit from its effects again. "Make sure you don't get followed." I snapped on the stunning watch and walked down the stairs.

In an orderly country like Germany, it's expected that the patrons follow the rules in public places. When I marched into the kitchen, one of the cooks stared at me, shocked. "Don't worry," I said, "this branch has gotten a fine review. I will tell Mr. McDonald himself that everything is fine here."

"*Vielen Dank,* Madame," he responded.

After I walked out of the "employees only" back door, I laughed at myself for saying such a stupid thing. On the other hand, if he worked in the place and still thought that the old man was alive, then he was certainly a pathetic creature.

Though no one would know that I had come out of the back door, I decided to practice evasive procedures for an hour. Interestingly, when I placed myself in "suspicious mode," the term I coined for worrying that everyone around me wanted to kill me, I found a lot of possible candidates who could be my adversaries. One bicyclist stood out rather distinctly because he stood by a phone booth when I entered a clothing store, and was still there when I got out ten minutes later. Taking a bus ride a few blocks, and then turning around and riding the other way eliminated any questionable characters.

I got to our bench about five minutes early. Sensei pulled around the corner in a dark blue Mercedes with diplomatic license plates. I walked over and leaned in the open window. "Nice job losing the tail," he said. "Yousef couldn't keep up with the bus. Come on, now, you drive."

I removed my coat and took over the controls. When I sat down, I let my skirt ride up to focus his interest on my legs. Sensei didn't try to hide his glances at my new face and body. He directed me out of town, to a safe house we would use for the remainder of our time in Germany.

Once I felt comfortable behind the wheel, I took the opportunity to get some clarity from my teacher. "Is it safe to talk in here?"

"No one's listening but me."

"What is our relationship with Yousef and Madame Moreau?"

"They have been part of my team for years," Sensei explained. "We've been through a lot together since we started doing intelligence work against Iran. Your cousin is one of the smartest men in the kingdom and has always handled our communications and research requirements. Only recently has he gone into the field under cover. He surprised all of us with his ability to assume a new identity. He says that when he plays the part of someone else, he completely changes his character to the new one. That's why he doesn't stutter now. But once he's back in the palace, you can be sure that he'll start up again. He used to sit in hotel rooms with computers and radio equipment, but now he's developing."

"And Madame?"

"She may seem gruff, Sara, but ... Well, actually, that's just her personality. She grew up in Switzerland. Her father was an Iraqi diplomat who fell for a Swiss nurse. When she got pregnant, he married her as a second wife. That lasted only a few years since living in Iraq, which was much more religious then, was difficult for a freethinking woman. She returned to Switzerland, but was not allowed to bring her daughter. That was the last time your Madame ever saw her mother – age eight."

"No wonder she's grumpy."

"She became the woman of the house in many ways. And those responsibilities taught her to demand high standards from herself and everyone around her. She eventually got a job in the palace library as a translator. She knew many European languages and impressed a young captain."

"Was that you?"

"No, it was when I was still in university. Your father was the one who spotted her as a rising star and arranged for her to join the diplomatic corps."

"What kind of diplomat was she?" I asked.

"That's more of a euphemism. Half the people in the diplomatic corps of any country are just spies. You're a diplomat, too." He pointed his finger to the entrance ramp of the autobahn and I veered on. After a few minutes, Sensei said, "This car has a 'sixth' gear. Give it a try."

Right away, I pushed down on the heavy clutch, grabbed the steel ball on top of the gearshift, and pushed it to the right and down. Pressing heavily on the gas, my left foot slowly began easing. The car switched smoothly into its fastest gear. At 150 kilometers per hour, the engine hummed quietly. I loved the rush, and was impressed that people were still passing me. Sensei pushed a cassette into the tape player, raised the volume, and then sat back as Beethoven's ninth intensified the sense of speed.

Lowering the music with the control on the steering wheel, I continued to probe. "So if we're all spies, what's our mission now?"

"Right now, my goal is to get you ready for a deep cover assignment. You've been training, and will continue for a few more years. I want you to feel comfortable working with our team, and they need to see that they can trust you, too. I'm sure you can imagine what would happen if one of us were caught."

"Why don't you tell me?"

"When a plan goes bad, Sara, people can die. And the way to that death is sometimes through torture. When a person is beaten for weeks on end, he sometimes lets critical information slip, like where his co-conspirators are located. If a German agent broke every bone in my body, one by one, in order to find out where you were, do you think I would tell him?"

The image of seeing my teacher beaten and broken disturbed me. I slowed down and moved to the right lane. "You would never betray me, Sensei. And I would sooner die than expose you to any danger."

"I know. You and I have a very special relationship. Over time, you will have the same commitment to the others. Just like they will have for you."

It was hard to imagine that I would let someone break my bones before turning in Madame. She was a bitter, old teacher who had smacked me months earlier. I believed that Sensei's wisdom would illuminate my path towards camaraderie with her. "What sort of deep cover do you mean?"

"We need more intelligence about the plans of the United States. Not so much now, though it would help, but later." Sensei pointed to an exit off the highway and I followed a sign toward Nürburgring. He continued, "You will be planted in a university in the States. There, you'll learn the hard sciences that can help us develop better defenses. And on top of that, you'll develop connections with students who come from high-powered families, and who will themselves become senior decision-makers one day."

"You're sending me to America for school? I never thought I'd end up there."

"As soon as we finish up here, we'll head to America to arrange for your admission to Princeton University. They have some formalities that you must pass in order to enter there next September. In the meantime ..." I cut him off.

"In the meantime, how is your son?"

"Well, thank you for asking. He's been traveling, as have I, but I got a short telegram from him a few weeks ago letting me know that he had been having mixed successes in his boxing matches, but is trying hard."

The answer seemed totally honest, but strange. I hadn't wanted to bring up the beating that I had witnessed, but then I realized that perhaps I had seen someone else.

After being on the road for a total of only twenty minutes, we pulled into the parking lot of the Nürburgring racing track. A greasy-looking old man with a very round, bald head greeted us inside. Without warning me, Sensei introduced me in English, "Hans, this is Leila Amal from London."

"*Es ist ein Vergnügen, Sie zu treffen,*" Hans started to greet me politely, but Sensei cut him off.

"She doesn't speak a word of German. You'll have to teach her in English or French."

"Very well," the host responded. "It will be my pleasure, Ms. Amal."

Sensei explained that Hans Ostheim was one of the top trainers of German racing car drivers. He looked more like a mechanic who should tune a transmission rather than train a driver. "We have some gear you can try on, Ms. Amal. Choose something comfortable." He pointed me towards some helmets and gloves on the other side of the room. As I went over to check them out, Hans asked Sensei in German, "What are you doing with such a sweet flower?"

"She's my cousin's daughter. For her 18th birthday, he gave her three wishes. Learning to drive like a professional was one of them. Anyway, I'm doing him a favor and he's paying. She wants to learn to handle a car at high speed, and also some of the police techniques of both chasing and avoiding being spotted when you're following someone."

"How much time will you be here?"

"Until Thursday. So we should have a full three days."

We didn't start driving until later in the afternoon. Hans was quite meticulous in his approach and taught me how to dismantle certain sections of the engine, change tires, and repair minor problems. He proudly informed me that unlike in other countries, German drivers must have a great understanding about the mechanics of a car before they can get their licenses.

During the days, I spent hours driving at high speeds. It's hard to describe the scenery around the track because it all zipped by at 200 kilometers per hour. Maintaining control of the car as it went faster required squeezing the wheel with all my might. The view at such speeds narrowed, so it seemed like I was in a tunnel. Hans kept reminding me to glance quickly into my mirrors. "Even though you are driving one car," he explained, "you must have a view of everything going on around you."

We practiced high-speed turns, identifying what racing drivers call "the line." The line represents the best way to enter a curve, cross the apex, and then exit with as much force as possible. The burned rubber marks on the track from the thousands of previous cars made it easier to spot the crucial guiding line.

He showed me how to make use of the aerodynamics of other cars around me by "slipstreaming," or "drafting." When I tailed another racer closely, his car would act like a battering ram, softening up the air for me. We practiced racing, slalom driving, evasive maneuvers, and more. Quitting time was around four in the afternoon, which was plenty for me.

At the conclusion of the second day, Sensei asked me if I wanted to go back to the safe house, or if I'd prefer to go shopping. "What for?" I asked.

"I'd like to see a designer I know."

I was impressed with Sensei's style, so I smiled, and when we got into his car I grabbed his hand and squeezed it. "It sounds like fun," I told him.

After driving a short distance, he pulled on to a dirt road and crossed a field. At the other end, I saw a rundown-looking shack with a man outside watering neat rows of red and yellow gerberas. There were several old cars parked in front, also in an orderly line. Sensei pulled the Mercedes to a spot adjacent to the others in the series, maintaining the order. He got out first, and I watched as he walked over to the man. I stood by the car before going closer. Showing respect to the older gentleman, Sensei waited until the man offered a handshake. They spoke to each other for a moment before summoning me.

When I was introduced, I offered my hand to Dr. Baldwin, which I had learned was the appropriate German etiquette for a woman meeting a man. He was a round man, with very short hair and scruffy cheeks. His palms were wet, either from watering the flowers or from sweat. His grip was as firm as Hans'. "Come along, Doctor Hasim," he said to Sensei. He laid his hand on my lower back to escort me towards the car. "We will go for a drive." He put me in the back and Sensei in the front passenger seat. To my surprise, Dr. Baldwin then put a life-sized mannequin into the driver's seat. He attached its hands with Velcro to the steering wheel and the back of its head to the headrest. "You can control the car from your side. All you need to do is to drive around the field here and I will follow you," he told Sensei. He turned the ignition, and Sensei started to drive slowly, getting used to the opposite controls.

"I thought we were going to visit a designer," I said.

"Dr. Baldwin is one of the finest."

"So why are we driving in circles around this field?"

Sensei glanced over his shoulder, and I looked out the back, to see that Dr. Baldwin had begun driving another car behind, staying about a car's length away from us. "I'm not really sure, Leila," he finally answered.

"Well, he doesn't seem too interested in design. He hardly looked at my outfit, and frankly, his attire was nothing special." I laughed to myself that my teacher always had different names for me: Fatima, Sara, Leila. What would be next?

"He doesn't design women's clothes."

Suddenly we were assailed by an odor of smoke. "Sensei," I called, "Stop! There's a fire." Sensei jammed on the brake and both of us jumped out of the car. Dr. Baldwin pulled slowly up behind our car and stopped. He walked to the dummy in the front, pulled it out, threw it on the ground, and started stomping on its head to put out the fire.

"You like that?" he asked.

"What have you got?" Sensei asked, "a fire doll?"

Our host lifted up the doll and showed us the slightly burned face. The paint on its mouth and nose looked like a child's drawing, but the eyes were both black and very round. "I did that from my car," he asserted. "While following you, I locked onto the eyeballs of Frankenstein through your rearview mirror. Then I blinded him."

Sensei smiled broadly. He was very impressed with the technology. "You have a laser in your car?"

"It's solid-state, so it won't break all the time in bumpy terrain."

"This is phenomenal, Leila," my teacher explained. "He's got a powerful laser in his car that tracks the eyes of the driver in the car in front of him. When he activates the laser, it blinds the driver, causing him to crash."

"Actually, the laser is relatively weak. We're not burning down missiles; we're just destroying some tissue. Better still, there is nothing a medical examiner would ever find in an autopsy. Even if the car doesn't catch fire, which of course makes the kill more spectacular, no one would ever check to see if the retinas of the deceased were burned."

"What if the enemy doesn't look into his mirror?" I asked.

He brought us over to his car and showed us a small light attached to the top of his windshield. "It flashes a few different, pretty neon colors to catch the attention of the target. As soon as he looks at it... zap! The laser pulse can inflict terminal damage in under one second."

"That's incredible," I complimented him. "And you made this?"

"That's right, my dear. I am the designer."

I looked at Sensei knowingly, realizing that we weren't buying clothes that day.

"How much?" Sensei asked.

"A hundred fifty thousand dollars."

"I'll take two for two-fifty," my teacher bargained. "I'd like to have one for my wife."

"Two seventy-five?" Dr. Baldwin proposed.

"No. Two-fifty, and that will include training and immediate delivery."

"Very well," the seller conceded. "Shall I install it in your Mercedes?"

"No thank you." I'd like you to teach my wife and I how to do it ourselves so we can take care of it and move it from car to car whenever necessary."

We spent hours learning the design and installation of the laser. Dr. Baldwin had designed the package to fit between the metal roof of the car and the fabric inside. Only a small section peered out through the front to create the flashing distraction and deliver the deadly pulse. Just like a tape deck, the device drew power from the car's own electric system. We installed and removed the device several times from different auto models. At around 10:30 p.m. that evening, Dr. Baldwin packed two metal briefcases with the weapons and thanked us for the business. "I have many more ideas, Dr. Hasim. Come again soon."

As we drove back to the safe house, Sensei congratulated me for learning so quickly. "If you don't work out as a spy," he joked, "you can always become an auto mechanic."

We finished off the week at Nürburgring. Sensei beat me in our final race, but it was close. I thanked my driving instructor, who said, "I hope you won't ever need to use these skills. And don't forget to strap in."

We went directly to the airport, once again passing the crowds by using all the diplomatic doors. Sensei had packed our bags and brought the laser systems, as well. He carried them himself, leaving the clothing for the porters. "Please come again," the German airport sign said, "*Adieu.*"

The official jet we flew in was larger than the last one, and it took over eight hours to reach our destination. Since I no longer had to play the part of a devout Muslim, I could enjoy reading some of the newspapers and magazines. My escapades in Germany had tired me out, however, and I slept most of the way.

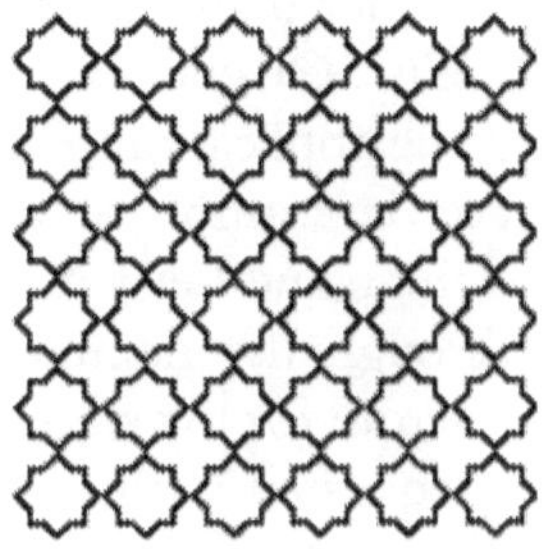

Chapter 8

Yousef had prepared all of my university applications a few months earlier. Though I hadn't realized at the time, my exam at the U.S. embassy was the SAT, a college entrance test. Having received top marks and presented excellent paperwork, I was invited for an interview. Sensei told me that he had not used any political influence to ensure my acceptance to the school, but I suspect that he may have helped since there was a major donation during my freshman year endowing an Islamic Studies chair.

We landed in Newark and got similar diplomatic treatment as in Germany. A limo took us to a bed-and-breakfast outside the university, and several suitcases of new clothes were unpacked for me. A buyer from Neiman Marcus, a ritzy New York store, came to help me try on some of the outfits. He advised me to wear a very conservative below-the-knee dark blue skirt, and a thin sweater. "You look like a member of one of the famous Princeton eating clubs," he told me. He coached me on how to present myself in the interview, and reviewed American dining and business etiquette.

Sensei drove me to the interview the next day. He chose a BMW rather than the limousine to demonstrate some humility. On the way, he handed me a file with a copy of the application so I could familiarize myself with the description of who I was. "I'm glad I get to keep the name Leila Amal. It has a nice sound." I read through the document. "These are some essays that I wrote for my studies," I noted.

"The school requested writing samples. Yousef was going to do them for you, but when we reviewed some of your own pieces, we determined that they were more appropriate."

When I skimmed through the other pages, I noticed a problem. "It says that I grew up in London. What if they ask me about it?"

"Just talk in generalities. London's a town just like any other. You've got noise, pollution, politics, scandals, and… Well, try to avoid the subject if the discussion gets too detailed."

"But what if they catch on? What about my accent?"

"Try to make it sound a little British," he responded.

"Please tell me you're kidding."

"Americans are so provincial that they don't even know there's a world to the west of Manhattan. Mention London Bridge, and they'll think you own the city. Don't worry, Leila. They'll never know. Anyway, your English certainly sounds more European than American, so what will they know? According to your dossier, your mother was French and your father was Iraqi, so if you have some imperfections in English it makes you sound realistic."

"Yes sir," I conceded.

In the end, I met with the head of the School of Engineering and Applied Sciences (SEAS). He was much more interested in telling me about their program than in hearing my stories of growing up under the watchful eye of Big Ben in the Queen's hometown.

With funding in the tens of millions of dollars, he explained how their department facilitated research by its staff, and encouraged participation by the graduate and undergraduate students. I had him focus specifically on the chemical engineering and the mechanical and aerospace engineering departments. He also said they were developing interdisciplinary studies to allow students to focus on areas such as engineering biology and robotics. I realized that with the data they would give me, I'd be well equipped to train scientists back home.

As we wrapped up, he said, "I do hope you will join us, Ms. Amal. You seem like quite an enlightened young woman, and I am sure you would fit in well here."

When I returned to Sensei, he let me know that the meeting had been a technicality, and that if I wanted to sign up, the school was ready to accept me. I smiled and told Sensei, "Sign me up for September."

To celebrate, Sensei said we'd go out. At our B&B, I changed into less formal attire, and then we went to a beautiful restaurant in our chauffeured car. Afterwards, Sensei said that he wanted to meet someone at a pub up the road. About five miles away, we pulled into the parking lot of a creepy-looking bar. There were over twenty motorcycles parked outside, and bikers were getting very drunk both inside and outside. We went inside and straight to the bar. "You stay here," Sensei said, "and have a drink. I'll be back soon."

He went towards the couches in the back, where a man in a suit was leaning back. It was noisy from the brainless music that they played, but I saw the man greet Sensei happily. I didn't want to stare at them, but was able to follow the whole interaction in the mirror behind the bartender. Sensei picked up a menu from the table and looked at it while leaning back on his couch. For a moment, he let it drop onto his chest, and then handed it to the other man. The man then opened the menu, hiding whatever was inside, and when he put it down, he straightened his jacket. Though they were subtle, I knew that Sensei had passed him some envelope or documents.

"You smell delicious, Baby," a hairy man said to me as he came too close. "I know you came in with that suit over there, but why don't you leave with me? I'll take good care of you."

"You remind me of a Kurdish bandit that I met in the hills of Baghdad," I replied. "And he also promised to take care of me. What can you do that he couldn't?"

"I don't know what he offered, Baby," he said, putting his hand on mine and sliding it up my arm, "and I don't know nothin' 'bout Kurdish, but I can show you the stars in the sky!"

I pulled my arm away, but he kept holding on.

"I am sorry, sir, but I have to ask you to stop touching me."

"Come on, Baby," he encouraged, "Lemme be your Kurdish." He kept touching me, and though I didn't want to disturb Sensei's meeting, I moved my hand on top of his, as if I were going to hold his hand. Once in place, I positioned my thumb by his pinky and my other fingers around his wrist. In one quick application of pressure, I twisted his wrist around, causing him to lose his balance completely and fall off his stool. He hit the ground with a heavy thud and, in fact, I felt a little bad because he seemed so dumb and I had outsmarted him with a simple ju-jitsu trick.

"You college bitch!" he yelled as he got up. I glanced over at Sensei, who spotted us, but for some reason didn't come over. As I turned back around to confront the biker, my driver's arm was already wrapped snugly around his throat. As a well-trained bodyguard, the driver escorted the assailant painfully to the exit, and then firmly pushed him out.

When the driver returned to make sure I was safe, he stuck out his hand to shake mine. As I returned the grasp, he placed a small item in my hand and whispered, "Put this morphine solution in the drink you serve to Dr. Hasim's partner over there." It was a ring that had a small compartment by the knuckle. I slipped it on and looked at Sensei. He and the other man were smiling proudly at me and laughing. They seemed to have liked the show that I put on. Sensei held up two fingers to me and mouthed, "two beers."

I ordered them from the bartender, and as I picked them up, I slid open the tiny door on the ring. A small amount of the sedative poured into the drink that I gave to the second man moments later. "Well, thank you, lovely lady," the man said, and I returned to my stool. In the mirror, I saw how he kept eyeing me. About ten minutes later, Sensei indicated to the man to wait for a moment. My teacher then came over and sat next to me.

"In a few minutes, the drug will take effect to knock Ken Peters out. In the meantime, go introduce yourself to Ken over there. Make nice to him, Leila. *Very* nice. He thinks that you are a gift that we're giving him. When it gets a little too steamy, excuse yourself to wash up. The bathroom is over there. Got it?"

"Okay. But where will you be?"

"Just go. Don't worry about the details."

I walked slowly over, looking deeply into Ken's eyes. It was clear how excited he was that my focus was on him. Even though we were in a public restaurant, he must have felt that no one cared about who we were. Perhaps the morphine had started taking effect, giving him a sense of relaxation. "You really are one beautiful woman. What's your name, honey?" he began.

"Oh, come on, you don't really care about my name, do you?" Placing my leg next to his, I reclined on the couch. With such soft cushions, my body rolled halfway onto his. He had kept one hand on the seat and began to rub me as I touched his cheek and snuggled closely to his ear. I whispered some of the more erotic lines that I had read in *Cosmo*. He placed his other hand on my leg, and started exploring my body.

"Oh, yeah, 'honey.' That's a fine name for a sweet lady like you." He tried to get his face close to mine, but I purposely maneuvered away. He kissed my neck as I teased him a bit more, loosening his tie and rubbing his shoulders. I made quiet noises to make him feel like he was pleasing me. "What if we go to my hotel down the block, honey?" he asked.

"Mmm, that sounds nice," I replied. I placed both my hands on his cheeks, probed his eyes and made him think that I was about to give him the kiss that he wanted. I could feel the rapid pulse in his neck as I slid my fingers slowly down. "Let me go wash up and then I'd love to see where you can take me." With a wink, I pushed myself off the couch, and headed for the washroom. Neither Sensei nor my driver was around. I turned back to look at Ken and blew him a kiss.

"I'll be waiting for you, honey," he called out as I went into the ladies room. In the back, there was an open window. I walked near it and heard someone whistling "Honeysuckle Rose," a song that Sensei had quoted to me on our night back in Germany. A manly-looking woman approached me, saying, "Hey girl," but I ignored her. I pushed the window open and climbed out into Sensei's waiting arms. "Where you going, bitch?!" were the last words I heard as I left the restroom.

The driver came over to the back of the bar where we were standing and handed Sensei a camera. "I got it, Dr. Hasim."

"Thanks," Sensei answered. Then he turned to me and said I had done a great job. "Ken works as a planner for the State Department. It's kind of like being a diplomat," he explained, using the euphemism for spy. "He's a pretty solid man, and we've helped him on many occasions with data on Iran and Saudi Arabia. By our supplying him the right information, he has impressed his superiors and moved up to a trusted position near the White House. Parts of his memos often appear in the President's daily security briefing."

I listened closely as we got into the back seat of our car, and Sensei continued, "As you know, we're finding it impossible to deal with the Kuwaitis at this point, and President Hussein is fuming that the Emirate ignores all his gestures. The papers I just gave Ken were a series of correspondence between Quassay and Prince Ahmed Bin-Salimon. They prove how intransigent the Kuwaitis are, and they help to build our case against them. We'd like those documents to spread around Capitol Hill, and frankly, if someone there doesn't leak them to the press, we will."

"Why get the Americans involved at all? Do they really care?"

"In general, the average American wouldn't lose a moment of sleep if we simply took back all of the Kuwaiti territory. The U.S. President, on the other hand, seems to have more of an imperialistic focus. We don't know how determined he is to manipulate us, but we're not about to accept client status from the Americans like the Europeans or Israelis. If they see that we are both strong and justified, they will stay out of our battle."

"But we're not in any war now," I noted.

"Not yet."

After spending Ramadan in Iraq, Yousef took me to London to continue my schooling. I had a private apartment on The Edgware Road near St. John's Wood, close to the Regents Park Mosque. My days were spent studying with tutors, learning the culture, and exercising. Sensei visited a few times, but tensions on the southern border of Iraq were monopolizing his time. He arranged for a former SAS officer to prepare me in some of the more violent martial arts. He liked to call them "practical artwork."

In July, I got a fax from Sensei with instructions to set up accounts in several offshore banks. With all of my perfectly forged documents, I flew to the Isle of Man and opened three different accounts. When the bankers asked me how much money I would send in, I wasn't sure what to say. I told each of them that I expected an inheritance from my grandfather and assumed it would be well over a hundred thousand dollars. They gave me a form with a SWIFT number and all the bank transfer instructions. Using a secured fax line, I sent them to Sensei.

Four days later, I got a call from each of the managers of the bank thanking me for my business. Since Sensei had been keeping out of touch, I didn't know how much he had wired. It turned out that he had sent $800,000 to each account, giving me control over $2.4 million. "How would you like that invested, Ms. Amal?" they asked. I told them to put it on deposit until further notice.

Yousef and I spent about two weeks touring London by foot. He wanted me to have a strong sense of the city so that I could easily pull off the cover of being British when I returned to the States. When speaking to Londoners, I listened carefully to their pronunciation and tried to imitate it closely. After a while, I adopted a fairly basic British accent, certainly enough to fool an American.

At four in the morning on August 1st, 1990, Yousef came into my apartment using his key. "Leila," he called through my bedroom door. "Get up. We have to go." I hopped out of bed, put on my robe, and came out to get the story. "It looks like there will be a war, so we've got to move on."

"Someone is attacking London?" I said with surprise.

"No. It's back in Iraq. Our uncle had a big argument with the head banker of Kuwait about the repayment of loans they made to Iraq during the war with Iran. The banker started demanding repayment now and infuriated the President."

"Which banker?" I inquired.

"I'm not sure exactly. I think he was from the Sultan family, and right now the President is calling his generals together." I knew my uncle hated that family since they controlled so much money and oil, but never came together to support pan-Arab causes.

"Is it safe to go back home now?" I asked.

"We're not going back to Iraq. Dr. Hasim ordered me to take you to New Jersey now in case there are travel problems as a result of the war."

"What if the war doesn't happen?"

"First of all, Leila," he began, "even if the war doesn't materialize, you'd have to get to Princeton anyway in the next few weeks. And secondly, the war is going to start, probably within hours." He looked around my apartment to see if there was anything important. "Take your computer, grab a few clothes, and let's go. Our plane is being fueled up right now."

As our British-registered transoceanic Lear Jet taxied to the runway ninety minutes later, I listened to the BBC: "Reports from the defense ministry say that intelligence sources have spotted Iraqi dictator Saddam Hussein's elite Red Guard massing troops on the border of Kuwait." I smiled to myself. The Kuwaitis were getting what they deserved, and I hoped my uncle would finally reclaim all the land that rightfully belonged to the Iraqi people.

It wasn't until the next day in the United States that I was able to hear the news. In a sweeping victory, Iraqi troops conquered Kuwait. My uncle called to immediately absorb the losing country under our flag. In one of the proudest moments of our history, the BBC called President Hussein, "by far the strongest leader in the region." The rest of the world seemed upset, but I figured that with the intelligence that Sensei had passed to the CIA in the bar in New Jersey a few months earlier, the Americans would basically ignore internal Arab politics.

The United Nations, on the other hand, was quick to condemn us and demand our withdrawal from Kuwait. They talked a lot, however, but tended not to do anything. The United States, surprisingly, ignored the information we had passed to them, and initiated their "Desert Storm" force to extricate our forces from their new positions. Within a week, George Bush was already announcing military plans against us.

"What about the papers you gave to Ken Peters?" I faxed in one line to Sensei, but he didn't respond.

As I settled into my cozy apartment a few minutes away from the campus, the Western imperialists reveled in their plans to destroy Iraq. It became clear within days how the weaker Arab nations would kowtow to the pressure of the Bush war machine and his terror squads. Rather than support the pan-Arab move that we were making, the Arab League decided to send Egyptian, Syrian, and Moroccan troops to fight side by side with the United Nations. "U.N. Unwanted Nobodies," I joked to myself.

I felt so helpless, basking in the warmth of the demonic country's educational core while my comrades were burning in the heat of battle. My apartment, established originally as a resting place for Iraqi diplomats, was well equipped to make me forget the harsh realities back home. Along with several bedrooms, plush carpets, and a well-stocked bar, though, the TV kept playing RNN. I realized the Americans had no idea of ideals and meaning in life. If they could capture a soundbite and sell advertising around it, they'd broadcast it. RNN tried to find a moment of suffering, a glimpse of heroism, or footage of some high-tech missile that could kill hundreds of people instantly. They framed a defensive war, a fight where the most massive forces in the world crashed down upon a sovereign power, as some sort of battle for freedom. After a while, I determined that anything they aired probably was false.

On the first day of college, I dressed in the stylish clothes that had been bought for me, shut the TV, and drove my new motor scooter to campus. In accordance with directions from Yousef, I registered mostly for chemistry and political science courses. The class in Middle East politics was rather timely, and I found that I tended to agree with the professor in class discussions while the loud-mouthed neo-conservatives argued that President Bush was some sort of modern day messiah. "Perhaps he's trying to orchestrate the book of *Revelations*," I commented one day after one of the more outspoken Aryans, Arthur Reese, praised the use of extra-powerful bombs called "bunker busters."

"You're worried about a few more ragheads getting evaporated while we make the world safe for democracy?" he chided me.

"There are a lot more of those ragheads in the world than idol-worshippers like you!" I called back.

Reese jumped up from his chair and pointed a finger at me. "You...," he began.

"You! Mr. Reese," the professor interrupted, "should please be seated." The snake slithered back to its hole, but tried to frighten me with its staring eyes.

Later that week, I went to find the professor during his office hours to apologize, but instead met up with the teaching assistant, a graduate student named Effi Stein. He had spoken in class with a slight accent, so I decided to try to catch him off guard. "*Slichah,*" I began in Hebrew, excusing myself and then asking if this was the professor's office: "*Zeh ha misrado shel ha moreh?*"

He looked up with a smile and then greeted me in Arabic, "*Salaam aleikum.* The professor got called away for a consult, so I'm covering for him. You're Miss Amal, right?"

"That's right."

"Perhaps I can help," he gestured for me to sit opposite him at the desk.

I could feel a blush warming my cheeks. "I just wanted to apologize for my outburst in class the other day. Could you please just tell the professor that?" I started to get up, afraid to overstay my welcome.

"You mean with Arty Reese? Don't worry, Leila. He's a schmuck and everybody knows it. He thinks he's God's gift to Princeton and happily degrades everyone around him."

I sat back down. "I thought so, but I didn't want to get on the professor's bad side so early in the year."

Effi explained that as a well-known teacher of Middle Eastern studies, Professor Beck often consulted for the State Department about the balance of power in the region. He had done extensive research on the religious revolution in Iran as well as the Iran-Iraq war. During the early '80's, Beck had been asked to join a CIA training team that was helping strengthen the Hussein regime. He served with the title of "cultural liaison," which I suspected was another euphemism for spy. "Would you like to get a coffee?" Effi offered around 4:00 p.m., when the scheduled hours finished.

Twice a week for the following month, Effi and I met at the same time and enjoyed coffee. He had taken over lecturing because the professor was invited to stay in Washington and participate in the President's advisory counsel. Though he lacked the same depth of knowledge as his mentor, Effi presented the coursework well. He understood the mindset of the peoples from the region where history started.

I ended up getting a much better grasp of the role that Israel had played in the past century, creating a democratic state in the midst of more traditional societies. Effi had studied in Brandeis University after he finished serving in the Israeli Defense Forces. As a native Israeli, he had been drafted into the army after high school. He opted to stay for four years, instead of the mandatory three, since he got accepted into an elite commando squad called the "*duvduvan*," which means "cherry" in Hebrew. He finished college in his mid-twenties, and was now getting his academic career going with the position at Princeton. His goal was to get his doctorate and then work in a political policy think tank.

"It's hard to save money," he confided, "since I go back to Israel a few times a year to join my army unit as a reserve soldier. The other T.A.s often get jobs to earn some extra cash. But I've got other responsibilities."

"What do you actually do there?" I inquired.

"My job is to gather intelligence and sift through it for the decision-makers."

It took a while for him to warm up to me, but I made an extra effort to become friends. After he felt he could trust me, he told me his family history and recounted some of his army stories. With fluent Arabic, he had been able to work undercover in some of the Palestinian hotbeds to gather information and occasionally arrest wanted terrorists. After he described how the PLO ran the whole area, I was further convinced that the whole Palestinian cause was a sham. Though the principle of replacing Israel with a Palestinian state had always been paramount in my house when I was growing up, the fact was that from the leadership who ordered suicide bombings down to the street merchants who supported them, there wasn't a shred of nobility in the people themselves. Why set up another despotic regime in the Middle East when there were already so many others? One way or the other, though, I had always thought that with the Israelis and Palestinians killing each other, there seemed no real reason to get in the way.

Meeting Effi, however, changed my mind. I had never spoken to someone so passionate about democracy and about how a well-balanced culture leads to true intellectual and economic growth. Effi noted the futility of having peace treaties with dictatorial countries like Syria because when that particular leader is replaced, the country has no reason to keep its promise. When he mentioned Iraq, however, as another evil empire, I held back defending my uncle.

Effi clearly had no idea how Saddam had transformed Iraq from a pathetic religious society into a prosperous and vibrant country. Though I explained that Iraq was one of the few Arab countries that educated its women and had a truly beloved leader, I had to protect my cover as a British woman of Arab descent, so I didn't defend my cause too strongly.

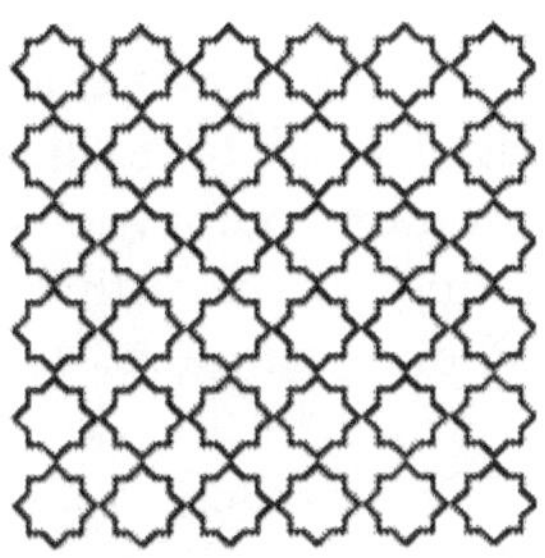

Chapter 9

"Since you live off-campus," Effi asked one afternoon, "have you had the chance to get involved in any of the social activities here?" He told me how the different "eating clubs" of Princeton all had their own atmosphere. One of the "old money" clubs was scheduled for a party that Friday night, so I decided to go.

Since I hadn't made any real friends, I asked Iris Wolfe, a shy girl whom I had met in chemistry class, if she wanted to join me. She lacked the grace that a lot of the other girls had, wearing the same jeans almost every day and keeping her black hair in a braid. Her goal was to be a researcher, so she remained content buried in her academics. However, with a little cajoling, she agreed to come along.

Around 10:00 p.m. on Friday night, I picked her up and we scootered over to the club. "Please bring a helmet for me next time, Leila," she told me disapprovingly when we arrived. I shrugged apologetically.

Iris had tried to dress up, wearing black slacks instead of her usual jeans. Her baggy, green turtlenecked sweater hid any semblance of a figure that she might have had. I straightened the necklace she wore with the Jewish star on it since it got tangled around her collar. I tried to follow the Princeton look, and wore a more preppy-looking outfit with white Keds. Walking up the path on the cold evening, I heard loud music and occasional shouts from inside. Just as I reached for the door, it came crashing open. Arthur Reese rolled through, holding two beers, and ended up looking right at Iris. "Who the hell are you?" he asked with a drunken tone. She stared at him for a moment and then tried to walk around him. "Hey, bitch!" Reese shouted, trying to impress his two other intoxicated companions. All three wore similar, expensive leather jackets, and they quieted down to hear her response. I could see her getting nervous. Reese's blond hair was a mess, and he put his arm over her shoulder and started to pull her in. "Don't just ignore me like I'm a tree!" he ordered.

I pushed his arm away from her, catching his attention. "Leave her alone. Let's go, Iris."

Spotting her necklace, he shouted, "Why don't you take her to the Temple down the block? That's where she belongs on Friday night, with all the other Jews."

"Yeah, right," I said, trying to avoid escalating the situation. The three of them blocked the entrance, and we couldn't easily get around them.

"Let's go, Leila," Iris said.

I stared at Reese's blue eyes so that he would know I wasn't afraid of him, but acceded to Iris's request. Holding onto her arm, we walked down the stairs. As soon as I touched her, I realized I had made a terrible cultural faux pas. Growing up in Iraq, it was normal for girls to hold hands, but as soon as Reese saw us, he blurted out, "Hey guys, let's watch the dikes. They're giving us a live show."

Iris immediately pulled her arm away, also surprised by my mistake. "Sorry, Iris," I whispered. We couldn't just walk away, though, since a number of guys came outside, curious to see Reese's fantasy.

"Come on, Iris! Go for it with the Arab!" Reese began. I could feel my heart beating faster, but I employed my breathing techniques to calm down. I certainly didn't want any fight to break out. As we walked over to my motor scooter, though, he kept following us. "Let's see, ladies. I'll bring my camera!" he kept shouting as we got to my vehicle. As I was about to get on, his tone changed. He grabbed the handlebar and yanked my bike over, breaking the side-view mirror.

"Hey," I yelled.

"Yeah, hey to you, Arab! Everyone looks at you anyway. Kiss your lesbo lover so we can get a good look."

I bent down to pick up my scooter, but he put his foot on it. Seeing him precariously balanced, I took the opportunity to swing my leg around and knock his other foot out from beneath him. I connected firmly above the ankle. A moment later he fell onto his behind, spilling beer on his jacket. He shook his head to gather his senses, and then stood up to the laughs of his comrades. I had picked up my scooter and positioned myself next to Iris on the other side of it.

When he surged towards us, Iris bravely commented, "You're going to beat up some girls to impress your friends?"

He wasn't deterred. "He's not going to beat up any girls tonight," I told Iris. He got a head start on us, though, and pushed my scooter over again. This time, Iris tripped and her leg got caught underneath. She wasn't hurt, but was stuck. I pried the heavy machine off her leg, but with both of us on the ground, Reese had an easy target.

He stomped towards us with his two friends in tow. "Since you're lying down together," he laughed, "why don't you get started now instead of waiting until you get home tonight?" He nudged me towards Iris with his foot on the back of my head. I grabbed his leg and held tight.

Suddenly, I heard a familiar voice. "You're a schmuck, Reese." I kept holding the leg, but the rest of the body went limp. Wearing a suit, a tie, and a blue-and-white knitted yarmulke, my friend Effi showed up and knocked Reese squarely across the jaw. By holding his foot, I had caused him to lose his balance. The impact on his face must have caught him off guard. Right away, though, Reese got up and, with his cohorts, came at Effi.

"This used to be a pretty good school, but now the kikes and the ragheads are all bed buddies," Reese asserted. He thrust his thick arms directly towards Effi's chest. Effi backed up and shook his head slowly from side to side to try to stop the fight. With the next double punch, though, Effi ducked down, turned around and grabbed both arms of his assailant. Staying low, he flipped Reese over his right shoulder. As he threw him, he stood up, making his target hit the ground from a greater height. Drunk and in pain, Reese didn't move.

"Let's trash him," one of the Reese boys said to the other. Remembering the move that I had seen Sensei's son use on him almost a year earlier, I spiraled around on the ground, put one foot in front of one of his legs and scissored my leg closed, causing him to trip forwards. He put his arms down to stop his fall, but as he pushed himself back up, Effi drove a powerful punch between his shoulder blades. He collapsed on the sidewalk.

"Don't embarrass yourself, too," Effi said to the third one, holding up his hand like a policeman directing traffic. He looked at his two friends who were getting up, and then saw a campus security car approaching. Like a mannequin, he remained still. Though the guards were not real police, they were armed and could call the police, and then we'd all end up in trouble.

"What's going on here?" the first guard asked as he got out of the car.

We all stood quietly, looking around at each other. The guard recognized Reese. "We got a call about a disturbance, Arty. Do you know about it?"

Reese brushed off his clothes. "Nothing's going on here, Tony."

The guard looked at Iris and me, and then at Effi. We didn't say anything. "Let's have a quiet night, friends," Tony said and he walked back to his car.

When the security vehicle moved away, Reese turned to his buddies. "Let's go. I'm sick of being around these foreigners." He looked at us, "While American soldiers are risking their lives to protect the world for democracy, you freaks think you can come and live here! You probably support Saddam Hussein and his terrorist regime."

I chose that moment to say nothing and just walked away, wheeling my scooter with me. *If only he knew how right he was*, I thought to myself. "Thanks for your help, Effi," I said, gratefully.

"No, Leila, thank you," he responded. "You're one tough fighter."

I turned to Iris. "I'm really sorry I brought you here."

"I appreciate that you thought of me. But I can really see this isn't the place for me. I find the library much more relaxing than the eating clubs," she responded.

"Can you help me with this?" I asked Effi, wheeling my scooter towards him. It was heavy to push, and I wanted to walk with him for a while.

He brought his fingertips together by his mouth, smiled, and said, "I can't do that now."

"I'm sorry," I replied. "Did you get hurt in the fight?"

"Not at all. It's just that it's Friday night, which is Shabbat, the Jewish Sabbath. It's prohibited for Jews to engage in work on the day of rest. Pushing a motorcycle, or even touching it for that matter, would constitute a violation of Jewish law."

"Beating up Reese must have taken some effort. Was that prohibited according to your rules?" I queried.

"Taking down a few drunk clowns is hardly work, Leila. And anyway, a more important and overriding rule in *halachah*, which is the Hebrew word for Jewish law, is the requirement to protect a life. As I was walking home from Stevenson, the kosher eating club, I spotted Reese starting up with you and I decided to help out."

"Do you mind if I push the bike while we walk back toward campus?"

"The laws of Shabbat only apply to Jews. Feel free."

Iris interjected, "I think we're not both going to go for the walk. I'm going back to my dorm. See you later, Leila."

After Iris left, Effi and I wandered amongst the beautiful Princeton buildings. I locked up my scooter and walked under one of the arches. An all-male, *a capella* singing group was giving a concert, which echoed fabulously inside the stone passageway. Effi was taller than most of the students there. I enjoyed feeling like his date that evening, and we wandered around for hours before he escorted me home. "I have to get back to synagogue early tomorrow morning," he said as he bid me goodnight.

As an orthodox Jew, he took his religion seriously, and much more thoughtfully than the Muslims that I knew in Iraq. My family and associates in the palace were certainly not part of the religious sector. Practicing Muslims prayed a lot and dressed more modestly. It never made much sense to me, nor to them, I think. It seemed like a well-tuned cult that gave everyone a sense of belonging.

Effi's approach to his Judaism, on the other hand, focused on the development of a peaceful society, where scholarship and good deeds were praised. He explained that on the holiday of Passover, Jews all over the world recount the story of the exodus from Egypt. Grandparents would tell parents, and parents would pass on the same story to their children generation after generation. Every year, the recollection of how God cast the Ten Plagues on Pharaoh and his people would be repeated in millions of Jewish homes. "How do you think that started, Leila?" he asked rhetorically, "You think one day someone just made up the tale of the parting of Red Sea and convinced millions of desert wanderers that they had seen it, too? It would have been impossible to start that rumor unless it actually happened. And today, in whatever Jewish Seder you attend, you'll hear people recount the exact same events as they really happened."

Having never thought of the Bible as an historical study, I hadn't ever considered the possibility that it was real. Effi explained how so many archeological digs had proven that Biblical events actually did occur. He stirred my interest enough to check out a few books on the topic of Judaism. In any case, just talking with him was fascinating, so after that Friday night I arranged to meet with him frequently.

About a week later, after finishing a long chemistry lab, I dropped by his office. He was on the phone, writing notes frantically in both Hebrew and English on a white pad of paper. "Yes, Professor," he said several times, "I understand, sir. I'll get you that information right away."

When he hung up, I greeted him, "Hi, Effi."

"Oh, Leila. I'd love to talk now, but I have to check out something for Professor Beck."

"What is it?" I inquired.

"I'm sorry, but I can't talk about it. Maybe we can get together later?"

"Would it be okay for me to call you?" I asked, leaning over his desk with a smile. I took hold of his pad of paper, and leaving his notes in place, I tore out the second page. "What's your phone number?"

I wrote it on the piece of paper, folded it up, and then placed it carefully in my purse. As I dug around in the crowded handbag to find a safe place for it, I grabbed a small and flexible metal card and palmed it in my hand. "I just had a really hard day and I need a shoulder to cry on," I started saying as I put my hands behind my back and walked around the desk to him. I peeled off the paper that covered the adhesive and, to Effi's surprise, I wrapped my arms around him and gave him a hug. He paused for a moment, and then patted me on the back. "I'm sure it'll be fine, Leila. And I really want to hear about it. But you have no idea how important this job is for the professor. I'll call you as soon as I finish."

As he spoke, I attached the tiny, sticky microphone to the inside hem at the back of his jacket. I forced myself to bring a tear to my eye, and when we released, I backed up and thanked him for the hug. "I'm just far away from everyone," I said, "and sometimes I just need to feel that I have a friend. Good luck with your work." I waved the tips of my fingers towards him and left.

I closed his office door and pulled my Walkman out of my purse. I set it to the radio setting, and tuned into the FM station to which the transmitter was set, and hit the record button. I could hear some papers shuffling as I picked the lock on the office next door. The British trainer who had taught me martial arts the previous summer had also shown me more sophisticated lock-picking techniques than just using a credit card in the slot of the door.

Once inside, I locked the door and sat close to the dividing wall. The transmitter was very low power, and I had to stay within about 40 meters to pick up the signal. At first, Effi didn't say anything. On the desk in my borrowed office I found a sharpened pencil. Very lightly, I rubbed the sharp point over the page that Effi had just given me with his phone number. Since it had been the second page in his pad, the pressure of his pen on the first page had made a slight indentation on the second. The pencil rubbing brought out the words that he had written, and I was able to decipher his notes. I think he wrote in Hebrew to keep people from peering over his shoulder. Though my reading skills were slow, I had time to study each word.

He had obviously written down the questions that the professor wanted to know. "Where is the bunker where Saddam is likely to hide? How long will Saddam's supplies last in the bunker just north of the Baghdad palace? How many people would Saddam bring to the bunker? Would there be civilians?"

I sat still for over half an hour. The phone in Effi's office rang and I listened carefully on my headphones. "I can't talk now, *Ima*," he said. "I'll call you Sunday."

It was late afternoon, and though the office I was using seemed secure, I figured the guards would come to lock up the building soon. At 5:30 p.m., Effi called his chief. "Professor, I went through your notes as you said and I think I found the information that you wanted." He paused, "Yes sir, I can tell you now. No one is here. Regarding location, I don't think Saddam would be in the Dora Farms palace or bunker. Even though that residential palace isn't used much, and it might seem more secret, it's still too close to Baghdad. He's also probably bringing his top brass with him, and the bunker under that palace is too small."

Effi listened for a moment, and though I couldn't hear the specific words of Professor Beck, I could hear mumbling sounds. Effi replied, "No kidding, Sir. You were in that bunker as a cultural liaison?"

Effi continued, "I see you have sketched out some maps of the area north of Baghdad. On one of them here, you circled Samarra. It's a little south of Tikrit."

As soon as he said the name, I was sure they were on to something. About fifteen years earlier, my uncle had ordered the creation of a major chemical weapons facility around Samarra called *al Muthanna*. Yousef had taken me to check it out a few times and I met several of the researchers. Sensei used it once to test my training in covert surveillance and quick entry.

Thinking about one particular trip with Yousef, I looked in my purse and wrapped my hand around the gift that I had gotten while I was there. The director had given me a cassette that contained a small compartment with a large dose of sarin nerve agent. "Be careful, young lady. You could wipe out a small city with this," he told me as he explained how to snap open the compartment that would heat up and then release the gas within five minutes.

The "pesticide" facility made the nerve agent Tabun in the '80s. When the Iranians were pushing too close to our border during the war, our troops fired canisters of the toxic brew on the battlefield that gave us the upper hand. That was another time the U.N. got upset with us. They tried to document our viciousness for being the first country to ever use nerve agents in battle. My uncle took that as a compliment.

"Based on your notes in the margin, Professor, Samarra seems like a probable candidate. Wait, here's a map of the facility. You have written on it in pencil. I could fax it to you, but the writing is very light and I'm not sure it will come out. It refers to this facility, which is about 75 kilometers from Baghdad." Effi read ahead for a moment. "You have a complete security map here. Let me give you the details. The total perimeter is surrounded by a fence, about 10 km by 10 km. There is a second fence around the testing area. Both fences are two meters high and topped with barbed wire. There is a north and west entrance, both with armed guards. They have tire slasher barriers, and each entrance has serpentine barriers so vehicles have to slow down and zig zag through." He went on to accurately describe the storage facilities, the bunkers, the production areas and many details. I could tell by the answers Effi supplied, that the professor would be turning over this information to the military advisers at the Pentagon.

"What do you think they'll do with the scud missiles there?" Effi asked. He was quiet.

"Hit Israel? My whole family is there. Do you really think the missiles will reach that far?" I knew that Israel was always a target for my uncle, especially in retaliation for their bombing raid on our nuclear power plan in 1982. However, I didn't expect the revenge to come now. "That sarin gas could kill hundreds of thousands of Israelis!" Effi said.

When I had last left Samarra, I had seen plans to fit the missiles with gas delivery systems. However, there were many technical problems with the devices the scientists were trying to use. Anyway, the use of gas on Israel could force them into a nuclear response, which I was sure the President would try to avoid.

Down the hall I heard the two security guards doing the final evening check on the building. There was no safe hiding place in the office where I was, so I pulled a black mask out of my bag, tied my hair back, covered my face, and prepared to leave by the window. With this critical information I had to make sure that I could report back to Yousef or Sensei. I was now sure where the Americans would strike next, and also where they would not. If Effi knew I was there, or even suspected that anyone had heard his conversation, all of this information would become useless.

I continued to listen on my Walkman to understand as much of the plans as I could, and I climbed on the desk to reach the small window high on the wall. It was painted shut, and wouldn't budge. As quietly as I could, I popped the glass with my handbag. Unfortunately, it made a shattering sound just as the guards were checking the door to the office. I heard one say to the other, "Did you hear something, Tony?" I pulled myself up and looked outside. There was no ledge either up or down.

With a jump off the desk, I rolled onto the floor to keep my landing quiet, and hid behind the door. I pulled a special, very thick magic marker out of the side compartment of my knapsack and took off my Walkman, leaving it in "record" mode. I was wearing leggings underneath my skirt, which I unzipped and let drop to the floor. I'd need strong kicks to win a quick fight, and keep it so quiet that Effi, next door, would not hear a thing. The guard's key slid in the door and the handle twisted. "Where's the light switch, Tony?"

"It's on the other side of the door."

My first victim walked around the door and could hardly see me crouched down in the dark. When he got completely on my side of the door, I drove the palm of my hand up into his groin with all my strength. The pain knocked the wind out of him as he dropped to his knees. The only sound he made was a brief grunt as I covered his mouth with my right hand, taking a firm grasp of his jaw. My left hand was anchored over his ear, and I pushed both hands together, snapping his neck. His lifeless body fell limp, and I lowered it to the ground. As he descended, I drew and cocked his revolver.

"You okay, Dave?" Tony said, walking into the room all the way. Once he was inside, I pushed the door closed, turned on the light, and pointed the gun right in his face. He turned pale and nearly fainted when he saw his partner on the ground. I kept the gun pointed right at his eyes so he wouldn't think to even look in my direction. Even though my face was covered, I didn't want him to have any sense of who I was. To disguise my voice, I whispered hoarsely, "Turn around now or I'll kill you, too." He complied. I pulled his gun as well. Sticking my leg between his legs, I pushed them apart.

As a former cop, Tony must have sensed that when I had one leg off the ground to frisk around his ankle, he could take advantage of me. He swung around, bringing his arms up to a fighting stance. I simply pushed his arms a little further, using his own momentum against him, and launched a powerful roundhouse kick straight to his face. His glasses flew across the room, but he made little noise as he toppled. I opened the back of my magic marker and pulled out a small rag. It was doused in chloroform in the sealed pen. Turning my head away to avoid breathing the fumes, I covered his mouth and nose with the cloth. In a few seconds, his tense body relaxed. I pulled the cloth away before killing him.

I had not wanted to break the neck of the other guard, and did not want to take the last breath from Tony, either. However, I had mission-critical data that needed to be transmitted back to Iraq. I sat on the floor, looking at both bodies; one dead, one barely alive. Tony had a wedding ring on and a mustache. What if he woke up?

I tried not to look at the dead one.

Yousef and Sensei were both out of the country. My only contact was Madame Moreau. I remembered Sensei's words about being a team that helps each other, so I waved the chloroform cloth in front of Tony's face again, just to keep him sleeping and ran up to the top floor of the building.

The halls were mostly dark, and no one seemed to be in the building. There was a payphone that I used to call a computer that I had set up in the chemistry lab. It was designed to answer calls and then reroute them using another one of the university's thousands of phone lines. It wasn't perfect, but would make a trace unlikely.

"I have a problem," I said in French when Madame answered the phone. "One of my birds has flown, and one has a broken wing."

"Euthanize the broken wing," she ordered, and then took my location.

I polished my fingerprints off the phone and returned to the room and found Tony lying on his back. He had rolled over and was struggling to open his eyes. Following orders, I held the cloth over his mouth for a minute and watched his soul leave his body. He was yet another casualty in the Americans' war against my people. Despite the knowledge that I was doing my job well, I was pained at the loss of life. I reviewed my steps since entering the office and then cleaned everything that I had touched. I checked my Walkman, but Effi had obviously gone since there was no more sound. After packing it up, I waited by the door. Keeping it open a crack, I monitored the hallway. Thirty minutes later, a cleaning lady came down the hall pushing a large cart. As she approached, I recognized Madame and let her in.

"It looks like you eventually learned how to do something useful," she said looking at the two corpses. It reminded me of the scolding I had once received from her for cheating on my homework.

"I have information that I must relay immediately to the palace."

"Okay, child. I'll clean up after you. Be off."

I strolled carefully out of the building, and raced back to my apartment to relay the tape's contents to Yousef and Sensei.

After copying the cassette and securing the copy in the floor safe, I sent an encoded fax to Sensei's contact in Baghdad. The fax printed the confirmation that the paper had been printed on the other end, but there was no response. I clicked on the TV to watch the news and pass some time. The ring from the fax machine woke me about two hours later, and a brief document came through. It took me about ten minutes to interpret the code, which directed me to a payphone about twenty minutes away.

At 2:00 a.m., a payphone by the side of the New Jersey Turnpike rang. I picked it up and mounted a digitizing mouth and earpiece. I keyed in the code that we would use for the first two minutes of the conversation, and then said, "Who's there?"

"It's me, Leila," said Sensei. I thought I would cry. The comfort of hearing his voice made me feel like a child who gets hurt and acts very bravely until he sees his mother. At that point he breaks down, relieved to be in the comfort of someone he truly trusts. After the security guard episode, I had no comfort from Madame, but I knew Sensei would validate my feelings. "It's hard to talk now, my dear," he concluded, "What has happened?"

"I intercepted and recorded a conversation between a researcher and a military adviser. They were discussing their strategy for tracking the President."

"Plug in the recording to this secured line and play the tape on fast speed. I'll record it here and then analyze it offline."

"Are you sure this is a safe transmission? It will take about thirty minutes to play the tape, even at the fast speed."

"It should be fine. You weren't followed, were you?"

"No, Sensei. Can we at least talk while the tape copies?"

"Do you have another telephone security device?"

I told him that I didn't, but he said that as long as we speak cryptically, it should be okay. While I copied the tape, I gave him the phone number of the adjacent pay phone. He called and I mostly told him about my classes, though I didn't mention Effi. I realized that even though nothing had happened between Effi and me, if I were to have brought him up, Sensei might be jealous. I felt torn inside because I did consider Effi a good friend, and somehow he had partially replaced Sensei as far as an emotional comfort. On the other hand, I assured myself, Effi was really an espionage target, a Zionist who could feed me the information I needed to protect my uncle.

As the tape breezed by at double speed, I could hear the high pitch sound of Effi saying, "Hit Israel? My whole family is there."

"Sensei," I said, "How will our cousins be affected?" I referred to the Israelis that way since like us, they considered themselves descendents of the prophet Ibrahim, though not through his son Ishmael. "Will we deliver them a package?"

"I suppose we'll send them something, since it's hard for us to deliver a nice present to their big brother."

"Something wet or dry?" I asked, referring to whether the scud missiles would include a nerve gas component.

"Wet."

I wasn't sure what kind of response the Israelis would have if attacked with gas. However, I did not see why Effi's family had to get involved in our fight with the Americans. "I believe they will send us a package, too, my teacher. And since our cousins have such a good sense of humor, I bet if we send them something wet, they will send us something hot."

"Why do you say that, my dear?" he asked, trying to figure out why I thought there could be a nuclear response if we used gas.

"I'm getting a great education here at Princeton. I believe I have developed some good insight."

"I understand, my dear. I will review our plan with the team. How's the other line doing?"

As I checked the recording, I spotted two headlights in the reflection in the phone. I had seen them a few minutes earlier, and they were still in the same place. It seemed unusual that at such a late hour, someone would stop in the rest area and keep his lights on. The recording was nearly finished, but I thought it was dangerous to stay any longer. I, too, must have appeared suspicious, using two phones in the middle of the night with wires dangling from one of them. "My teacher, I have company."

"Disconnect now," he ordered, "and go north on the highway."

I stuffed the equipment in my backpack, and hopped on my motor scooter. Crossing over a grassy partition, I got onto the New Jersey Turnpike heading towards New York. When I glanced over my shoulder, my suspicions were confirmed. The parked car had zipped out of the parking lot and made an illegal U-turn to switch towards my direction. Under the bright lights of the parking area, I saw two people inside a black sedan with New Jersey license plates. I had no idea how they thought to track me there. Who would have leaked information? In fact, I wasn't sure they knew who I was, but perhaps it was more of a routine check. I was sure that the recording hadn't been intercepted since the digital encryption technology had been bought from a CIA agent only a few months earlier. In case I got caught, I replaced the cassette from my Walkman with a Sting album that I had copied from a CD.

With my weak engine, outrunning my assailants would be like a child trying to run away from a German Shepherd. My headstart caused by their having to turn around from the southbound side to the northbound lane put me around a mile ahead of them. But I knew they'd catch up soon. Late at night, the road was rather empty. I caught up with a truck that was hauling cars in the right lane. By pulling around to his right side, I rode in the shoulder and hid from my assailants. I was concerned that my red taillight would expose my position, and I couldn't shut it off by flicking off my headlight. With my helmet in hand, I twisted around and with three solid whacks, I broke the light.

The wind blew my hair all around, and I couldn't get my helmet back on. I tossed it to the side, not wanting to lose my concentration on the road while dealing with it. I then wrapped my hair around my hand and stuffed it down the back of my sweatshirt. That held it for a few minutes, and allowed me the time I needed to destroy the incriminating cassette. Bending the case between the handgrip and the brake lever of my motor scooter, I cracked it open. I pulled on a piece of the actual tape inside, and let the case drop onto the pavement. The whole spool unwound, leaving hundreds of meters of stretched out recordings to fly away with all the other garbage on the road.

I stayed close to the truck, using it to shield me. After several more miles, I couldn't see them. I assumed that they had passed me while I was dismantling the evidence. A few minutes more, and I veered off the highway to another rest stop. I parked near the restaurant and stood beside my scooter. My body was shaking from all the action and the high speed — it was surely faster than such a small motor was meant to handle. After inhaling a few deep breaths, I headed inside to go to the bathroom.

Though it was around three in the morning, there were about twenty patrons in the roadside eatery. My throat was dry and my hands ached from squeezing the handles of my bike for so long. I ordered a coffee and a bowl of vegetable soup as I sat at the counter. One old trucker nearby nodded his head politely. "It may start raining soon, young lady," he warned. "Drive safely."

With a smile, I responded, "You, too." We chatted for a while. He told me his name was Douglas, but his trucker handle was "Big Doug." I told him I was Dana. After about ten minutes, two men in suits came in. They spotted me right away and walked casually over. One of them was Ken Peters, the CIA agent that Sensei had me seduce for some pictures a few months earlier. He and his partner sat down on either side of me.

"Let's talk outside," Ken said.

"I'm sorry," I said, "I don't want my soup to get cold."

"Let's go," the other one ordered.

"I can't do that just now."

He put his hand on my shoulder and was about to grab my wrist, when Big Doug intervened. "You leave that little lady alone."

"You stay out this, Pops," Ken said. "This is police business."

I knew that they were trying to work unnoticed, so I decided to increase the volume. "You're no cop! Show us a badge!" I screamed.

Ken took hold of my other hand, and they both tried to pull me out. "We'll show you the badges outside," he said.

I mouthed the word "help" to Big Doug, and he stood right up. The two men were well trained, and I couldn't move my arms at all. Big Doug stepped into our path, but as we passed him, Ken's partner swung his elbow sharply into the trucker's chest, causing him to gasp, and trip backwards on to a chair. They marched me straight out to my motor scooter and demanded the tape.

"I don't know what you're talking about."

Ken rummaged through my bag, found the keys, and unlocked the storage compartment. He popped the cassette out of my Walkman and then brought me over to their car. Ken sat up front and his partner pushed me in back.

"Who were you talking to before?" Ken's partner began his interrogation.

"I'm not sure," I said stalling.

"What is so valuable on this tape that you're willing to die for it?"

I chuckled, "I'm not going to die for it. Who are you?"

"Don't be a smartass, lady. I'm asking the questions."

"Well, I already know Ken pretty well," I smiled, sure that if he didn't already recognize me, Ken would realize who I was.

"Just shut up," Ken said, "and answer the questions." He had trouble getting the cassette into the tape deck of the car, and then hit rewind before it started to play any music. I was lucky he didn't immediately notice that there was only music on it.

I struggled to break free, but Ken's partner held both my wrists tightly and said, "Just sit still. In the middle of a truck stop off the New Jersey Turnpike is no time to start pissing off two tired cops."

"Enough with the cop story," I said. "You're CIA. Who do you think you're fooling?"

He shot the back of his hand up towards my face and his knuckles stung my chin. I figured I had another half a minute until the tape got back to the beginning; then they'd realize it was not the real one.

I was afraid that that would lead to some serious torture.

"We know about your connection to the terrorist leader Gamal," Ken said. "Was that who you were talking to?"

"No, Ken," I said condescendingly. "I was talking to your wife."

Smack – another hit to the head. When he punched me above my ear, my head jolted towards the door and the other side of my head hit the window. I remembered that Sensei had taught me never to show emotions when being beaten. Breathing slowly and deliberately could help me concentrate on separating my mind from my body. An American officer in Vietnam had been caught by the North Vietnamese and subjected to the vilest torture. He was determined not to submit to their demand to publicly denounce America's war effort. As a punishment, they bound his arms and legs in precarious positions, and beat him for hours on end. After over a year in solitary confinement he was released, having never submitted to his captors. I had read his story months earlier. He had eventually become a professor of aeronautical engineering at Notre Dame University. His steadfastness inspired me on many occasions, and I tried to concentrate on his strength as I prepared myself for a brutal session with Ken and his comrade. I was sure they would kill me if I didn't give them what they wanted– and even if I did tell them, they'd have no further use for me and would probably kill me anyway.

Then I heard the click of the tape reaching the beginning. "Now let's listen," Ken said.

I knew the first chord of the music would lead to more abuse when they realized I had swapped the tapes. Suddenly, the driver's window was smashed as Big Doug jammed the muzzle of his shotgun into Ken's side. "Don't move, punk, or your friend's wasted," he threatened. Neither man moved, but their eyes met when the music started. "Get out the car, Dana, and get going. I'll keep these guys here 'till the real cops come."

"Goodbye, gentlemen. Enjoy the music." I ran back to my bike and started towards the exit of the rest stop. I decided to keep going north. As I circled around, I glanced at the car that Big Doug was guarding and saw the man in the back make a quick move. I saw Big Doug's arms jolt as he pulled his trigger. A fraction of a second later, the back seat lit up with the blast of the second man's gun as he shot Big Doug in the head. His body collapsed on the car, almost as though he was leaning against it. The shooter got out of the car and pointed his gun at me. I swerved and banked vigorously to avoid falling into his line of sight, and since I was already far away, he got into the driver's seat of his car and started to come after me. I zipped onto the highway and hoped to find a new means of escape.

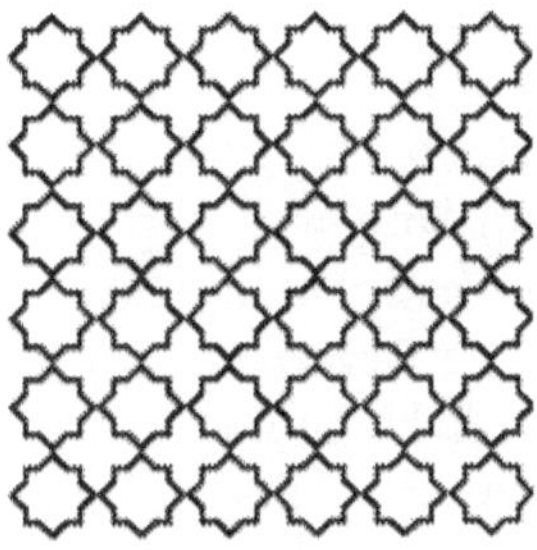

Chapter 10

I had a small head start on the highway, but I knew that it would only give me a chance to choose my lane before the car would catch up with me. There was a moving truck further ahead, but it was going very slowly. With no choice, though, I scurried to its right side and prayed it would obfuscate my pursuer's view of me. Moments later the truck began to slow. The CIA agent had put a police flasher on his roof, and that made the driver start to pull over. As he was near stopping, I pulled ahead to find another decoy.

The biggest car on the road was a tow truck, so I decided to try using that as a shield. It was going rather slowly, too, and I figured that maybe the driver had also seen the police lights. When I looked closer, though, I saw that the driver had the light on inside the cabin and was waving a small banner. It had the three distinctive stars of the Iraqi flag. Was this why Sensei had told me to go north?

I glanced in my rearview mirror and saw that there were only a few hundred meters between my assailant and me. Ahead, someone else was sitting next to the tow truck driver and had put a piece of paper on the window. Written in Arabic, it said, "Come to my right and grab the net." The truck stayed in the right lane, and I sped up on the shoulder. Just as I reached it's side, the CIA car reached me. He couldn't squeeze onto the narrow shoulder, so he just stayed right behind me. The passenger of the tow truck threw a large fishing net out of the window, and attached part of it to the frame of the vehicle. As I got close, I could see the face of my savior. I inched even closer and threw my bag into the window. Madame caught it and then yelled to me to hurry up. Stretching my left leg onto the ledge of the truck, I grabbed hold of the net and hopped off my bike. Since I pushed off it a bit, it immediately lost balance and crashed into a railing where it bounced off the side and slid into the door of the car behind me.

My arm took the brunt of the hit as my body swung on to the frame of the tow truck. At 50 miles per hour, the impact of even small movements seemed magnified. Though I had a hard time controlling my direction, I was safely entwined in the net, and Madame was able to pull me in through the window. As I tucked my legs inside, the driver gave an order with slurred speech. "Strap in." I hardly understood, but Madame buckled herself and I did the same.

The driver glanced down to confirm that we were secure and then he jammed on the brakes. He turned the wheel sharply to the left, making the back end of our car swing towards the right. Our tail collided with the CIA vehicle's hood and made a crunching sound even louder than that of the skidding of the wheels. Our truck then lurched ahead, and I watched our opponent swerve back and forth a few times until he got back on track.

His lighter vehicle had the advantage of being more agile, and he tried to slide up on our left. "Let him pull up close," Madame shouted to the driver. She put her hand out to me and said, "Give me your gun."

"I don't have one with me, Madame. It's in the safe."

"You stupid amateur," she snarled. "Do you think we gave it to you as a collector's item?"

She formed a tight fist and punched the air in front of the driver's face, indicating to him that he should ram the car. He cut sharply left, knocking the opponent into the railing, and then pulled away to prepare for another assault. Our driver's window then crumbled as a bullet passed through it and pierced our windshield. A small spider-web appeared in the middle of the glass, and the wind made a whistling sound as it rushed into the car.

A short bang on the brake pedal and our truck paralleled the car. Like before, our driver thrust the wheel left and this time we pinned the car against the railing. We rammed into him yet again as we pulled away and then immediately crashed into the side of his car again. Our driver checked the rear view mirror, and seeing a clearing, screeched to a halt while spinning the wheel all the way to the left. We spun around, facing against the traffic on the Turnpike. He floored the gas pedal and turned on the yellow rotating light on top. In his slurred voice, he instructed Madame to take the Q-beam light from the floor and plug it into the cigarette lighter.

We had to maneuver quickly to avoid head-on collisions with other cars, but so did our pursuer. He had turned around and continued his chase, following directly behind us. Up ahead, I spotted a truck in our lane. Our driver was keeping his eye fixed on the mirror to track the car. "Watch out for the truck ahead," I warned. He ignored me.

The assailant shot out our back window, putting another hole in the front glass, too. The oncoming eighteen-wheeler blasted his horn, but we stayed in our lane. "Shine the light out back," our driver ordered in his awkward speech. Madame flicked on the 200,000-candle power beam, nearly blinding the CIA driver. Watching him squint and cover his eyes, I heard the Doppler effect on the truck's deep horn, making it scream to an ever-increasing pitch. Just as we neared a head-on collision, we swerved to the side, narrowly missing the rolling thunder. Madame kept the beam squarely focused through the front window of the tailing car.

I'm not sure whether he saw the oncoming truck. Seconds later I saw the whole street light up with the flame that burst out between the two engines. The truck skidded for a while, but I could no longer see since we crossed through an "authorized vehicles only" passage and joined the traffic moving in our direction.

"Go get her motor scooter about four kilometers back," Madame shouted at the driver. Then she turned to me, "Do you know who that was?"

"I'm not sure. I guess he was a CIA agent."

"Don't guess, Leila. Think. Who was following you?"

"There were two of them at first. The one who got shot back in the parking lot was Ken Peters, who I believe was a CIA operative. It would follow that the second one was his partner."

Madame looked worried. "You killed Ken Peters?"

"No, I didn't kill him. There was some truck driver with a shotgun who helped me escape. I didn't see the whole thing, but as I pulled away, I think Ken got shot. In any case, he was in the car when it crashed. So if the bullet didn't kill him, the car crash must have." I then recounted the story of the beginning of the chase.

"You have an uncanny ability to ruin years of work," she scolded. "Ken was one of our best contacts in the U.S. government. You could have avoided being caught by not stopping for a rest. You think that you can just run away from the CIA and then stop for a coffee?"

"I, I..."

She cut me off. "Even if Ken caught you, you knew that we have enough information on him to stop him from hurting you. Why didn't you just play along for a little while?"

There was no point in defending my actions. Surely she would submit a damning report to Sensei, and hopefully he'd forgive me for participating in the death of one of his contacts.

The driver returned to the place where my motor scooter was destroyed and picked it up. Since we were in a tow truck, no one assumed anything was out of the ordinary. Five or six emergency vehicles sped past on their way to the accident we caused. We also returned to the rest stop where I had been picked up. Madame surveyed the area for about ten minutes to see if any surveillance cameras might have caught me on video. She spotted one, but said that it was only pointed at the cash registers, and that I would not have been filmed.

As I waited in the car with the driver, I tried to talk with him. I realized then that he was virtually deaf. Madame later explained that his father had been a chef in charge of one of Saddam's kitchens. Kurdish spies captured the chef and his son and ordered the chef to poison Saddam's food. He was so loyal to the President that even when they tortured his son, he would not agree. They tried torture through sleep deprivation, blasting loud music whenever either of them dozed. To increase the pain, they affixed a headset to the boy's head and wrapped it on with duct tape, completely covering his whole head, except his mouth and nose. They increased the volume so strongly that the father could hear the pounding even though he was on the other side of the room.

He finally complied, unable to cope with the torture of his son. They supplied him with a small dose of sodium fluoro-acetate to sprinkle on Saddam's main dish. As was often the custom, he personally served the meal to the President. Captain Gamal, at the time a lower rank, was dining with the President. He noticed that the chef looked rather nervous. After asking the President to wait a moment, he then instructed the chef to eat some of Saddam's meal. The chef tried to talk his way out of it, but Gamal cocked his gun and placed it to the back of his head.

The chef downed the food, eating slowly until he was ordered to speed up. After about five minutes, his face started twitching, and he asked to be excused. Gamal didn't look too good at that point, having had someone else eat the President's food. But as the chef began to leave, he bent over and vomited all over the floor. He could hardly breathe, but he managed to say where his son was being held prisoner. He died a few minutes later. On autopsy, the toxicology report identified the poison, and the cause of his death was recorded as respiratory failure due to pulmonary edema.

Though the President was incensed at the attempt on his life, he was more angry at the Kurds for torturing an Iraqi boy. To show his respect for Gamal, he asked him to a lead a rescue team. Choosing to go alone, Gamal waited until 3:00 a.m., sure the captors would be asleep. He slipped in through the window of the apartment they were using and slit the throats of all four Kurdish spies while they slept.

Gamal rescued the boy, who suffered permanent and almost total hearing loss as a result of the explosive sounds to which he had been subjected. Feeling sorry for him, the President allowed him to get training as a driver, and eventually he got assigned to the embassy in the United States. Madame explained that he had taken some special driving courses in Germany, and I felt a little closer to him, knowing that we had both probably learned similar techniques.

They dropped me off about two blocks from my apartment, and I walked home. I was sure I would lie in bed, unable to sleep, thinking about the excitement. I took a long bath, after which I lay down on the couch. I remembered how I had once snuggled up to Ken Peters, and how I saw the manly desire in his eyes. *Goodnight, Ken,* I thought to myself, feeling a little sad. Maybe I should have done something so that he wouldn't have gotten killed. Surely when Sensei told me to ride north, he didn't know who would be chasing me. I fell asleep confused.

My 6:00 a.m. alarm clock was a self-inflicted torture. Going for a run hardly seemed sympathetic to my tired body. By a newsstand nearby, I read the headline of the local Princeton daily, "Two university guards dead after fatal car crash." Smiling headshots of Dave and Tony looked nothing like the corpses I had left on the office floor. Madame must have dragged their bodies out of the building and staged a realistic accident. *Boy, she's good*, I thought. My feet pounded into the ground. *And, man, I'm bad.*

With a faster pace, I emptied my mind of the human factors of the previous evening. Jogging – almost sprinting – was like entering a long, narrow tunnel. I focused on getting to the other end, and I could not see anything on either side. When I emerged from my hour-long run, much longer than usual, I showered and dressed, transitioning from one of Sensei's killers to an Ivy League college student. The only crossover was a Colt Detective Special, a .38 snub-nose revolver with a shrouded hammer that I strapped in an ankle holster under my jeans. Madame was right – guns are no use when they are locked away.

As the new semester got under way, I focused on my studying to direct my mind away from the war. However, while reading, I always kept RNN droning in the background. About a week into the new courses, one news item caught my attention. Someone at the Pentagon had leaked that U.S. forces were preparing for an immediate attack on the

Samarra military installation. I was in a lecture hall when the actual assault happened that afternoon, but there was a fax waiting for me at home that simply said, "Your uncle says thank you." Days later the U.S. government admitted that faulty intelligence or an information leak had led them to believe that they would find Saddam at that chemical weapons facility. Though I only found out much later, my uncle used the tape that I sent and found refuge at the Dora Farms retreat. My first mission was a real success.

On Thursday afternoon, I bought a coffee on the way home – a double latte. I called the Guernsey bank that held some of my money. "This is Leila Amal," I began.

"Good day, Ms. Amal," the receptionist seemed unusually happy to hear from me. "Mr. Hardwick was awaiting your call." She passed me through to the bank manager.

"I'd like to thank you for the considerable con-fidence you have placed in us," he began with his English accent.

Slipping into a slight accent, too, I played along. "We've been very pleased up till now. Do you have any suggestions for me?"

"As you know, Leila. May I call you Leila? As you know, we are not licensed investment advisers. But if I could make a suggestion as a friend, I would take about at least a third of the million and a half that just came in and place it in a time deposit. That way, you'll know it's safe."

I was amazed that so much money had been deposited. Last time Sensei sent any money my way, he put equal sums into three different accounts. Shocked by the huge amount, I just listened to Mr. Hardwick droning on. When he finished, I told him that it sounded really great and gave him the okay to place the balance of the money in the investments he was describing.

"I will fax you the trade confirmations. Have a good day."

Immediately, I checked with the second off-shore bank, which also confirmed that $1.5 million had been wired into my account. When I got the same news from the third bank manager, I asked him to transfer a hundred thousand dollars to my local Princeton bank. "Tuition has really gone up in America," he commented.

"So has the cost of new car," I smiled.

As I headed out to go car shopping the next morning, a fax of several pages arrived. It was from Mr. Hardwick, confirming the various securities that he had bought in my account. Not really understanding the details, I copied the essentials and faxed the same information to the other bank managers and asked them to purchase the same investments in my accounts there.

Having over five million dollars in offshore bank accounts, I considered that I had several options. What would happen if I created a new identity, shuffled the money around, and then disappeared? When "Leila Amal" was created, I was hardly consulted. Saying that I refused the assignment would not have been possible. Where would I have gone? But with more experience and seemingly unlimited assets, I didn't need permission. If my uncle heard that I had absconded with his money, though, I'd be on the run for the rest of my life. The Mukhabarat would eventually track me down and maybe even kill me. Perhaps Saddam himself would do the honors. Though I admired him greatly, I recalled the story that at the tender age of 11, he shot one of his teachers. From the Tikriti clan, he adhered strictly to the codes of swift and severe punishment.

I had thought about asking Sensei why this money was being put in my name, but then I decided to leave the topic alone. He surely had his reasons, and I trusted him. "He must trust me, too," I thought, as I realized that his faith in me was worth more than anything.

As I stepped out of my building into the icy cold air, I spotted two well-dressed Arab men watching my apartment entrance. Their thick black mustaches exposed them as Iraqi. My heart skipped a beat, and I considered running. I realized, though, that if they were here to hurt me, they would have slipped into my home. I stopped and stared back for a moment. One of them looked at me and then whispered to the other. "Leila?" the second one called.

"Yeah."

"Catch!" He tossed his car keys high in the air. I thought it was some kind of trick to distract me, so I just stared at him and let them drop in the frosty grass nearby. Both men began to laugh loudly; one of them began coughing, and they strolled towards me.

"Leila," the first one began. "I'm Tariq Mohammad. I work at the embassy. You can pick up your car keys."

I bent down waitress-style and snatched the keys, never taking my eyes off them. "What do you mean 'my keys'?"

"President Hussein wanted to send you his best wishes. He thought you might like a Mercedes." There were two, brand new Mercedes parked across the street. "I thought you'd like the black one."

My uncle was known to generously reward people who helped him and, like my father, I was now directly feeling his largesse. People never realized how giving Saddam Hussein could be. Similarly, many had spread rumors about the magnitude of his cruelty to his enemies, but I figured that that was also Western propaganda designed to influence public opinion against our regime. As a joke, I responded, "Black's a nice color, but not for a girl. I would have preferred the blue one."

The next set of car keys flew towards me. This time I caught them. "Can I have the other keys back, please? Tariq asked "We need to drive back to New York now."

This unusual encounter lasted less than two minutes. As they drove off, I found myself standing on the road beside a royal blue 1991 Mercedes 500sl. It reminded me of the regal carpets in my uncle's palace. I had been planning on putting the $100,000 to work on a new Porsche, but I didn't want to appear ungrateful for my uncle's gift. Besides, the two-door, sporty Mercedes seemed more sophisticated than the overly flashy Porsche.

That afternoon, with a new toolbox in hand, I parked the car at the far end of one of the university's parking lots. There were very few cars around, since most of the students had gone home for the break. I spent all afternoon installing the laser system that Sensei and I had bought in Germany. When I had done it with Sensei, he did most of the hard work. But he had made sure that I understood the details, obviously preparing me for this day. For most of the time, I kept the engine idling to keep me warm inside. The windows fogged up after a few minutes, giving me more privacy to work. When it was all set,

I sat in the driver's leather bucket seat and burned a few holes in oak trees nearby.

When Effi contacted me for the first time in the semester, I heard warmth in his voice. "Hey, Leila. It's great to talk to you. Did you fly back to England for the break?" His words, slightly elevated in pitch, sounded genuine.

"Tickets are real expensive around New Year," I told him, pleased with the hypocrisy of my comment.

We got together almost every day and spent hours watching RNN together. After talks froze between U.S. Secretary of State James Baker and Iraqi Foreign Minister Aziz, Saddam himself appeared on TV, dressed in his army uniform and Rolex watch. He made huge speeches, instilling faith and pride in the Iraqi people. Effi commented that Saddam's flamboyance would be crushed by the massive force of over a half million allied soldiers. Days after his remark, however, Saddam launched a strike against Israel. At the request of George Bush, the Israelis absorbed the hit and withheld any response.

I could see how desperately Effi wanted to return to his country, to show support for his friends. I noticed his smile of relief as the news announced that the scud missile we sent lacked any poison gas. I wasn't sure if it was true – perhaps it was just a cover-up. On the other hand, maybe Sensei took my report seriously and decided not to risk the wrath of Israel's nuclear arsenal.

In any case, I tried to call Effi to propagate the ruse of being a good and caring friend, but he suddenly became increasingly scarce and unavailable. After a few days and dozens of phone calls to his home and office, I finally got through to him.

"Leila, thanks for calling," he said to me, "but I'm terribly busy, I'm afraid. My friends and family back in Israel are frightened, and Professor Beck has asked me to do some extra research for him."

"Where is Professor Beck?" I wondered aloud.

"He's down in Washington on call to the National Security Council. But Leila, I am so very busy at the moment. I can't talk right now. Can I call you later?"

"When?" I asked. I also wanted to ask about this extra research and what it might include, but I refrained.

"When I can," Effi replied, "okay?"

Something made me ask him where he would be in the next few days. I was surprised when he responded that he would be in the office for the rest of the day and then, that night, he would be traveling by train to Washington to deliver some very important papers to Professor Beck.

Contemplating Effi's clandestine behavior, I decided to don the black-as-pitch jumpsuit given to me for secretive operations like the one I was about to embark upon, utilize some of the skills I learned in spy training, and sneak into the Professor's office to see what I could glean from any unused information possibly left behind.

After the sun set that evening I placed a series of calls to Effi's office. After six tries without an answer and a phone call to the train station to double-check that his train down to Washington had left on time, I figured it was safe to assume his office was empty and that Effi had finally left for the capital.

Using my student identification card, I easily walked onto campus and entered the faculty building, making my way to Effi's office just down the hall from Professor Beck's. The building was deserted by the time I arrived, aside from a wandering security guard immediately outside the building. He must have assumed nothing was amiss because he didn't even pass me a momentary glance. Once I arrived at Effi's office, I used my library card to pry open the flimsy lock by sticking it into the crack between the door and the wall, forcing the door to pop open quickly and easily. I stepped into the office, closed the door, and flipped on the overhead light. The desk inside had a mess of papers strewn around and piled high on top of books and across shelves lining the walls. I didn't know exactly where to start or even what I was looking for, but I was sure that I'd recognize something of value once I discovered it.

Slipping on a pair of soft, suede Isotoner gloves, so as not to leave a trace of fingerprints, I started to rifle through the messy stacks of papers all around the office. Most of them were photocopies of clippings from American and British newspapers about the progress of the war against Iraq; some papers were faxed copies of newspaper clippings from Zionist newspapers such as *Maariv* and *Ha'aretz*, all of which claimed my uncle's regime was doomed to collapse, leaving a vacuum in his wake in my homeland.

Beneath many of those publicly accessible papers, there was a series of faxes and previously sealed documents sent directly to the office from the Kiryah, the Israeli high command in Tel Aviv. Thanks to my newly-developed proficiency in Hebrew, I was able to translate the words of the pages quickly. According to these papers, the prime minister of Israel, Yitzchak Shamir, as well as the top brass in the military, had authorized the ready deployment of nuclear weapons systems throughout Israel in the event of a chemical, biological, or nuclear attack from Iraq. Orders, these documents reported, had already been issued to Israeli military commanders in the field authorizing retaliatory strikes against Baghdad in the event of a cataclysmic attack. This information was no surprise to me. I had already sent messages confirming this suspicion to Sensei back home. However, there was one document hidden in an obscure crevice at the side of Effi's desk, stamped, in Hebrew, with the enticing phrase "top secret," that really caught my eye.

The papers appeared to be the recorded conversation from a closed-door meeting between Prime Minister Shamir and his Cabinet ministers. From what I could decipher, the prime minister was under intense pressure from his Cabinet to actively deploy various options for a nuclear response, which he had already authorized, while, at the same time, demanding from U.S. President George Bush more patriot missile batteries to defend Israel from Iraqi scud attacks.

The Israeli Cabinet, according to these recorded minutes, had unanimously insisted that Shamir travel immediately to Washington to make it very clear to the American president that if he did not buckle to their demands, Israel would have no other alternative but to retaliate against Iraqi attacks. The Cabinet was clearly annoyed and irritated with the prime minister for capitulating to American war planners to effectively refrain from any tit-for-tat with my country. Some Cabinet ministers were even threatening to pull out of the ruling coalition, which was tenuous at best, in the hopes of replacing the government with a leader who would, in their words, "blow those Arab bastards to hell."

Earlier on, Madame had given me a small, handheld spy camera no bigger than a light bulb, and I used this camera to photograph this document along with all the others I felt would be of use to my handlers in Baghdad. I snapped dozens of photos and then snuck out of the office as fast as I could.

My departure was somewhat hasty; as I strolled nonchalantly out of the building, I realized that I probably didn't do the best job of locking up the office or covering my tracks. I walked briskly across the campus heading back towards my apartment. At one point, I passed the same security guard I saw on my way in; he smiled at me and wished me a good evening. I returned his pleasant gaze, but said nothing in return. Instead I made a point of shivering a bit, and I gathered my coat and scarf around me to indicate how cold I was. Once I got back to my place, I prepared the microfilm and called a scrambled line to the Iraqi mission at the United Nations. I left a vaguely worded message that would alert someone there to come out to my apartment within the hour to retrieve what I'd managed to find. They could then relay this information to my uncle, who was currently under siege in Baghdad.

After placing the call, I slipped out of my heavy clothing and fixed myself a hot cup of green tea. I turned on the television and lay down on my sofa to watch the biased programming of RNN. As usual, Barney Brandon was reporting about the progress of Coalition forces in the deserts of Kuwait and Iraq, all the while claiming tremendous victories for American and British forces, and showing images of mass Iraqi surrenders and defections. I assumed that everything I saw on RNN was a lie and wholly orchestrated by an unseen American propaganda machine meant to nurture worldwide support for the massive invasion of my homeland.

Shortly thereafter, RNN cut to a clip of a press conference beamed across the globe from somewhere in Saudi Arabia. At this press conference, General Andrew Boulder, the commander of all Allied forces in the Gulf region, claimed that U.S. and U.K. forces had effectively driven Saddam from the Emirate of Kuwait, liberating the tiny, oil-rich nation, "saving democracy from the tyranny of Saddam's thugs." I was appalled seconds later when footage was shown of a "smart bomb" blowing up a bridge somewhere in southern Iraq. I was further disgusted by General Boulder when he glibly described the events of that day to a room full of international reporters and press:

"If you see here, you'll notice a truck speeding away from the impact site on the bridge. The missile hit the bridge, destroying it with a big explosion, and this Iraqi clown here," the General pointed to a small dot driving away from the explosion, "must've got one hell of a shock to see the bridge he'd just driven across blow up in his rearview mirror." General Boulder and the rest of the international press then chuckled acrimoniously.

A few minutes later, there was a knock at my front door. I wrapped myself in my white silk robe. When I opened the front door, there was a man dressed in a red pizza delivery uniform; he was holding a large, square box emblazoned with the phrase "HOT FRESH PIZZA."

He said, "Your pizza has arrived, Madame."

"I didn't order any pizza," I told him. "Perhaps you've got the wrong address."

"No, Madame," he replied, "My name is Yasir. I've come from the pizza place, and I'm not making a delivery. I'm here to pick up a parcel." When he repeated everything he said in perfect, flawless Arabic, I understood that he was from the Iraqi mission. Just to be sure, though, I asked him something in Arabic.

"To go with God," I began, "is to go with greatness."

He replied correctly, "May Allah watch over you and guard you and the generations you will spawn."

"Very good." I smiled curtly and told him to wait just inside my foyer while I prepared the parcel. I retrieved the papers and the microfilm from my mini camera and came back to him. In hindsight, putting the papers into the pizza box and sending him on his way probably wasn't the smartest move. Moments later, as I locked the door after him, I realized how strange it might appear to someone watching my home that a delivery man would come to my door with a pizza and leave still carrying the pie. It was too late to correct the situation, however, so I turned off the lights around the house and climbed into bed for a dreamless sleep; just another amateur mistake.

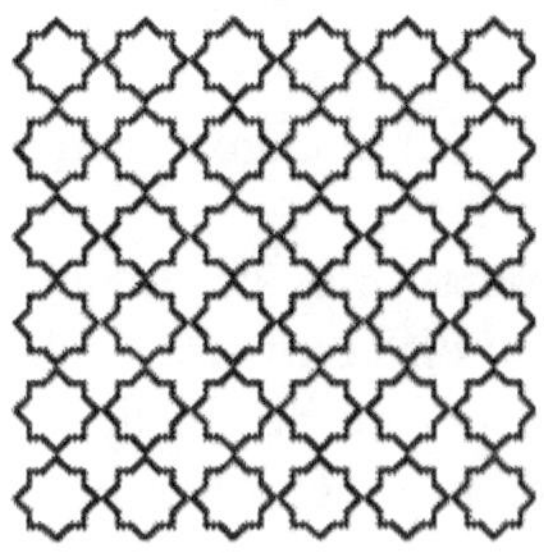

Chapter 11

A few days later, I received an unexpected phone call from Effi. "Leila, hey. Sorry to have taken so long to get back to you. I wanted to call and say 'hi' before I left."

"You're leaving?" I asked him, "Where are you going? Are you going to Washington again?"

"No. Actually, I just returned from there. I've quit my job with Professor Beck. I'm going to Israel. The war doesn't look good for my country so they've called up my reserve unit."

I made a mental note of this development. "Is Israel finally going to retaliate?"

"I don't know, but I'm in a panic being here while my family and friends are in the heat of the battle, enduring Iraqi scud attacks. Part of me wants to strangle Saddam with my bare hands, if only I had the chance to get at that Arab bastard!"

I was caught off-guard by his sudden outburst and felt incensed. I wanted to shout at him, "Watch it, Jew boy, that's my uncle you're talking about!" But I bit my lip and remained quiet. Instead I caught myself and acted compassionately. "Of course, Effi, I understand. You will keep in touch, though," I inquired, "won't you?"

"Of course. Let me give you all my personal contact information."

Effi gave me a series of email addresses, phone numbers, and two different street addresses in the Jerusalem suburbs before he finally said goodbye and promised he'd be in touch once he was settled in Israel. When I got off the phone with him, I made a point to transcribe all the information he'd given me, as well as pen a short report of my acquaintance and involvement with him. I then filed it all away with the plan of transferring the information to my handlers back in Baghdad.

The next ten days were somewhat uneventful. Everyone in the United States, so the national news had me believing, was on edge about "Desert Storm." And then, suddenly, the conflict quickly climaxed with the arrival of American and British forces in Baghdad. I remember skipping a few days of classes just to sit in front of RNN television news waiting to hear a report that the Coalition running amok in Iraq had finally captured and executed Saddam Hussein. But, in the end, the American president, standing side-by-side with the British prime minister, declared a cessation of hostilities.

Two feelings ran concurrently through me; first, I was thrilled that the war had quickly stalemated and the fighting, for the most part, had subsided. Second, I was surprised that the satanic president of the

United States had not made a direct attempt on my uncle's life to satisfy the American public's lust for Arab blood. Within a week, however, there were several news reports filtering in about an American-backed rebellion in the south of my homeland, near Basra. According to what I heard, the politicos were hoping for an uprising that would somehow overthrow my uncle's regime. As a result, I decided to keep my eyes and ears open around campus, and even paid a few unannounced visits to Professor Beck's office hoping to glean some information. Unfortunately, the professor was still on call in Washington, and his new assistant, a mean-spirited redhead named Katie Jefferson, proved time and time again to be unhelpful.

A few times I placed calls to Iraq's various stateside offices. I even made several attempts to contact both Sensei and Madame Moreau, as well as the Iraqi mission in New York, hoping someone somewhere would give me an assignment or provide my life and cover with some sort of daily purpose. But it was as if everything and everyone regarding my job just fell completely silent. As Desert Storm began to wind down, I found I had almost no energy to continue the ploy of my studies at Princeton. I still regularly attended my classes, but very often I would simply doodle, doze off, or daydream during lectures. For some of my classes, I just totally ignored any reading or outside work assignments.

About a month after the cessation of hostilities in Iraq, I received a call from Madame Moreau. "Leila," she said to me with a hint of scolding in her voice, "there is no time. You must follow any instructions you receive in the next few days to the letter. Our 'friends' are planning a large party for our family. It's meant to be a surprise, but you know how 'mother,' at her age, does not like surprises. Be prepared to act soon."

"Yes Madame." During the week that followed I sat by the telephone and waited patiently for further instructions from Madame, but no calls ever arrived. In a maddening sense of obligation, I refused to leave my apartment, filled with the many creature comforts that I'd come to love. I waited for days, and still had not received word from anyone connected with my uncle or my homeland. I imagined that the domestic American security services were probably watching the Iraqi embassy in Washington as well as the consulate mission in Manhattan. In addition, the Americans had probably tapped all the telephone lines.

After many lonely days, I decided to finally leave my home to walk to the supermarket down the street. I presumed that since I had yet to receive a phone call from Madame Moreau, the chances of receiving one in the half hour it would take to go shopping were quite slim. As I stepped out across my threshold, I noticed two men dressed in black leather coats, wearing dark Ray Ban sunglasses. From where I stood, I could clearly see the white radio wires dripping inconspicuously from their ears and ducking into their ironed-to-a-crisp white, starched, button up shirts.

Their equally dark black suits and shiny embossed faux Italian designer leather shoes exposed them as agents of some sort, probably sent by the White House, the Pentagon, or Central Intelligence to watch my movements through my windows. The thought that these two men, standing as plain as day and no more than a hundred yards from one another in rival doorsteps along the avenue, had perhaps seen me at my most vulnerable instantly crossed my mind. For all I knew, they, and the rest of the United States government, had seen me worrying and waiting for my next assignment.

I considered re-entering my home and attempting to contact my comrades, but realized that would put them in immediate danger. I thought back to the conversation Sensei and I had about giving our lives to protect each other, and I wondered whether the time had come. I started to stroll as nonchalantly as I could down the street, pretending to be totally oblivious to the two men. In hindsight, I doubt the mystery was lost on any of my neighbors or anyone else who might have been peering at the scene on the street that day; those two agents were as inconspicuous as an elephant on an ant farm. Nevertheless, I continued on foot down the street, watching them from the corner of my eye. First, one of the men darted out of a doorway and stole away to the other side of the street to duck into another doorway, sort of leap-frogging his way down the street in pursuit. The other agent tried poorly to stroll along about a hundred meters behind me but, in both cases, I could easily see that they were following me. Obviously they hadn't undergone the same rigorous training program as I had. Was Uncle Sam slipping in his security procedures?

As I reached the end of the block, I decided to walk faster as I crossed the street. As I had expected, the two agents also picked up their pace. I was wearing a pair of heels and I knew it would have been impossible for me to start running in those shoes. Instead, I ducked into a Korean-owned dry cleaner, hoping to shake off the agents.

"Hello," I said to the small Korean man inside. Removing my sunglasses, I asked, "Do you know where I might find a bottle of …" At this point my mind went blank; my eyes quickly scanned the room looking for something; I don't know what; to finish; "… starch?" It was a bad move.

"Starch?" The Korean shook his head, "We don't sell that here. Go down the street to the other cleaners' store. They might have it there."

"Okay," I smiled weakly as I glanced out the window. I saw both agents whisper into their shirt-sleeves and press microphone receivers into their ears. They came together directly across the street from the dry cleaners and stared at me head-on through the bay window of the shop. "Well, do you know where I might find some …" again I drew a blank; "…laundry detergent?" I slipped on my sunglasses and turned again to look out of the window of the shop.

"No," the man shook his head quickly. "I don't know anything. Why you come in here and ask stupid questions?" His mood and tone changed instantly, "We don't sell starch or laundry detergent. You go to supermarket or green grocer for that. You leave now!"

I was slightly flabbergasted by his sudden outburst. I said, "Well, in that case, don't expect me to bring my clothes here for a wash!"

"Good," he yelled at me, "We don't want your wash here! Now go, or I call the police!"

I wanted to reply, "Don't worry, the authorities are already here, just waiting for me right outside." In the end, though, I nodded my head curtly and pushed open the door, stepping out onto the side-walk.

I was right around the corner from a busy street, not far from the local market. I entered the shop in the hopes of giving those two agents a run for their money. Later on, I reckoned, I would devise a method to shake them off once I'd entered the shop, which I'd hoped would be packed with customers. Unfortunately, when I arrived, I saw that the market was virtually empty except for a small crew of Salvadorans working the cash registers. For a moment, I considered approaching one of the female workers and telling her a couple of men outside were following me, hoping some misguided sense of sisterhood on her part might inspire her to call the police. But I realized that would, in effect, probably turn out to be a useless endeavor since those two spies chasing after me were undoubtedly from the law enforcement agency. If the CIA knew where I lived, who I was, and who I reported to – if they really knew why I was in the United States to begin with – calling the police would be like summoning a crossing guard to fight against an elite squad of assassins.

I wandered into a back aisle, behind the cereals and the boxes of oatmeal, and tried to hide near the freezers filled with ice cream and microwaveable dinners. A set of dated Christmas bells rang as I heard the two agents push open the door of the grocery. I tried to look busy as I searched through frozen tenderloins of beef, but also listened carefully.

"Excuse me, I'm from Washington," I heard one of my trails explain to one of the checkout girls, "I'm looking for a ... friend. I think she might be in here."

As I listened, I imagined this spy taking off his glasses and smiling graciously at the Latino checkout girl. I rolled my eyes as I opened one of the refrigerators and took out a frozen leg of lamb. I figured that if I was cornered, I'd just whack them both over the top of the head, hopefully knocking them unconscious. Then, I could escape. As I turned to march down yet another aisle, I saw one of the agents coming towards me. When we saw each other, we both stopped dead in our tracks and just stared. His eyes remained obscured behind his sunglasses, as were mine, but both of us instinctively and slowly removed our glasses to glare at each other eyeball to eyeball.

"We know who you are," he stated, smiling smugly.

"I doubt that."

"We know who you work for, too," he added.

Sarcastically, I retorted, "I work for Hallmark. I write greeting cards."

"No," the American agent shook his head slowly, "you don't." He started coming towards me.

I held up the leg of lamb, "I don't know who you are but you're a strange man coming towards a lone woman." I held up the leg of lamb, the coldness beginning to numb my hands. "If I am who you think I am, then you'll know I'm not afraid to use this."

The agent lifted his shirtsleeve to his face and whispered into his wrist, "Agent Rodney, I'm going to need some assistance in aisle four."

A voice from behind me said, "I'm here, Lieutenant Dan."

I flipped around and, standing about two meters behind me, was the other American agent. He said,

"We don't want to hurt you; we only want to ask you some questions."

"Who are you?" I asked them as I stepped into a spot equidistant from the two of them, figuratively digging my heels into the store floor tile, preparing for some sort of showdown, "Where do you come from?"

"Relax, ma'am," said the first spy, the one called Lieutenant Dan, "we're from Washington."

"Big deal," I said.

"We're from the NSA," said the second agent, Agent Rodney.

"Oh yeah, show me some ID."

With due reverence, both men quickly produced black leather wallets, which they flipped open to flash some sort of badge that I, of course, barely saw; they could have been showing me their library cards for all I knew.

Agent Rodney spoke to me calmly as he held out his hands, "Now if you'd just kindly leave with us now, we won't hurt you."

"We don't want to cause a scene in here," said Lieutenant Dan.

"You've already done that." I said, "I heard you tell the girls at the front I was your 'friend.'"

"That's all we want from you," Agent Rodney smiled. "We just want to talk to you … as a friend."

"Well," I declared, "my friends don't work for the NSA."

"Excuse me," said the grungy-looking stock boy as he pushed a cart filled with fresh-cut meat down the aisle. His apron, stained with meat splatters, had a torn name tag and his voice sounded slightly famil-iar. He began unloading his stock onto the shelves, oblivious to our conversation.

"Come on, now," Lieutenant Dan held out his hands as if to prevent me from running away or escaping, and started moving towards me. "Just come along with us."

I slipped my sunglasses on and clutched the frozen leg of lamb. The two spies inched closer and closer at me, obviously ready for me to bolt down the aisle away from them, but they blocked any possible escape route. I backed into a wall of canned tomatoes and canned peas, gripping at the leg of lamb, this time with both hands.

"Please, miss," said Agent Rodney, "really, we don't want to hurt you. We don't want this to get ugly."

"Yeah, right," I stared at them. Both men were standing less than two feet away from me, "I'm not waiting for any trouble." I raised the frozen leg of lamb quickly while the two spies moved into my personal space. Neither of them had a chance to adopt a look of surprise on their faces as I took a swing. First, the frozen leg of lamb struck Agent Rodney on the back of the head; he fell into a wall of Lay's potato chips and Oreo cookies, and landed on the floor with a groan. When I turned to face the second assailant, I saw he was already on the floor with the stock boy on top of him. I was stunned that someone had helped me, and then, instantly realized why the worker's voice was familiar.

It was my beloved teacher, Sensei. He had appeared suddenly, it seemed, out of nowhere. I was thrilled to see him, and I melted into his strong, embracing arms. As we hugged, he kept his boot pressed firmly on the throat of the counter-spy that he had just defeated.

"Sensei," I cried into his shoulder softly.

"There is no time," he replied quickly, "we have to get out of here before the police arrive and start asking questions. Come!" Sensei snapped a vicious kick into his victim's ear to ensure we'd have time to escape, and then he quickly ushered me past the butcher counter and through an open door veiled with transparent plastic sheets dangling from the top. He pushed me into the back storeroom, which was filled to the ceiling with giant crates of canned goods.

"Sensei," I asked, "what is happening here?"

"They're on to us," he told me, "the Americans. Ever since the start of the war they've been observing our family and have been listening in on our phone conversations and watching the houses. It was impossible for me to contact you in the house since you were under constant surveillance. I knew that eventually you would have to surface to get food, so I got a job working here to wait for you. I had no idea our meeting would include American agents, but since they have come and ruined our reunion, we need to run. It's only a question of time until they get the rest of us." Sensei led me to a back door, which he kicked open and then shoved me through into the back parking lot.

"What do you mean?" I asked him, "Until they get the rest of us?"

His reply came in quick breaths as he moved me toward a black Mercedes, "The American police already captured Madame."

"Oh no! What have they done to her?" Although I sometimes hated her, the thought that she'd been taken away by those blasphemous Americans made me sick. "Did they shoot her?"

"We don't know," Sensei opened the passenger door of the waiting car, and practically hurled me inside before going around to the driver's side. "We don't know anything at all." Sensei stuck the key into the ignition and started the motor. "It's rather embarrassing." Putting the car into gear, Sensei added, "Especially for Madame."

Sensei sighed as he steered the car out of the parking lot, turning a quick left, followed by a quick right, and then another quick left; then he floored the gas pedal and drove onto the Garden State Parkway heading south at 75 miles per hour. "Sometime earlier this week, the police arrested Madame Moreau as she was trying to walk out of a grocery store in Pennsylvania. Once they took her in and looked over her documents and passport – all of which are fake because they were doctored by our expert friends in Czechoslovakia – they realized who she was. They've since locked her up incommunicado."

Sensei drove the car onto Route 17 and sped north. For a few minutes he sat in silence before he took out a pack of Marlboro Red cigarettes and lit one without rolling down the driver's side window.

"When did you start smoking?" I asked. I watched him inhale and exhale.

"When we lost the war."

"I'm sorry," I said, mid-cough. "What did you say?"

Again, Sensei inhaled dramatically. "You asked when I started smoking, and I'm answering your question. I started smoking when we lost the war."

"Oh," I nodded and stared out at the highway. "I didn't realize that's how you felt about our … situation …" I turned to look at him, "Sensei?"

Sensei sat silently and drove the car while angrily smoking the cigarette. I tried to concentrate on the dotted lines pasted along the highway ahead of us but found my eyes turning to stare at Sensei.

"Sensei," I stated, "you have to talk to me. What's going on? Where are we going now?" I searched his profile looking for something; more answers to more questions; but he just stared dead ahead, squinting his eyes. I asked him finally, "Do you believe we lost the war?"

First Sensei shook his head, and then he laughed. "Don't tell me you think we won the war? Even your all-powerful relatives back home couldn't pull off a lie that grand. No, Leila," Sensei glanced at me. "The Fatherland lost the war. Iraq has been conquered by infidels! Soon they will start to rape and pillage."

"No," I started to shake my head.

"Think of it, Leila. They could rape your mother."

"No," I raised my voice and screamed, "Oh God, no!" I cried.

I took a deep breath, "I'm sorry, Sensei." I slowly started to weep with pent-up emotion. "I don't know what's come over me." Sensei handed me a tissue. "I just need to calm down."

Sensei was driving faster than the posted speed limits as we crossed the line into New York. "Sensei," I asked, "Where are we going? I have a right to know!"

Sensei sighed, "We're heading north."

I looked at the signs along the road, "North to where? Schenectady?" I remembered learning that around the time of the U.S. civil war, the black American slaves sought their freedom by heading north. Here, too, we were seeking emancipation from those who wanted to trap and possibly kill us. The

Underground Railroad helped the escaping slaves find their way, but we were enemies of the Americans – there would be no one who would offer us refuge.

"No," he shook his head, "Vermont."

"Vermont?"

"Yes, we have to get out of this country as soon as possible. We'll cut across to Quebec from Vermont and hope they don't shoot us at the border."

I was stunned by the dramatic change of plans. "Who's going to shoot at us? The Americans? I'd think they'd especially want us out of their country."

"Be that as it may, the Canadians might shoot us just as quickly as the Americans. That's why we're going to a remote area out in the woods."

"And after that, what are we going to do?" I asked him, "Once we're in Canada, I mean?"

"Once we get some new clothes, we'll travel to Montreal and fly out of the airport from there."

"I see," I said as I nodded my head. "So," I asked him, "where are we flying to? Surely there isn't a flight to Baghdad."

"Of course not, Leila. We don't have the luxury of direct flights. The world is against us. Our only allies are in the palace, and I don't even think everyone there is going to be so happy to see us return alive. I don't know where yet, but don't worry." Sensei smiled a soothing smile at me. Touching my hand, he pressed my palm and fingers together, giving me a strong feeling of safety and determination, "I will work everything out. Your job is to act the part of the doting traditional wife."

"All right," I pressed my hand into his, "I trust you, my teacher. I will do as you say from now on."

"Good, Leila," Sensei grinned. "Very, very good."

We drove for hours and hours. At one point we crossed over the river and drove through a series of towns and villages called Fishkill, Wallkill, and the like, before we rounded the capital area around Albany. The towns' names reminded me of the feeling that was welling up inside me, that I wanted to kill something, too. I had worked so hard for my country, given up my identity, and risked my life; I was angry and I felt powerless. I prayed that Sensei would find a plan that would help me regain my strength and sense of purpose.

"Once we get off the New York State Thruway," he said, "we'll take the back roads to avoid detection from the authorities."

"Do you think they're looking for us?" I asked Sensei.

"Anything is possible," he replied. "I'm sure they know what we look like. Let's just hope they haven't put out a bulletin to the police."

"Merciful Allah!" I cried, "I am so nervous, so very nervous, Sensei." I shook my head, "And I'm hungry. Perhaps we could stop at a Burger King?"

"No, Leila," Sensei cut me off suddenly, "there will be no eating and no stopping, except for petrol for the car. We will eat once we reach our destination."

"Vermont is far away, Sensei, and I am hungry now."

"Leila, don't be so selfish! Think of all the children in Iraq who are starving at the hands of the invading hordes of infidels from America."

Rolling my eyes, I said, "Fine." I stared out at the passing trees and scenery, "In that case, give me a cigarette. I need to smoke."

"Smoking can kill you, Leila," Sensei said as he handed me the box. "Don't you ever read the warnings?" Half smiling, Sensei passed me his lighter.

I took the pack from his hands, along with the lighter, and scanned the small print of the warning on the side of the crumpled cigarette pack. "Well," I smirked, "why should I care about what it says? I'm not a fetus."

Sensei chuckled at that, and finally I smiled genuinely, grateful for a mutually appreciated moment of levity. "We'll stop in about an hour for some gasoline and then you can grab a bite."

"I imagine we will also need to change our clothes at the very least. I can't run across the border wearing a pair of heels, now can I?"

"I imagine not," Sensei shook his head. "We'll stop and rest a bit in Vermont."

"Where? In a hotel?"

"I have a friend with a cabin."

"A friend?"

"Yes, a true friend, a friend of our ... how shall I put it? A friend of your uncle's, as it were. He's very sympathetic to the plight of our people and very disgruntled about the invasion of the Fatherland."

"Oh?" I asked, "Who is this friend?"

"You'll see when we meet him."

"Is he American?"

"Yes, but not originally."

"Well," I asked, "where is he from?"

"Leila," Sensei turned to me, "you'll meet him in a few hours. Must you ask all these questions? Remember you are still in the battlefield, and silence is golden."

I was unhappy at how he spoke to me. "Please, Sensei, don't think that way about me."

"Why don't you rest?"

Sensei shifted into the left-hand lane and sped up. "The drive must be continued in silence. I must gather my thoughts. The journey ahead of us is treacherous and potentially dangerous. We will need our strength; we must nurture our perseverance now. Rest, Leila, rest. I'll wake you when we stop."

It was then that I realized I still had yet to light up. I placed the cigarette between my lips and brought the lighter close. I inhaled deeply, as I had observed Sensei doing and then, almost immediately, started coughing.

"Obviously," smiled Sensei, "you're not a natural smoker."

I knew he was right as I kept on coughing. In a fit of exasperation, I rolled the window down and tossed out the cigarette. I waved my hand in circles swishing away the remnants of cigarette smoke clouding around my face.

"That was quite possibly," I told Sensei, "one of the worst things I've ever had the displeasure of tasting in my entire life."

"Rest, Leila," he said to me, "just rest."

I coughed a bit more before I finally bunched up my coat and pressed it between my head and the window, propping it up like a pillow. Quickly I fell asleep. I don't know how long I was out, but, at some point, Sensei woke me up by shaking my shoulder to tell me that we were stopping to refuel.

"Sensei, where are we right now?"

"We're very close to the border with Vermont," he answered.

"So we're still in New York State?"

"Yes," Sensei nodded, "but only for about another half an hour or so before we cross over."

As I stepped out of the vehicle, I realized just how tired I was; the stress of the past few weeks sat piled upon my shoulders, weighing me down. In my mind's eye I saw the ancient Greek hero Atlas, bending under the weight of the giant globe on his shoulders. How long ago was it that I had read this tale in my uncle's palace. That was when I was another person, another character, another identity. Who was I now? And why was I so scared to be running away? My life had ended once before in the fake car accident; would it be so terrible if I died a second time?

When I returned to the car, Sensei offered me a bottle of Coca-cola and a bag of potato chips.

"Here," he said as he handed me the tasty items, "so you don't starve like our brothers and sisters back home in the Fatherland."

"Thank you, Sensei," I said and gratefully tried sharing them. Sensei refused to partake. An eternity later I heard, "Leila, we are here. We've arrived in Vermont. In just a few moments, we'll be at our destination." He veered off the main road onto smaller roads and then finally onto unpaved and dirt roads. It was cold, and snow and ice were dangling from the trees. I spotted a deer running away from the hum of the car's motor. Sensei pulled up to a secluded cabin hidden deep in the woods. The scene was pure Americana, something out of a clichéd Norman Rockwell painting. Sitting out in front of the cabin was an old red pick-up truck, trimmed with Vermont state license plates.

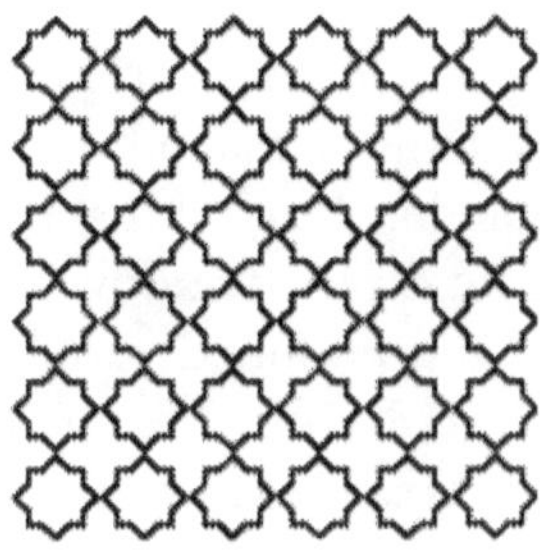

Chapter 12

"Who does this belong to?" I asked as we stepped out of our car and started walking up to the lone cabin in the woods. I noticed through the windows of the beat-up red truck, that the seats were covered with plaid flannel blankets. Sensei just ignored me as he stepped up to the porch and knocked on the thick wooden door. He knocked a second time. We waited as a moment passed; it appeared there was no movement in the cabin.

"Maybe your friend isn't home right now," I said to Sensei.

"Don't be stupid, Leila," he replied. Sensei glanced over his shoulder, "His truck is here. If he's not inside, he's out hunting grouse."

I asked him, "You mean to tell me my uncle has friends in Vermont who hunt grouse?" I shook my head for a second, "I'm not even sure I know what a grouse is."

Sensei knocked on the door more loudly and stepped to the side to peer through a porch window. He tapped lightly on the window and called out, "*Aki, Aki!*" an abbreviation of the word *Akhim*, one of the Arabic words for "brother" or "dude."

"Do you see him?" I asked.

Sensei shook his head. "It's dark inside." He tapped lightly again on the window and then stepped over to the door and pounded very loudly. He called out once again, "*Aki! Aki!*" Finally, a light came on and Sensei stepped back over to the window to peer through before smiling widely. "Here he is."

I waited a few seconds until an older man with dark hair graying at his temples opened the door. He stepped across the threshold of the cabin and embraced my teacher.

"Al-Hasan," he held him tight, the way a father would hold a son who has finally returned home from a distant war, "*Salaam aleikum*. It has been far too long." Never before had I heard anyone use Sensei's real name. When Sensei and I had first met, He had introduced himself to me by his full Arabic name, Al-Hasan bin Ibrahim Gamal, but then he had immediately insisted I call him Sensei.

Sensei was equally as pleased to see this older man. He hugged him and whispered, "It is good to see you as well, dear friend."

"I didn't know when to expect you," said the man. "When you called, I was on my way to class and the message my secretary gave me later was very cryptic."

"Well," Sensei smiled at the man, "you know how the business works better than I do."

The old man smiled and nodded, "Yes." He then turned to look at me, "And who is this?" This man was clearly an Arab. When I looked into his deep-set, dark-brown eyes, I sensed that he had grown up in plain view of the majestic beauty of the Iraqi desert, back-dropped by the rugged mountains of Mesopotamia and the banks of the River Tigris. I could tell, just by looking at him, that he was one of us.

Sensei said, "Let me introduce you to Fatima."

At first I smiled at the older man, but then I glanced in utter surprise at Sensei when I heard my true name. Oh, how I'd missed that name.

"Fatima," continued Sensei, "has been a student."

"Hello," I said, not knowing whether it was appropriate to offer the older man my hand. "May Allah protect you and all who enter your house, sir."

"Oh," he scoffed as he held out his hand, "don't call me sir. Call me Basil."

"All right," I uneasily and nervously shook his hand, "Basil."

"Fatima," Sensei added, "allow me to introduce you to Basil Mahmoud Farouk."

"Dr. Basil Mahmoud Farouk," said the older man, correcting Sensei. "I never miss a chance to impress a student, especially one as stunning as you. How do you do, Fatima?" Basil took my hand and kissed it like a refined European gentleman.

I smiled and warmed up to his demeanor quickly, as the whiskers of his dark-haired mustache tickled my knuckles and the tops of my bejeweled fingers. "Very well, thank you."

"Let's go inside," said Basil. As we entered his cozy cabin snuggled in the wooded forests of Vermont, I felt the irony of the situation: Iraqi spies, enemies of America, seeking refuge in what could only be described as true American accommodations. I could almost smell the apple pie in the oven and hear the game show on TV. But Sensei's voice quickly brought me back to reality.

"Basil," Sensei went on, "is a distinguished professor of Arabic linguistic studies at the State University of New York at Albany."

"Oh," I smiled, impressed with the professional, academic moniker. "An intellectual; well, I must say I'm honored."

Basil closed the front door of the cabin, taking a few seconds to bolt, then double bolt, it. "Don't let his fancy words fool you. I'm a legitimately decorated Arabic language teacher at SUNY Albany but, just between the three of us, I'm also an Iraqi sympathizer. But please don't repeat that to anyone."

"Great," I smiled at Sensei, "I guess." I liked the older man's attitude and look. He was dressed in a pair of American blue jeans, a plaid flannel shirt that, oddly, generally matched the patterns on the blankets lining the seats of the red pickup truck parked out front. For shoes, Basil was wearing a pair of Native American-style moccasins without socks.

"Basil used to help out our local intelligence agencies," Sensei began.

"But then I left in the late 1960s to upstate New York, a few years before the Woodstock concert."

"So, as you can see," Sensei was quick to tell me, "you're in good company."

"That's good to know," I said. I asked Basil, "Were you in the service?"

Basil's reply sounded almost flippant, yet stand-offish: "That's a genteel way of asking if I was a spy, like you and Al-Hasan here."

"Well, I … uh … you know," I turned to Sensei nervously, not knowing how to backtrack from the faux pas I'd obviously made in front of this distinguished professor.

"Oh heavens," said Basil, "where are my manners?" He smiled at the two of us and asked, "Can I get you something to drink? Some wine perhaps? I've got a great bottle of Chardonnay, but if that's not to your liking, I've got a half-bottle of Merlot and a Shiraz out around the back."

"Yes," answered Sensei, "I know Fatima and I would both love a drink after that long drive."

"How was the drive?" asked Basil as he sauntered over to the kitchen. "I heard, Fatima," he said as he opened the door of the white refrigerator, bending over to pull out a wrapped-in-plastic cheese platter adorned with pieces of fruits and vegetables, "that you hit a Fed over his head with a leg of lamb, knocking him out cold before leaving him to rot on the floor of a supermarket." Basil raised an eyebrow and looked at me directly and pensively, as if brimming with questions.

"Well," I demurred, "people can get vicious over shopping carts."

Basil stared at me long and hard before he broke out into a wide grin. "Let's sit in the salon and enjoy our reunion," he led the way, "even if it's not under ideal circumstances."

We made a solid dent in Basil's wine collection. Our laughter flowed as easily as the beverages themselves. I found the old man to be coy and mysterious; how did a former Middle Eastern spy end up wearing plaid flannel and moccasins with no socks, have a beat-up red pickup truck, and hide out in an old cabin in the rural forests of northern Vermont?

After a rather short period of time, I could tell that Basil intentionally dodged my many direct questions. For example, I asked him point-blank who he had worked for back in the sixties, and if the Americans knew about him. Drunkenly, I tried to get the distinguished professor to open up to me.

"Ha," Basil also laughed, "I retired over thirty years ago, and no one anywhere has ever given me trouble." I sat up a little straighter and, despite my inebriated self, tried to understand Basil's comment – "retired." I never thought one could retire from being a spy. I always felt as if this task was forced on me, and now, faced with the possibility of capture, I felt as though I was condemned to be a spy until my demise. Even if I took all the money that I had tucked away in offshore bank accounts and started a new life, I would always be looking over my shoulder. I shuddered at the thought and forced myself to focus on the conversation. I wanted to learn more about Basil – about what he did, why he did it, and how and why he stopped doing it. He continued, "Not the Americans after the Lockerbie bombing, not after the explosion at the Marine barracks, and not when Hussein took over Kuwait. They never call on me and, really, why should they? The Americans are so fickle! Up until August of last year, Iraq was an ally."

"Allies?"

"Yes," Basil sipped from a flute filled with sparkling champagne. "Politics makes for strange bedfellows; the marriage between Reagan in Washington and Hussein in Baghdad was, simply put, a marriage of convenience. A tragic misalliance, if you ask me; Iraq and the United States were necessary evils for each other."

"So," I interjected with a question, "you worked for the Republic of Iraq?"

Basil clicked his tongue and shook his head, "And now," he proceeded to speak slowly, "now Saudi Arabia is the close ally and friend."

"So then," again I had to ask, "you worked for the Saudis?"

Basil again clicked his tongue and shook his head, "Fatima, if I'm a professor of Arabic, that means I would have to speak in the very best Arabic. If I speak with a Beirut accent-"

"Aha!" I held up my hand, "you worked for Lebanon!" I must have been a bit drunk.

"-Then I would sound different," Basil finished what he was saying, "than someone from Morocco."

I shook my head for a second, "Morocco?" I turned to Sensei, "Is there such a thing as Moroccan spies?"

"But then," said Basil, "there would be the age-old debate, the Cairo dialect versus the Damascus dialect. Which is more appropriate as the proper form of modern Arabic? Now I don't know, so you tell me."

I thought it over for a moment and then made a list; Basil Mahmoud Farouk had made references to potentially being in the employ of Iraq, Saudi Arabia, Lebanon, Morocco, Egypt, or Syria.

In the end, I just blurted out, "Okay, so tell us then, Basil. Who did you work for? Syria? Egypt?" I burped and giggled, "Bahrain?"

"No," Basil laughed as he poured some Zinfandel into my wine glass, "Certainly, most definitely not Bahrain."

"Kuwait, then?"

Basil shook his head and said to my Sensei, "She sure is persistent, this one. But not so subtle."

"So," I pleaded with Basil, "who did you work for? The Syrians?"

Basil's answer was said half-seriously and half-jokingly: "What does it matter, Syria, Iraq, Egypt; we're all pissing in the same pond, aren't we?"

"No," I slurred as I shook my head from side to side, "I don't think we are pissing in a pond at all. I wholly disagree with you totally." I hiccupped, "I don't think of my homeland-"

"The Fatherland," Sensei interjected.

"The Fatherland," I corrected my drunken self, "I don't consider the land of my birth to be a pond worth pissing in."

Basil laughed, "Of course not. You're right. Your country is in a field by itself." He continued to laugh and turned to Sensei, "Who is this girl? Where did you find her?"

"She's royalty." Sensei added, "And I trained her, along with Madame."

"Really?" Basil nodded as he turned to look at me again. "I see."

Later that night, after drinking my way through at least a bottle or two of wine, I finally passed out on the sofa in front of a television broadcast of *Late Night*. The next morning I was yanked out of the bliss of slumber too early. Sensei shook me awake around four in the morning, long before the sun crested over the eastern horizon.

"Fatima," he said, "we must dress you properly today. We're leaving for Quebec in a few hours."

"Quebec?" I rolled off the couch and stumbled into the bathroom to brush my teeth and hair.

When I came out, Sensei was waiting for me in one of the bedrooms. He told me to undress quickly, "Strip down to your panties." I'll admit that I was a little tired, and still feeling very groggy after the previous night's drinking. Although I felt his command was odd and indecent, the fact that I was hung over and dead tired lulled me into complicity. I slipped out of my clothes and, before I knew it, I was standing before Sensei almost completely naked.

"Here," Sensei brought out a large black *burkha*, complete with a head covering, that would totally hide my face. "I will help you to put this on. You'll wear it until we're safely back home."

"A *burkha*?" I asked Sensei, "How on earth did you find a *burkha* out here in the middle of rural Vermont?"

"Basil had one hanging in the guest room closet."

"He did?"

"Yes," Sensei's tone did little to hide his annoyance, "He has a fetish for religious Muslim women, so he dresses girls up in this thing. Unfortunately for him, you and I need it more immediately or, I should say, you need it to cross the border into Canada."

I put on my clothes, pulled the *burkha* on top of them, and wrapped myself in the black fabric. "What'll we be doing in Canada?"

"We're going to the airport in Montreal and flying out." Sensei added, "We need to get as far away from the United States as soon as possible. That's why we need to leave the country today."

"Will I get a new identity for this journey?"

"Of course you will, Leila," replied Sensei. "You know how the game is played." Sensei helped me to wrap myself up in the *burkha*.

"What will my name be?" I asked as I pulled the head covering over myself, totally obscuring my face as well as my vision. "Am I to be Leila, or Fatima, or a different name?"

"Yes, of course, Fatima."

From behind my Muslim facemask, I rolled my eyes. I was getting confused.

"And," Sensei continued, "you will also get a new nationality today, but that's only temporary, along with your new name."

Sensei zipped me up and patted my back through the thick, black velvet fabric of the all-encompassing *burkha*. "Today, you're an Algerian."

"Algerian?"

"Is something wrong?"

"Well, no," I shook my head, but Sensei wouldn't have known because it was totally hidden behind the *burkha*. "I've never been to Algeria. I don't think I've even flown over Algeria in a plane."

"Perhaps tomorrow," Sensei told me, "you will be from a different country."

"Yes," I nodded, "perhaps."

There was a knock on the door, "Hello, may I come in?" I recognized Basil's voice.

"Yes, Basil," answered Sensei, "You may enter."

Basil stepped in and took a look at me dressed in my all-black *burkha*. "Well, well, well, what have we got here?" he whistled as he scanned me up and down. "Very nice. This is a great look for you, Fatima."

"Hmm," was all I muttered under my breath.

Sensei said, "Is the car ready, Basil?"

"Yes," Basil nodded, "everything is set and ready to go. In fact," Basil took a moment to glance at his watch, "we need to get going if you want to reach the border before sun up."

"Yes," Sensei nodded, "we must leave now." He clutched my arm right above the elbow and practically pushed me out of the room. "You will again play the part of a dutiful wife and doting mother."

"Where are our children?" I asked him.

"Back in Algiers," said Sensei as he shoved me through the small cabin out onto the old wooden porch.

"Then why are you pushing me around, Sensei?" I asked him, "What has come over you?"

"Be quiet, Fatima," he said. "We don't have time for this nonsense. Also," Sensei was quick to add, "you are, in case you haven't already noticed, supposed to be a devout Muslim woman, so you can't speak to anyone except other Muslim women. I will do all the talking for you. All you have to do is remain quiet until we have reached our destination."

"What kind of Islam am I supposed to be adhering to?" I asked Sensei. It was then that I noticed my teacher had also transformed; gone was the slightly debonair master spy that had rescued me back in New Jersey. Standing before me now was a frumpy, dressed-down man in a plain button-up shirt tucked tightly into a pair of wrinkled khakis. Sensei looked rather simple and ordinary, like a devout Muslim man that works as an engineer in a Western liberal democracy, such as Germany, Sweden or, in our case, the United States.

Sensei released his tight grip from my arm, "Just move quickly."

Basil came out of the cabin at that moment. "Okay, let's go," he said as he closed and locked the door.

As I glanced out, I noticed three cars parked in front instead of the two that were there the night before. Next to the old red pickup truck was the car that Sensei had driven the day before and, next to that, was a brand new, black Jeep Grand Cherokee with slightly tinted windows.

"Where did that new car come from?" I asked them.

"I picked it up early this morning," answered Basil.

"You bought a new car at this hour?"

Basil went over and opened the driver's side door, while Sensei opened up one of the back doors for me. "Well," said Basil, "I didn't exactly buy it. I borrowed it from the Persian dealer off the highway that heads up to Burlington. He's a good friend of mine and, just like the three of us, he's also pissed off about the Americans running amok in Iraq."

In the darkness of the night, Basil drove us over to the highway and then about halfway across the state, heading further north the whole way. It was cold outside, and it appeared that the temperatures would continue to drop the closer we got to Canada.

Eventually Basil turned the car onto a small dirt track that, like the road that led us to his secluded cabin in the woods, also cut through the forests of northern Vermont. Then, much to my surprise, Basil suddenly put the Jeep into four-wheel drive and took the vehicle further into the forest itself, steering over fallen trees, dead animals, and rooted stumps.

"Soon," Basil declared, "we will cross over into Canada. Let's hope the patrol is still asleep."

As luck would have it, we had absolutely no trouble whatsoever passing over the border. Basil clearly had driven up this way before. He navigated through the backwoods of southern Canada for over an hour before he finally got us on to the highway. About seven-and-a-half hours later, we arrived on the outskirts of Montreal.

"I have a friend who'll meet us at the airport with a pair of airline tickets and some fake Algerian passports," Basil told us.

"We'll fly on, then, to Algiers?" I asked.

"No." Basil shook his head, "Who the hell flies to Algiers?"

"But," I said to them, "you told me that my children are waiting for me back in Algiers."

"Like I said," said Basil, "That's just your cover."

"Yes," I nodded my head, "I understand that. But tell me where we'll be flying to, if not Algiers? Surely there isn't a direct flight to Baghdad from Canada!"

"No," Sensei shook his head, "surely not."

"Today," answered Basil, "you will be flying Alitalia to Rome."

"Excellent!" I said excitedly.

"The most infidel of all cities," Sensei continued, "We're probably not even getting off the plane or, even if we do, we certainly aren't leaving the airport."

"Actually," Basil interjected, "that's not true. You and Fatima will need to stay in Rome for at least a night so that we can get you a new set of passports and airline tickets."

"Oh my," I exclaimed, "I'd like to visit the Coliseum, the art museums, and the Vatican."

"No, Leila," Sensei said, "you'll go nowhere near the Vatican." He turned his head to glare at me. "Is that understood?"

Since he could only see my eyes through the slit in the black fabric draped over my head, I glared back at him, making little or no effort to hide my growing frustration. Ever since he'd rescued me from that supermarket near Princeton University, he'd been getting on my nerves. I didn't have the foggiest idea as to why he was treating me like this. However, I soon chalked it up to anxiousness on his part for I was also on edge. But, like the good diplomat he'd trained me to be, I went out of my way to hide my fears.

"But," Basil held up his hand, "don't take my words as gospel. I really don't know what will be happening to you in Rome. There's a chance everything I've told you so far is completely false. You may get there and, for all I know, be whisked away."

"Whisked away to where?" I asked him.

"I don't know," Basil shrugged his shoulders, "maybe you and Al-Hasan here will be carted off to an Italian jail or something. Better yet, maybe you'll be deported back to your homeland, which should make the whole journey easier and, might I add, cheaper, in the long run."

Sensei declared, "Let's hope that doesn't happen to us. I don't want to end up arrested like Madame."

"For your sake," added Basil, "I also hope that doesn't happen."

A few moments later, we pulled into the multi-level concrete parking structure located opposite the international departures terminal. Basil graciously offered to wait in line while Sensei and I went to wash up. When I came back from the bathroom, I rejoined him at the ticket counter.

The line for the Alitalia counter hardly moved an inch, and the check-in hall became decidedly more crowded as more people from many nations, speaking dozens of languages, crowded around Basil and me. At one point, a swarthy man with a thick mustache and correspondingly bushy black eyebrows appeared next to us. This man stood rather close to me; so close, in fact, that I could smell his scent of cardamom and Moroccan jasmine. He was an Arab.

This man, also, was dressed simply and modestly in a pair of plain brown wool pants and an ordinary dark blue sweater. On top he wore a generic windbreaker emblazoned with the label, "Members Only." Poking out above the vee cut of the neckline was a wisp of curly black chest hair.

Without uttering a sound, he stood alongside Basil and me for at least ten to twelve minutes. As my anxiety regarding our upcoming departure consumed me beneath the totally restrictive *burkha*, I realized that Sensei had still not returned from the bathroom. I was about to signal to Basil to go search for him when, all of a sudden, the swarthy-looking Arab leaned over to say something to him. I watched the two of them as they talked for a couple of moments, and then Basil shook his head and chuckled. The Arab man then turned and leaned in, close to me.

"Of course," he talked quietly Syrian-accented Arabic, "no one is going to speak to you. I will tell them it's against your marital vows and your religion, but you must remember to respond to the name 'Nanoor' because that is what's written in your passport."

Immediately I knew I had heard this voice before, despite the Syrian accent. Although he was speaking in a hushed tone, it was clear enough for me to recognize that this was Sensei! His disguise was so convincing that it initially fooled even me! I smiled at him in recognition from behind the darkened veils of my *burkha*.

The pace of the queue picked up tremendously as the line for the Alitalia check-in slowly but surely surged forward. Soon enough, Sensei and I, posing as Algerians with our false passports, were standing at the counter speaking to an Alitalia Airlines representative. As Sensei booked us into a first class upgrade, I looked around and noticed that Basil had disappeared.

A few moments later Sensei and I were handed airline tickets and a pair of boarding passes, and we were on our way to Rome.

Our carefully doctored Algerian passports proved to be flawless as we passed through customs and entered Italy. Sensei hailed a cab outside the airport and in perfect Italian told the driver, who had a burning cigarette dangling perilously from his lips, where to drive us. We found ourselves right outside the front door of a fashionable apartment block. Sensei paid the driver and helped me to gracefully emerge from the backseat of the taxi. As the warm outside air hit me, I realized I was very, very tired.

My desire to sleep, however, was not to be immediately satisfied. Instead, Sensei helped me to the ornate front door of the building, which opened as we approached as if someone on the inside had been watching us through the peephole. On the inside, standing just within the foyer, was a demure Japanese girl dressed like a flight attendant. She wore a gray unfitted suit that smoothed over the possible contours of her body. It was trimmed with maroon buttons and a matching cap beneath which her hair was piled into a bun. In accordance with what I presumed to be Japanese culture and hospitable protocol, this tiny Asian woman bowed her head in deference as she stood off to the side of the entryway, allowing Sensei and me to enter the museum-like building.

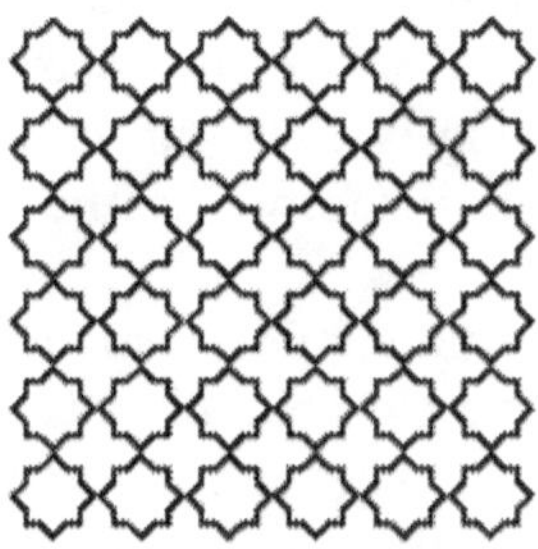

Chapter 13

Immediately upon entering, Sensei quickly left my side, disappearing into what looked like a kitchen or some kind of office right off the front hallway. The Japanese girl, extended her hand towards the steps and, led me upstairs to a decorated bedroom suite that had an elegant bathroom complex lined with mirrors. The room looked expensive; in fact, everything looked extravagant and rich, cushioned in a multicolored variety of velvet suede. The carpet was a soft kelly green, probably designed to look like grass and, in direct contrast, the ceiling and the top third of the walls were painted a rich dark green.

The Japanese girl talked to me in flawless Arabic as she showed me around. Ushering me into a wardrobe area consisting of a series of closets, she presented me with the brand-new selection of clothes hanging there.

"These are the clothes you are to wear during your stay here in Italy," she said to me. "Please now," she pronounced the words sternly, "change from your present ensemble into something more … appropriate … more … Italian … and in accordance with the … purpose of your … stay."

I thought she spoke like a robot. Perhaps, I thought, something was wrong with her. "And just what," I wanted to know, "is the purpose of my stay?"

"There's no time," she responded. She walked over to one of the closets and yanked open a set of doors, Gucci and Yves St. Laurent. "Here," she reached down into the closet and pulled out a pair of patent leather boots, which she tossed at my feet. "You must always wear these."

I looked at the boots and gasped. They were so ridiculously tacky. "I can't possibly wear those boots with Italian haute couture, can I? They don't match anything!" I stood my ground firmly, placing my hands on my hips. "Surely you can't be serious?"

"I am serious," she snapped back at me. She shook her head and waved a finger in my face before she angrily pointed at the boots lying at my feet, "You will wear those boots, and you will like them!"

"But … but …" I just didn't understand all of this at all, not in the least; "… but why?"

"Because," she retorted, "there is a radio signal, an electronic homing device hidden in the heels in case you are abducted by the enemy."

Despite my fashionable objections and reservations, I slipped on a yellow pant-suit designed by Versace and then threw a pink Balenciaga scarf around my neck. The finishing touch: I slipped on the boots; they reached up almost as high as my knee. At one point, I strolled over to a full-length mirror to take a look at the looming fashion disaster this Japanese servant had forced me to wear. I didn't know which was worse, this or the *burkha*

"This," I cocked my head to one side, "is the look of Italy?"

"Yes," snapped the girl, "but it's not yet complete. Here," she walked over to a small vanity cabinet, and pulled out a small leather case, which she opened in front of me. Inside was a pair of Gucci sunglasses. "You will wear these while you are living in this dwelling and when you go out into public areas, such as the opera, which you will claim to be in love with."

"What?" I asked her, "What did you just say?"

"You love Italian opera," replied the Japanese young woman. "If anyone should ask you, you love Italian opera. That's part of your cover."

"Well, okay then," I said as I took the sunglasses from the case and put them on. Their lenses were as dark as they were huge, and they practically covered half my face. Glancing at my reflection in the mirror, I took a good look at myself. I was dressed in yellow and pink, with a pair of high-heeled, shiny patent leather boots. This absurd look was topped off by these giant, oversized sunglasses. I thought I looked like a cheaper, trashier, continental version of Jackie Kennedy Onassis.

"Who picked out these clothes?" I asked. It was truly bizarre, arriving in Rome dressed like a religiously observant Muslim, and now, after less than two hours outside the airport, I was suddenly wearing an ill-fitting, yellow pant-suit.

"Like I said before," answered the girl in measured tones, "you love Italian opera. That is all."

"You're beginning to sound like a robot."

"I don't care," came the reply. "Instructions for your distinct appearance whilst in Rome were sent to us by your friends in Baghdad. Now, no more questions or comments. You ask far too many questions."

Suddenly in the background, a small bell rang out and the Japanese dark eyed woman clapped her hands in the air. "You," she said sternly, pointing a menacing finger at me, "are now expected downstairs for dinner with the others!"

"Oh, okay, then," I remarked quietly, "I just hope it will be more fun down there than up here."

"Your flippant attitude has not gone unnoticed." The bossy young oriental woman shook her head and placed both hands on her nearly absent hips, "I'll be sure to have a word with that gentleman who brought you here." She turned on her heel and led me out of the bedroom suite, scolding me all the while. "This chip on your shoulder is very much unappreciated."

She led me downstairs into a dining room and, upon my entrance, it was clear that the bell that had been rung earlier had been just for me. I was the last dinner guest to arrive. The other diners, who were all men, were already sitting around the table. Each of them sat in silence and stared down at his plate.

The Japanese woman pointed to an empty seat between Sensei and some bearded Muslim man wearing a white turban. Apart from Sensei, I did not recognize anyone there. As I took my seat, I noticed that none of the men acknowledged me, not even slightly or involuntarily; not one of them dared to look up.

Once I was seated a server, came over and forced a cloth napkin into my lap. Dinner was presented most efficiently. Red wine was poured into green glass goblets, and a square of lasagna was put onto our plates next to a simple pile of cinnamon-flavored carrots and some grains. The bearded man with the white turban who was sitting next to me ate the lasagna. It soon became apparent by the way in which he looked at me that despite his traditional religious appearance and despite the fact that he did not touch his wine glass, this Muslim was anything but devout.

The room was filled with an uneasy silence that, at least for me, was totally unnerving. After the lasagna, the plates were collected by an orderly troupe of servants all dressed in the same way as was the Japanese girl who took care of me. The servants returned to the table with a purple sorbet, which was scrumptious. A minute or two after I had taken my first bite of this dessert, I began to feel slightly nauseated and very, very sleepy. It suddenly became a chore to keep my eyes open and my head up.

"Oh ..." I groaned sluggishly, "I don't feel well."

"You should get her upstairs, Hasani," declared the big fat man seated at the head of the table. He was so fat and ugly that I'd made it a point not to look or stare at his repulsiveness.

Sensei nodded and said, "Yes, sir," right before I fell over into his lap. "Come, Nanoor," he whispered, "Let's get you to your room."

The next thing I knew, I was lying on the queen-sized bed in the suite upstairs. Sensei was standing at the foot of the mattress. The room became very blurry, but I felt him lie down next me. He began touching me, but I could hardly move my arms. As he rolled towards me, I passed out.

I must have woken up hours later and, when I was finally able to open my eyes, I sat up in the bed to see that I was no longer in that ornate bedroom suite in Rome. Somehow, I had been transported from the cozy confines of wealth, to a bed located on the inside of an airliner. I couldn't quite remember what had happened between Sensei and me, but I felt uncomfortable, and somehow wronged.

I glanced around the aircraft; sunlight shone through the round windows, and a flat screen television mounted to the wall showed a map, a plane, and the route flown since takeoff. On that map I saw the plane was just flying over Bulgarian airspace heading due south, southeast, presumably towards Turkey and then Syria. It was suddenly obvious that our destination was decidedly not Algeria, but was somewhere in the Middle East.

Across from the bed, there was a desk with a swivel chair that had its back turned towards me. "Where am I?" I asked loudly.

Slowly the chair behind the desk turned around, and Sensei grinned at me. "Hello, Fatima. I trust you had a pleasant sleep?"

I tried to shake the groggy, sluggish feeling from my head but it only made me feel more drowsy. "I don't know," I mumbled. "How long have we been airborne?"

"Relax, Leila," said Sensei, suddenly switching my name. "You've been unconscious, sleeping like a baby."

"Where are we?"

Sensei turned to glance at the map, "Somewhere just south of Russia."

"Where are we going?"

Sensei turned back to me and smiled softly, "We're going home, Fatima. We're finally going home."

"We're flying to Iraq?" Hope filled my lungs at the prospect of being able, for the first time since the American invasion, to check on my family, even though I had not spoken to a real blood relative in a very, very long time.

"No," Sensei scoffed, "of course not. Oh no, we're on board a private plane bound for a secret airstrip located just inside Jordanian territory, fifty miles away from the border."

The plane banked quickly to the right, and the sudden change in altitude made my head spin. I groaned. "How long was I out for?"

Sensei replied slowly, "You've been out cold for three days."

"Three days?" I pressed my fingertips to my temples. I felt a headache coming on quickly, "What did you give me?"

"Relax, Leila, it was just something to make you sleepy. But you're all right now; I made sure nothing happened while you were sleeping."

"Rest, Leila, rest." Sensei moved from the chair behind the desk and came to sit next to me on the bed. "I can close the windows and make it dark in here if that will help you sleep."

"I don't understand," I shook my head as Sensei embraced me with his big and powerful arms. I felt warm and secure in his embrace; he wanted to protect me, I could tell. "Why was I drugged in the first place? It was the sorbet, wasn't it?"

"Yes," Sensei nodded as our fingers interlocked. "You know that our great and majestic leader, dearest Saddam Hussein, never eats food unless it is of his own choosing, like it would be in a cafeteria or salad bar. He does this to specifically avoid being poisoned or drugged like you were. But, rest now, Leila. You're safe. As part of the plan, we wanted it to happen; we wanted to dress you up like a whore with those giant, ridiculous sunglasses and then knock you out like that in order to sneak you aboard this plane."

"But why, Sensei, why?" I pleaded with him, "Why like that? I don't understand."

"We needed you to look like a dead whore ... for diplomatic purposes."

I looked at Sensei with complete and utter disbelief, "Really, Al-Hasan" I made it a point to place emphasis on the 'al' in his real name. "Diplomatic purposes ... is that the best you can come up with?"

Sensei smirked and shrugged his shoulders. "It worked, didn't it? You're here now, on this plane, and we're there." He turned and pointed at the map on the flat screen television. "We're wherever that is right now and you're okay." Sensei gently cradled me in his arms, "And you're not wearing that ridiculous outfit. It was all part of the plan, and the plan went off without a hitch. Now you're tired. But we have a few hours before landing in Jordan. I suggest you take a nap." Sensei gently lowered me onto the bed, arranging the pillows softly behind my head and pulling up the silky bed sheets.

"Yes," I closed my eyes as my brain tuned out. "Perhaps I should sleep it off. I am very tired."

"Yes, Leila, rest."

Within seconds, I fell asleep. Hours later, Sensei woke me up and directed me to a shower in the bathroom of the aircraft to freshen up. We landed at a remote air base somewhere in Jordan, just as the sun was setting beneath the horizon. This time around, though, there were no passport controls or doctored passports. In fact, I was able to pick my own clothes to wear and, when we got off the plane, we just came down the steps and walked over to a waiting van with dark, tinted windows. Later, as we pulled away in the vehicle, I looked back up at the aircraft. Sensei and I had flown to Jordan in a blue and white L1011 neatly displaying the markings of Ariana-Afghan Airways.

"Oh wow," I mumbled as I looked up at the larger-than-expected-aircraft, "I didn't think it to be so big!"

From there we were spirited across the desert. We traveled over sand dunes for about ninety minutes before we stopped at a hidden oasis. Sensei and I switched out of the van and hopped into an ordinary military jeep. It was driven by an old Bedouin with missing teeth, strong body odor, and an enterprising spirit.

The driver refused to converse with me directly, but spoke to me through Sensei if there was any need. He told us, about fifteen minutes into our journey, that we were coming up to a generally unmanned strip of the Jordanian-Iraqi border where we would join up with the main Damascus-to-Baghdad-and-Basra highway. This well traveled road, the Bedouin told us, was where all the humanitarian aid workers and supplies traveled into Iraqi territory. It was widely known by the nomads in the area that both the American and British armies, as well as the collection of military forces and agencies crisscrossing the region, were using the routes of humanitarianism to smuggle in weapons and chemicals to later use on Saddam and his minions. Therefore, decided the driver, it would be natural for a couple of spies, such as us, to get across the border at that point, too.

"That's how all the other spies get into Iraq," quipped the old Bedouin man.

Something, however, did strike me as unusual.

"Sensei," I asked, "if this man knows we are spies for Saddam, which I am assuming he does, then doesn't that mean that all the desert people out here would also know that we are spies? Don't they talk to one another?"

"Yes, yes, yes," Sensei shushed me, "that's why we have to buy their silence and their secrecy. But really, who cares? Once we're inside Iraq the situation will change dramatically."

"Oh yeah?" It was my turn to scoff, "How do you figure?"

"Let me just say that once we cross over into the Fatherland, the scales will tip in our favor."

As we neared the highway, we pulled into a mobile weigh station. According to the U.N. oil-for-food program, all trucks entering and exiting Iraq had to be weighed by Jordanian officials, whereupon the results of these measurements would be cross-referenced by some arbitrary overseers located in Geneva. That is how the United Nations elected to keep track of all shipments into and out of Iraq, and that's how they determined if anything was amiss. Sensei eventually negotiated our way onto a truck marked with an Alia logo. He later told me that Alia was a front company that was overcharging the Australian federal government for the privilege of shipping in monopolized shipments of wheat. In reality, however, everyone in the desert knew that Alia, on

Saddam's behalf, was bilking the people back in Canberra for its own financial benefit.

"The wheat," Sensei explained to me as we settled into a corner in the back of the Alia wheat truck, "will later be either burned in a furnace, poisoned, or eaten only by Saddam and the rest of the Iraqi hierarchy."

"That's horrible!"

"No, Leila, it's laughable. Everyone knows about it. Saddam knows what Alia is doing, since he told them to do it. And the Australians know full well they are funneling money to our leader in Baghdad. Even the United Nations knows. And they, more than anyone else, should know about it, since they monitor the program."

"But what about the Jordanians?"

"What about them?" Sensei added, "What the Jordanians don't know won't hurt them. Look, Leila, if this wheat scandal were to become public, it would only harm the Australian government. Don't worry about this 'wheat for food for oil' story. Just don't think about it. Think about going home, Leila. We are finally going home."

Sensei and I eventually reached the border and, ducking from coalition forces, we drove straight through the night until we met up with the train that carries the oil from the south of Iraq to the north of Syria. As the sun was rising, I took a good look at the land, and I knew we were in Iraq; it smelled like there had been a war. I held back tears as the train moved on, deeper and deeper into my country. Images of American and British destruction, and the lingering scents of all types of weapons hung in the air. I didn't like it and I wanted to personally punish those responsible for this evil change in my peace-loving homeland!

By midday, Sensei and I parted ways with the truck just outside a random coalition checkpoint and walked through the wild desert for about four kilometers. It was extremely hot but, thankfully, Sensei had advised me earlier in the day to drink lots of water. Later, with the bright sun at its height, Sensei and I rendezvoused with some loyal Iraqi desert peasants who took care of us, piling Sensei and me onto camels and then shepherding us across what was left of the desert.

When we were close to Baghdad, the peasants took a sharp northward turn and, instead of leading us into the heart of the urban capital, they snuck us north to the eastern edges of the desert close to Tikrit, where they hid us in a Bedouin tent while we waited for nightfall. Once the sun set and the temperature dipped to a comfortable coolness, one of the desert peasant trackers asked us to dress in black and then he snuck us into a palace, a secret mountain fortress hidden somewhere in the mountains north of Baghdad, near the Tikrit region of Iraq.

Inside, it was clear that the palace had once seen better and brighter days. Portraits, pictures, and priceless artifacts had been knocked off the walls or pedestals as a result of intermittent bombing raids, the rugs and carpets were covered with clutter, and messy from soldiers' boots. Despite the disarray, the inside of the edifice was alive with excitement. Everyone was speaking loudly, if not yelling. Almost no one noticed Sensei and me as we suddenly stepped into the foyer. I personally took a moment to take a look at the various portraits propped up against the many empty walls of this once beautiful palace. One painting was of a bare-chested Saddam Hussein, complete with rippling biceps and glistening nipples, standing triumphantly on a human mountain made up of Iraq's many sworn enemies. Another portrait showed Saddam sitting topless in a veritable garden of Eden surrounded by many luscious, eagerly awaiting maidens, some of whom were fanning him with giant peacock feathers and holding out silver platters filled with grapes and baklava.

"My God," I whispered under my breath, "either this man has one hell of an inferiority complex, or he is totally motivated by a lust filled with self-confidence, self-pity, and arrogance. But," I reckoned, "he is my uncle, my leader and I do love him." I tugged on Sensei's sleeve and pointed up at an image of Saddam Hussein, complete with a dagger between his teeth and a leopard-print loincloth, hunting a Bengal tiger, and said to Sensei, "There's only one Saddam like my Saddam!"

Sensei must have felt either my sense of wonder or my feelings of being ill at ease that were the result of our sudden entry into this secret palace hideaway. He clapped his hands together twice loudly, before proclaiming at the top of his lungs: "*Allahu Akhbar!* God bless the Republic of Iraq and God bless our fearless leader, Saddam Hussein!"

Everyone and everything in front of us came to a sudden and immediate halt. Soldiers and guards running around with guns and papers stopped and turned to look at us. Many faces, upon seeing Sensei, went from an angry, aggravated growl to a suddenly happy and pleased look. People rushed over and surrounded us. They came to Sensei, singing praises to his name, slapping him on the back, embracing him with bear hugs, kissing him on both cheeks, and asking him about the grace and glory of Allah's protection. Things started to happen very quickly, and movements around the room became a general blur to me. I was marginalized and pushed out of the way as men and soldiers, and even a few harem girls I saw sauntering around in the back, all came up to Sensei to congratulate him for his work overseas during the invasion of the infidel Americans.

"Quick! Come!" shouted one of the more official looking men. "I will tell our leader and he will order a feast! Tell me, Al-Hasan, where is the princess who defeated the evil Americans who wanted to rape her and steal her unborn baby?"

Sensei nodded towards me. "That's the princess," Sensei pointed directly at me. "She is the one who killed the American with a frozen leg of lamb!"

As one, all the men in the foyer turned to stare at me in silence for a few seconds. Then they all burst into wild, welcoming grins and gave me the same welcome that they had just given my teacher. I assumed that all these people had not had the joy of experiencing the grace and glory of Allah's protection and most of them were curious about it. Also, many of them had never been outside Iraq and, after their initial reaction to my presence had subsided, they quickly started asking about the world beyond the borders of our homeland.

"Was it really filled with people who are evil infidels who want to kill Iraqi Arabs and peace-loving Muslims?" one of them asked me.

"Well," I replied, not knowing exactly which particular incorrect answer they most wanted to hear. "Yes," I declared. "They are all evil and they all want to kill each and every last one of us, and then they want to rape and kill your wives and your daughters, and then they will brainwash your sons to kill you all while you sleep soundly in your beds!"

Everyone in the room, apart from Sensei and I, gasped. And then, but a moment later, they all burst into cheers and praised my name. "You are one of the brave Iraqis, blessed with the grace and glory of Allah's protection, and because of Allah's magnificence, you have helped Iraq defeat the evil American infidels and kept them from raping and pillaging the fatherland and from deposing our beloved and fearless leader, Saddam Hussein, blessed be he. And," added as afterthoughts, "blessed be you! Not only has Allah granted you his unwavering protection, he has also granted you unlimited and breathtaking beauty that must captivate the millions who will one day gaze into your eyes; you sparkle upon the earth like the stars in the multitude of the Milky Way."

Quite a compliment, I thought, but it was getting ridiculous. Soon, a bunch of men ushered Sensei and me down several corridors, deeper into the palace. I was pushed into a dressing room and given a beautiful, yet conservative gown to wear. One of the harem girls showed me to a bath and supplied me with a variety of milky lotions and scented creams followed by miles and miles of soft, warm cotton toweling. When I finished bathing she then helped me do my hair and make up. Shortly after, I was cleaned and freshened up and, just as in Rome, sent to have dinner with the men. But this time I was brought to a lounge room where I met Sensei, who handed me a sniffer of brandy.

"Fatima," he whispered into my ear, "there is a treat for you. You are receiving a special state welcome for your services to the mighty Republic of Iraq. That's why we've been dressed like this. What is happening next is a formal ceremony ..." Sensei, dressed in a gray, silk Valentino suit, sipped from his crystal glass filled with Irish sherry, which smelled strong on his breath.

I heard the bolts of the double doors at the front of the room unlatched and then the doors opened. Standing just beyond the threshold of the room was my fearless and humble leader, Saddam Hussein.

"Fatima, my dear," his voice was surprisingly soft and sexy, almost musical. "I have waited for this moment for a long time. I've wanted nothing more but to thank you for your services to the Iraqi people and to me personally. Did you get the automobile I sent you?"

"Why, yes," I blushed as he took my hand into his, his palms were soft and warm and slightly moist from perspiration, as if he were an eager teenage boy meeting a pop star idol from England. "Yes, I did, dear Uncle."

"Excellent," Saddam smiled, showing off yellowed-white teeth. "And did you enjoy the gift of the automobile?"

"Why yes," I giggled. "Yes, I did."

"Excellent." Saddam Hussein turned towards Sensei. "Ah," he nodded, "Al-Hasan, once again you have made the people of Iraq proud. I understand you trained this..." Saddam motioned towards me, "exotic goddess how to protect the homeland and how to protect me."

"Yes, master," Sensei nodded and looked at the floor. Now that he was acting so modestly in front of our leader, I realized that I'd never seen him acting towards anyone with such extreme and sincere deference.

"Excellent," Saddam embraced my Sensei warmly. He kissed him on both cheeks. "Come!" Saddam wrapped his arms around my shoulders and Sensei's. "We shall dine! We shall have a huge, magnificent banquet in your honor, Al-Hasan, and in your honor, Fatima. From now on you shall be called Leila Minsk. That is the name that I have given you and I," here he pounded his chest, "I am President Saddam Hussein! President of the holy people and the holy Republic of Iraq! Long live Iraq and long live the benevolent Saddam Hussein!"

"Yes, sir," I smiled up at him.

"This banquet …" Saddam waved his hands around in the air, "…this banquet will not be in your honor." He pointed at Sensei, "and definitely not really in your honor, either, Leila Minsk; oh no… It shall be in my honor, for I am the one delivered from the heavens to mighty, earthly Iraq, and I am the one who has single-handedly defeated the infidels from raping our women and sodomizing our young boys! For I shall dine tonight in the presence of all of the invited, all of you!" Saddam pointed at the masses that had gathered in the palace. "The banquet shall be in my honor!"

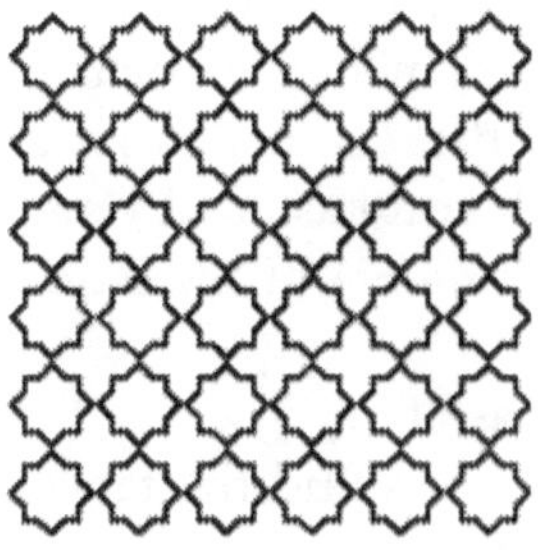

Chapter 14

A short time later, a banquet was served in a large, garish dining room. There must have been almost a hundred people seated around the gigantic oak table. At the meal, and after many rounds of champagne, Saddam, with glassy eyes and slurred speech, rose to his feet to toast none other than, once again, himself!

Graciously, Saddam bestowed a special blessing on Sensei, a blessing, Saddam declared, that only he could deliver: "I am thrilled that you, Al-Hasan, and your trained princess, Princess Leila Minsk ..." a drunken Saddam gazed at me longingly. "I am thrilled that you and Princess Leila here have worked hard to thwart those stupid American infidels from trampling down my glorious kingdom. ... May Allah watch over you and protect you. I, Saddam Hussein, leader of the Iraqi people, bless you and send you on your way to happiness and," he continued, holding up his finger, "I agree to assign Princess Leila's unborn sons, yet to be conceived, to important posts within the government." Saddam smiled at me and winked and quipped, "Perhaps your eldest will be our Iraqi ambassador to Paris or Moscow!" Saddam snickered for a moment and then held up his glass and screamed at those seated around the table, "And now drink; drink you bastards! Drink it up!" He angrily threw the contents of his fluted glass down the back of his throat.

And then, as if on cue, all the various Tikriti land sheiks, sitting around the table rose, lifted their glasses, and declared their allegiance to Saddam Hussein. Noisily they sat down. Then acting slowly like a poorly rehearsed Arabic version of a tragic Greek chorus, the sheiks stood up again, one after the other, to praise the Iraqi leader shamelessly:

"May God bless the holy Republic of Iraq and bless His holy Iraqi people!"

"Long live the Republic of Iraq! God's greatest gift to the world and to the freedom and peace-loving people of Islam! Bless God, bless His prophet Muhammad, and blessed be all those who bless Saddam Hussein, His holiest of holy majesties!"

"God grant Saddam the eye of Allah, so that he may live for ever and ever!"

Next they began to trash the United States and the other member states of the U.N. military coalition: "Hellfire, hell fury, damnation, and ruinous destruction will rain down like thunder upon those who wish to kill and destroy holy Iraq and holy Saddam Hussein!"

"May the Allah-blessed Saddam Hussein live for ever and ever because he, and only he, stopped the evil empire of the United States from invading Holy Iraq!"

"Long live Holy Iraq!"

They squealed and pronounced many blessings and salutations on Saddam Hussein, as though they were generously pouring olive oil on hummus. Once they were done with that, they cursed the American president and General Boulder.

"God, destroy the most evil of evil Western infidels. May the fury of Allah rain down destruction against the evil Zionists occupying Palestine. Allah should destroy the evil regimes of the Kuwaitis and the Iranians, who plotted to bring the American and British troops to Iraqi soil in order to rape and pillage the women of Iraq and to enslave Iraqi boys whom they will, no doubt, neuter to be made into loyal, God-hating eunuchs. God destroys the evildoers who dare to tempt fate and to destroy the holy Republic of Iraq and Iraq's eternally holy, fearless and beloved leader, His Majesty President Saddam Hussein!"

Saddam smiled with glee as he drank more and more, becoming increasingly intoxicated with liquor, arrogance, and power. I watched my leader intently as he gurgled down bottles of Dom Perignon that had been smuggled through the shared border with Azerbaijan. *So this is Saddam Hussein,* I thought as I stared right at him. His power and strength could not be seen, only felt. Fear of this mighty leader permeated the room. My uncle's power lay in the complete trepidation he imbued in his subjects. Reflections of the past few months crossed my mind and I began to more than understand —almost internalize the difference between the power of a democratic country and the ruthless dominance of a dictatorship.

After the party, Saddam ordered the handmaidens and harem girls to rush in and clear the table and then he came over to Sensei and me. He embraced Sensei energetically before he took my hand and kissed it. For some reason, I got the impression that this sort of behavior was not something that came naturally to him. In any case, Saddam also kissed Sensei on both cheeks, whispered something in his ear, and tapped him on the lower back before caressing him fondly for a brief moment. I thought the interchange to be very odd.

Moments later, Sensei, with a look of embarrassed horror, insisted that I must leave the premises. "Quickly, Fatima, you have to get out of here; and you have to get out of here now."

"But why, Sensei? What's going on?"

"Just go, before Saddam ropes you into becoming one of his harem girls. He told me he wants you. You have to leave, Fatima, now."

"But why, Sensei? Saddam just blessed me only a few minutes ago."

"Just go," Sensei pushed me, "Go right now, Fatima! He wants to sire the ambassador he spoke about a few minutes ago."

I took a second to look around the room. All of the men, religious and non-religious alike, were sparking up Cuban cigars sent directly to Saddam Hussein from his dear friend in Havana, Fidel Castro. One after the other they filed out, heading into an area off to the side of the elaborate dining room. Leaning at an angle to get a better look, I saw the other men step out of the area through an archway. I took a step closer so as to be in a better location to take a peek and, through this curved entrance, I saw the beginnings of an orgy well under way. The harem girls, naked on rugs, were looking up invitingly at the men. I saw Saddam Hussein, with a lit cigar between his smiling lips, slip off a suspender and growl like a mad dog in heat.

Sensei grabbed my arm suddenly and spoke to me sternly. "He told them we won the war! Now he wants to have a special party, and his goal is to spawn at least ten sons. If you don't get out of here, I fear that either he will rape you or he'll get one of his sons to do the job."

"Rape me?" I shook my drowsy head as images in my mind rushed back to that night in Rome.

"If you don't get out of here, that's what will happen to you."

"Right, well," I eyed Sensei directly and suspiciously, "I think you raped me. Did you not have your way with me that last night in Rome? Did you drug me and have sex with me while I was out in a coma? Why do you behave differently now? Aren't you still my teacher? My companion?"

"Leila," Sensei gently grabbed both my shoulders. "You have to understand ... this is a very tense situation we find ourselves in. I had to ... I don't know, act that way or else someone," he nodded towards the room filled with harem girls and chauvinist generals, "some superior or someone like that would have found out about ... you know... that we're ... like, you know... in love or... whatever."

"In love!" I smiled on the inside, "Sensei, do you mean to tell me that you ... are in love ... with me?"

"Leila," he started to push me as he tried to rush me from the elaborate dining chamber. "Just get out of here before something horrible happens."

My thoughts returned to that night in Rome, "What happened," I asked Sensei, "that last night in Rome? I never understood why you drugged me and did *that* to me."

"There were reasons, Leila, that I had to do that. I had to convince the others," here he nodded again to that room filled with moaning people, "that I was not in love with a student." Sensei scoffed to demonstrate how they would have scoffed, "It's just absurd! I can't have that, Leila. We can't have that, not if we are to be husband and wife one day."

"Husband and wife … oh Sensei!" I threw my arms around his neck and kissed his face and neck. "I am in love with you, too!" But then I pulled back from him dramatically and abruptly, "But that doesn't answer my question, Sensei. Why did you drug me and treat me like some lowly prostitute?"

"It's complicated, Leila, and tense, but in a nutshell, it went like this." Sensei took a deep breath and exhaled like a runner about to begin a sprint in the Olympics, "Our handlers in Baghdad wanted us to appear like a husband and wife. But the wife, who was supposed to be an Italian and not an Arab woman, was supposed to be ill, sick with some sort of mysterious, unexplainable disease."

"Right, okay," I thought about what he said, "that explains those stupid clothes but," I shook my head, "it does not explain the drug you must have slipped into my sorbet."

"Of course," Sensei smiled, "that was to make you appear laid up with some sort of … I don't know… malady. It was decided, in an effort on their part to prove to me that you, my student, meant nothing to me. Even though you did valuable work for the kingdom, these men see you as nothing more than a sex object. If I didn't 'claim' you – as it were – they would have had their way with you. I knew I would be gentle. If it weren't for me, you would be one of the whores on the floor in there. We dressed you up like a rich Italian whore and knocked you out with some Versed – you'll be fine, by the way, so don't worry – and then I made love to you."

Sensei paused. "Please, Leila, you must leave this area of the palace. You don't know what devils these generals are when they see a woman they want, a woman of your beauty."

"Yes, yes of course." I hurried out the door and raced back to my room. On my way back I realized how truly exhausted, after the feast and after all my travels, I was. I shook my head. "From Princeton to Baghdad. Who'd have ever thought?" I fell asleep very quickly.

The next morning, no one, not even Sensei, came to collect me. I decided to explore on my own.

The night before, the palace had been home to festivities and celebrations surrounding Sensei's return to Iraq. However, in what could have been only a matter of hours, the noisy Iraqi palace had been transformed into some sort of central command headquarters. An electronic display of satellite imagery was splashed across the walls and drawing tables throughout the foyers and halls. For lack of a better term, I was virtually invisible. No one stopped me or questioned my presence; in fact, no one even dared look my way, let alone acknowledge me. I freely wandered through the corridors past colonels, generals, and soldiers, and not one of them took any notice of me. I walked down to the main floor and then, simply out of curiosity, decided to retrace my steps from the night before back to the dining chamber.

As I stepped down the spiral staircase, I started to hear screaming and moaning, interspersed with the sounds of violent electrical shocks. Finally, when I entered what had been the dining chamber the night before, I saw that it was now an exotic torture chamber. In the middle of the room, a man had been stripped naked and tied up to a pole. Electrodes had been attached to his most sensitive areas, while an Iraqi guard screamed expletives at him.

"You dumb pig! Tell me where the Shia rebels are! Tell me now!"

The bound man was clearly too weak to talk, which greatly displeased the torturer. Glaring at his victim, he nodded his head to another guard who, in turn, flipped a switch that activated an electric impulse that ripped through the bound man.

"Now," said the persecutor, "if you don't say what the general wants to hear, we will take this cattle prod," he held up an enormous implement bursting with white electrical lightning, "and we'll sodomize your wife or," the guard grinned nastily, "shall we bring in your daughter?"

"No," the man whispered while spitting up blood. "I told you I do not know where there are any Shia rebels. If I did, I would have told you so by now."

"No," yelled the guard. "That is the wrong answer." The general who had been standing quietly in the shadows now walked over. He stood in front of the prisoner and punched him twice in the teeth before ordering an underling to flip the switch, thus sending him into convulsions. The prisoner shook as if he were having an epileptic seizure. His bowels unhinged themselves.

The general grumbled and barked a series of harsh orders at his subordinates. Then he was handed another set of electrodes which he clipped to each of the prisoner's earlobes.

"Please," pleaded a woman crouching in the corner trying to protect her son and daughter; it was obvious that she was the prisoner's wife and the mother of his children. "You'll kill him if you keep that up."

The general swung around and quickly smacked the woman. Next, he grabbed her by both shoulders and yanked her across the room. He placed her about a meter and a half from the prisoner, her husband. Then, in one fell swoop, he stripped her naked by ripping off her traditional Shia ensemble.

"Look at your whore wife," the general spat and snarled at the prisoner. "Look at your whore!" The general pulled her hair and moved the electric cattle prod closer to her body. "What if I were to ..." the general laughed, but didn't finish his sentence, leaving many gruesome potential consequences in the prisoner's mind.

The man vomited suddenly, mostly on his naked wife. Some of the vomit landed on the trouser leg of the general's pants and also on the toe of his shoe.

"You stupid pig!" The general shouted into the prisoner's face and threw his wife to the floor. He raised the cattle prod over the prisoner and zapped it where it must have hurt the most. "He who dares to puke on my shoes, he who dares to oppose Saddam Hussein, the mighty God-given President of the Holy Republic of Iraq, majesty over his beloved people, deserves to watch his entire family die right before his very eyes!"

Just then, two other Iraqi soldiers wearing uniforms decorated with the insignias of the Republican Guard pulled up the prisoner's head and held his eyes open. I glanced to the corner as I heard children start screaming.

The general hollered, "Bring me the boy!"

For some reason, the guards in the room glanced at one another in hesitation. I imagined they must have been terrified of what the general would do next, but their feelings of apprehension didn't last long.

The general yelled, "What the hell is wrong with you? Bring the boy to me now!"

Two guards dragged the ten-year-old, kicking and screaming, over to him. The general grunted an order at the uniformed men who then undressed the boy. The child must have gone into in a state of shock for he was seemingly catatonic. He'd stopped screaming and now just simply stared at nothing in particular.

The general, in the meantime, grabbed a knife and another cattle prod. "Which would you prefer for your only son?" He leaned into the prisoner and snarled, "Should I have my guards do it to your son or your daughters? He who dares to vomit on me will watch his offspring pay the ultimate price!"

The prisoner's eyes rolled back in his head. A mustached guard took out a small vial of some sort and wafted it under the detainee's nose. That woke him up and he began screaming and yelling. He called out about a nightmare he must have believed had not actually happened.

The general ordered two guards to smack the prisoner further into consciousness, and then he growled, "After I am done killing your wife and only son, I will ravage your daughters before I kill them too. Make no mistake about it, you filthy pig. Saddam Hussein will hunt down every brother, mother, father, and sister, and every aunt, uncle and cousin of yours and he will kill each and every last one of them. And then, when he is done wreaking his vengeance upon the Shia filth of your family, he will kill every last Shia rebel in the country and then go after their families until Holy Iraq has been purged of the Shia scum!"

The general drew his razor-sharp sword and, with one powerful swing, decapitated the prisoner's son, sending the young boy's head flying across the room, eventually landing at the feet of his naked mother who collapsed in screaming and tears.

I was horrified and tasted bile rising in the back of my throat. I turned from the shadowy corner where I was hiding, trying to suppress my own need to vomit. I ran up the stairs as quickly and quietly as humanly possible, making my way to the palatial foyer. Thankfully, I ran into Sensei.

"Sensei," I said, "I have to talk to you now!"

"Call me Al-Hasan," he said as he shoved me into the corner of the foyer, hiding us behind a blossoming, potted plant. "You cannot call me Sensei here in the palace. Only Saddam is accorded with any such respect."

"Fine, Al-Hasan, but listen, we've got to get out of here. I just saw one of Saddam's spies chop off the head of a kid, and now I am beginning to see what I refused to see before. My uncle and all his clan are vile, worse than animals. We must leave this place immediately!"

"Fatima, what are you talking about?" He put his large, muscular hand over my mouth. "You are one of Saddam's spies. You and me. We're the one of the few who made it safely back to Iraq out of all of Saddam's spies around the world. Remember what happened to Madame? She was one of his spies, too."

"And that's exactly why I have to get out of here, Sensei. Out of Iraq. I can't believe what I just saw. I realize now that we're working for a tyrant. He's sick! That's why I've got to get out of here. *We've* got to get out of here, Sensei. You and me together. We need to get out of this palace and out of Iraq before we end up having the same fate as Madame, as every other Iraqi spy, and as that poor prisoner's son."

"Don't be ridiculous, Fatima. Even if your ramblings are right and aren't the result of being influenced by the American culture you were spying on, where could we possibly go?"

"I don't know." I shook my head and bit my lower lip and thought of Effi, the Israeli teacher's assistant whom I both befriended and stole data from at Princeton. Now, in retrospect, that was probably a bad idea. But I didn't say that aloud. Instead I said. "I know what we can do. We can go to Israel. I have a friend there. He is a Jew, and he will help us!"

"Fatima," Sensei looked at me in a state of bewilderment, "A Jew? What has gotten into you? That's just crazy talk – pure nonsense!"

I knew that convincing Sensei to abandon his entire life's work, a life dedicated to the Iraqi people and Saddam Hussein, would not be an easy task. To make matters worse, my plan was to find safe haven with the hated Zionists, our most despised nemesis. Yet I knew their value of humanity would extend to those willing to leave an inhumane dictator's rule. Jewish humanity, Effi once told me, can go beyond political boundaries and negate centuries-old traditions of hatred.

"Listen to me," I implored Sensei. "You think I want to go to Israel any more than you do, because I don't. But, while under cover at Princeton, my closest liaison was a Jew, for espionage reasons, of course," I assured him. "When I saw him last, he promised me that he would help me and anyone I cared about no matter what the circumstances. Al-Hasan," I continued my Academy Award-deserving performance, even shedding a couple of tears in the midst, "we are in dire straits right now. The most powerful man in the region wants nothing more than to rape me. You said before you loved me, Al-Hasan. You said before we will be husband and wife. What kind of lover allows his beloved to be violated by any man? What kind of husband tolerates such promiscuity towards his wife?!"

I knew I had put on a masterful, thespian display, but I was nervous for Sensei's reaction. Saddam Hussein could have him killed, or worse yet, tortured for treason. All I could provide was a physical relationship and, maybe sometime down the road, a few little Al-Hasans and Al-Hasanettes. I was more than willing to abandon the awful Iraqi regime but, then again, I was relatively new to the rampant corruption, lewdness, and terror that Sensei had probably witnessed a thousand times. I considered my blood ties to the regime ended as the peasant's blood splattered across the torture chamber. Would he choose to stay put, forcing me to escape to Israel on my own, or would his heart win out over his common sense and would he accompany me to the holy land of the Jews?

"Fatima," he answered after what felt like an eternity of silence. "I think your plan is utterly insane." His tone indicated that I would be finding my own way to Israel. "But," his voice suddenly sounded a lot more enthusiastic, "since the first day I laid eyes on you as your teacher, I knew there was something special about you. I'm not just talking about your ravishing good looks," he continued, "but your natural instincts have always been, as long as I've known you, extraordinary. The first time I recognized this was the way you handled yourself at the rappelling practice when those Bedouin slime attacked us. I could tell right then that you would not only be a wonderful agent one day, which you have more than proven to be, but my wife. I love you Fatima," he said as he reached over and kissed me, "If you think it's the right move, we're off to Israel!"

We embraced, and I felt settled. I enjoyed the comfortable feeling oozing throughout my body as the warm grasp of his defined body came in contact with mine.

I smiled as Sensei, now armed with an M-16 he had slung over his shoulder, grabbed my hand and yanked me through the front door of the Iraqi palace. "Let's get out of here," he instructed me, "and let's do it quick."

Once outside, a team of Republican Guards tried to apprehend us, but Sensei shot at them. He snagged the gun of the first fallen man and gave it to me. Planting the stock on my hip, I loaded a bullet in the chamber and took aim at as many Iraqi guards as possible. The parking lot out front was filled with trucks and military jeeps, and a single Mercedes Benz with three flat tires. The whole area quickly turned into a makeshift cemetery as we ran across the parking lot, firing away at everyone who even glanced our way.

Sensei commandeered a supply truck, and he pulled me into it while continuing to shoot at the guards who were crawling between vehicles. For a moment, I stopped shooting, and I realized that all the noise had stopped. Between us, we had successfully shot and killed every last guard.

Once we were safely on route away from the palace, I elaborated to Sensei on what I'd seen previously in the dining chambers-cum-torture dungeon.

Sensei listened attentively and, when I had finished, declared his disgust. "That's absolutely horrific, Leila. But I can call you Fatima now, or whatever name you wish to be called. And," Sensei turned to me with a sad look in his eyes, "As much as it pains me to say it, I'm afraid you were completely correct about Saddam and his regime. I've been duped since day one; we've been working for an evil dictator. You saw one of his guards decapitate a child. I saw one of them rape a teenage girl and almost kill her last night. I didn't want to tell you about it at first, but now that you've witnessed the horrors yourself, there's no point in hiding anything."

I could hardly breathe for a moment, both because I realized that Saddam probably would have done the same to me had I been that girl and because I was slowly beginning to realize just how evil Saddam could be. After my brief panic attack, I reassured myself knowing that Sensei and I, Iraq's two greatest spies, were in this together.

For two days we drove across the Iraqi desert, back towards the Jordanian border. With relative ease, we crossed into Jordan via back roads and, about a day or so later, we arrived in the suburbs of Amman. In the creepy motel where we stopped, I called the information operator in Israel.

Speaking in Hebrew, I asked for Effi's number. Once I had it, I hurried to the Swiss embassy, which I knew had a diplomatic desk for Israel within its compound. Alone, I met with the special-enquiries person and handed Effi's number to her.

"Please," I pleaded, "I must speak with him. Pass on my contact information. I have to get to Israel." I left the Swiss embassy and went back to the hotel room. The phone was already ringing when I got there. "Hello?" I answered.

"Is this Leila? From Princeton?"

"Effi!" I was delighted. "You don't know how wonderful it is to hear your voice." I decided that if I was going to have any chance at taking vengeance on Saddam and the awful Iraqis, I needed to be completely honest with Effi. I went ahead and told him the whole truth about being a spy for Iraq and that I had worked for Saddam Hussein.

"This may come as a surprise to you," started Effi in a soothing tone, "but we knew all that from the beginning. Professor Beck really works for the National Security Agency in the United States. They knew you were a spy even before you landed in the United States."

"They did?"

"Yes, but that's not important now. What can I do for you now? Have you finally become a turncoat?"

"Well, if you mean am I ready to stick it to that evil bastard in Baghdad then I guess, yeah, I've become a turncoat or whatever you want to call it."

"Good, my associates here in Israel and in the U.S. were hoping you'd come around. Tell me, are you there alone or is someone with you?"

"I am with my teacher, Al-Hasan. Do you know of him also?"

"Oh yes, of course we do. I was not simply Professor Beck's lowly TA. I also double as a Mossad agent for my homeland. We know everything about you two and the organization that trained you. In fact, we even know that you call Al-Hasan 'Sensei.'"

"Oh my," I was now flabbergasted. "How come I never picked up on all of this before?"

"We've been in the spy business longer than you, I suppose," reasoned Effi. "And you were way too obvious in your undercover activity. It never occurred to you that I left all those papers in my office for you to find? And you never even tried to find the video camera that recorded all your moves. You know, by the way, that you could get into a lot of trouble for what you did to those two guards. You shouldn't have killed ..."

"But can you help me now?" I interrupted.

"Can you get to the Jordanian side of the Allenby Bridge border crossing in the next twelve hours?"

"Yes, I think so."

"Good, meet me there in twelve hours. I will see that you and your teacher get across the border without any problems."

"How?"

"Don't worry, Leila, I'll pull some strings at my end. I've got more important connections than you ever imagined when we used to speak in New Jersey."

I said goodbye to Effi, eager to see him again, and thanked him profusely. Twelve hours later, Sensei and I arrived at the Allenby Bridge border crossing and, sure enough, Effi was there to greet us. Thanks to him, we had no trouble crossing into Israel.

Immediately upon seeing us, Effi couldn't help but exclaim his utmost respect for Sensei and me. "Leila and Al-Hasan, I am extremely impressed you had the courage to forsake your 'Fatherland' and come to Israel; now, I'll take you to Mossad headquarters for a debriefing. They will ask you what you want and how you think you can help us."

"I already have an answer for that," I quickly told him, "I want the Mossad to train and arm us, and then get us back into Iraq to shoot and kill my vile uncle before he inflicts yet more harm on innocent civilians."

Effi listened carefully and, after I was done speaking, arranged a series of meetings. Upon our arrival, the Israeli agents stripped us of our Iraqi documents and fake Algerian ones as well. They worked with me to improve my Hebrew so that I sounded like a real Israeli. They also helped Sensei brush up on his Hebrew and took us to a training center in the north, near the Sea of Galilee, where they showed us how to use a special kind of weapon.

"This gun," said Mor, the Mossad trainer, "is a normal gun; however, the bullet is special. It splits in five directions and, because it has been dipped into a uranium alloy, it can poison and kill only once it is inside the body. So, when you shoot it at someone, it goes in five different directions and poisons the victim, killing him quickly but painfully."

"Oh my." I looked on in amazement at the Israeli technology, far superior to anything I'd ever seen in Iraq.

"Wow!" was all Sensei could muster as he shook his head.

I noticed Mor was not wearing gloves, "Won't you get sick if you touch it with your bare finger tips?"

"No," he smiled and shook his head, "the uranium alloy is only activated when it enters a human body, not before. And, if it shoots through and comes out the other side, it automatically deactivates itself."

"Boy," Sensei continued to shake his head, "you Israelis sure are advanced. I wish I'd had this technology and not the antique weaponry we were given back home."

"Yes," said Mor, "in fact, we designed these bullets specifically to kill Saddam."

A little while later, Effi sat us down. "We know the two of you can get back into Iraq with our help. Once we drop you in close to the palace, your job will be to kill Saddam."

Sensei blanched and shook his head, clearly perturbed by the thought of assassinating the very man he devoted the majority of his life to protecting, a man he had risked his life for on countless occasions. "Do you think we are truly ready?"

"Yes," Effi nodded, "Israel has already alerted our friends in Washington about the operation. You'll leave tonight, and within two days, we expect your target to be eliminated."

"Well," I turned to Sensei, who was still trying to digest the shocking assignment handed to him. "I guess tonight is the big night."

Sensei and I were next taken to an office where we received instructions from Mor's and Effi's superior, a former top commando named Gil. "Here is a map of northern Baghdad. We'll drop you here, about three kilometers down the road from where Saddam will be for dinner this evening. You'll carry out a frontal assault, going in through the main entrance and taking out anyone who gets in your way. Next, you'll proceed to the smaller dining room off the kitchen, but remember to go through the kitchen, because that's where Saddam's bodyguards will be, as well as his doubles. If anyone looks like Saddam, be sure to kill him. We want the Iraqis to think twice before signing up for that job. The fewer Saddam doubles the better. In fact, be sure to kill anyone dressed in a uniform and armed with a gun. Helping a terrorist makes you a terrorist. We're going to firebomb the place. Well, actually, we won't. Washington will. We'll send them a radio message once we have received a foto-bit from the two of you advising us that the mission has been accomplished."

"What's a foto-bit?" asked Sensei.

Ignoring the question, Gil continued giving over our mission. "Click this button on the radio twice, and we'll know it's you and that you have successfully completed the mission. If something goes wrong, click this button only once."

"Right." I made a mental note of the instructions while I put the radio transmitter into my suede handbag.

"Okay," said Mor, "let's get the two of you onto that plane."

"Here we go," I eagerly smiled to Sensei.

"I feel like I'm finally ready," Sensei responded cautiously, "but I fear what will happen. Perhaps one of us might be injured."

"Oh stop it," I shushed him and scowled, "we've both done this sort of thing many times before. Saddam is just another man. We'll shoot him, click on this button twice, and then all will be taken care of."

"What," asked Sensei curiously "exactly happens when we click that button?"

"Oh, right, that's a good question." I turned to Effi, "Effi, what happens after we click this button twice to inform you of a mission accomplished?"

"We come and get you, of course."

"But won't the Americans be bombing the palace afterward?"

"Yes," he smiled, "hopefully we'll be able to get you out of there in time."

"Oh," I said a bit shakily. Something seemed ominous, but I only needed to recall the helpless boy Saddam's general had decapitated and I became hardened.

"Leila," Effi prodded me, "your jet is ready."

"Let's go." I looked at Sensei and was reassured by his little smile.

We were taken to a small airport where on the end of the tarmac was a big green 747.

"So the Jordanians will think it's an Aer Lingus plane from Ireland that's gone off course," explained Effi.

Quickly we boarded and moments later we were airborne, flying towards Iraq. About three hours into the flight, the Israelis placed parachutes on our backs and told us we were in for a treat. I wasn't too sure of the treat part but went to stand behind Sensei at the door and waited for the shove on my back. The blast of cold air on my face made all my senses tingle. Sensei and I glided slowly down into Iraq and found ourselves about two miles away from the palace. As we landed we encountered a pair of Iraqis who appeared to be peasants. We knew our jobs. We shot and killed them in case they might have been agents. When we spotted a truckload of Iraqi soldiers, we hid on the side of the road to avoid having to take them out, too.

"Sensei," I said, a bit cocky with the power of holding a giant gun in my hands, "this is kind of fun, in a sick sort of a way."

As night fell, we slowly approached the palace. When we were close, we hid behind an old Mercedes Benz in the parking lot, the one with three airless tires, and just waited. Once we analyzed the movements of the guards, we opened fire with silenced guns. They never even had a chance to lift their weapons in defense.

In the foyer, the soldiers were surprised to see us. Using M-16s, we rapidly, though loudly, dropped the four guards. I tried to suppress my smile, but Sensei gave me a thumbs-up, like I had often seen Siskel and Ebert do when reviewing movies in America, and I couldn't hold back. The rush of victory was pumping through my body.

Sensei ran down the hall, stopping momentarily on the way to shoot into the rooms just off the foyer. I quickly followed him and shot anything that was still moving. Any time I began to question my murderous spree, I recalled the gruesome, unspeakable events that I had witnessed in Saddam's palace. Why my killing was better than his could only be justified because hopefully, my calculated murders would prevent many more indiscriminate deaths.

We arrived at the kitchen and, just as the Israeli intelligence had predicted, there were three Saddam Hussein look-a-likes eating sandwiches. Right away I knew they weren't really Saddam, so I heeded my commands and shot them. Sensei also opened fire and, using his Uzi sub-machine gun, he shot down three cooks, a couple of maids, and a waitress dressed in a French maid's uniform complete with black fishnet stockings.

The guards, by this point, were on to us and, just as during our sudden escape a few weeks earlier, they started popping out everywhere. Sensei and I just kept shooting, eliminating all obstacles on our path to Saddam. After the last burst of fire from our guns, the kitchen became quiet. Death was all around us.

I wiped the sweat off my brow, "Come on, Sensei. I think we've cleared the place. Let's get Saddam!"

There was no answer.

"Sensei? Sensei?" I looked around the room, "Sensei?" I became hysterical suddenly, "Sensei, where are you?" I ran around the room until I suddenly caught a whiff of his cologne. His leg twitched for a moment as I spotted him under a table. I was horrified to find him slumped on the floor, a thin bullet hole right between his eyes. I fell to my knees and tried to cradle his head in my arms, "Please, tell me you're not dead. Tell me you haven't left me, my Sensei."

Sadly, it was futile for me to say anything; Sensei was dead. Completely dejected, I stood up, brushed myself off, and started to shoot my gun off at everything in my path. When I ran out of bullets, I grabbed guns from the scattered corpses. I began scouring the palace looking to increase the body count, but it was suddenly empty. It became clear to me that Saddam had escaped.

I took out the radio from my bag and clicked the button once. I left the palace and went to hide just beyond the parking lot. I waited for four hours before the Israelis sent in a helicopter, an American helicopter that is, and I was rescued. I was flown to the aircraft carrier *USS Nimitz*, where I was debriefed before I was returned to Effi in Israel.

"I'm sorry I failed you, Effi," I stammered, as I fought back tears.

"Don't worry, Leila, you did well. I'm so sorry you lost your friend."

"Thanks. I will miss him greatly."

"I apologize for moving too quickly, but perhaps we can talk to you about Plan B now," Effi began.

"Plan B?"

"Yes," Effi smiled, "now that your Sensei has, unfortunately, been murdered, you'll probably want to be the apprentice of a new teacher and we, here at the Mossad, still desperately want to get rid of Saddam."

"Don't we all?"

"Step into my office. We have to talk about this and, of course, there is some paperwork you will need to fill out."

I went into Effi's office with my emotions an absolute wreck. On the one hand I had just watched my beloved Sensei, the man who had trained me and helped me mature into a woman, lie lifeless in my arms. Yet I couldn't help but feel a little comforted

knowing that I was now working for the Mossad and, more specifically, for Effi.

No longer would my highly developed espionage skills be used for evil, helping the autocratic regime of the tyrannical Saddam Hussein. Instead, I would be able to assist a democratic, peace-loving country whose goal is the safety of all its citizens.

Under Effi's guidance, I was confident that I'd be able to take my spying to the next level. As an Arab-trained, Semitic-looking, attractive young woman, I would have opportunities as a spy that no Israeli agent could ever even dream of. I began to envision a future as a heroine coming back to Iraq and liberating its persecuted citizens from the torturous regime. I could picture the exact weapon and bullet I would use to end my uncle's despicable life; a life he used to murder, pillage, and rape innocents; a life he used to illegally amass enormous wealth and boundless power; a life he used to alienate me from my family, my country, and my now deceased Sensei.

Once again, I was starting a new life. This time, I did not die in a staged car accident. I knew there would be no obituaries mourning the death of an Iraqi spy. There was no one to remember me. I was already dead to my family, and the man I loved was also gone. There was only one other who knew about me, and only one other who wanted to know me. And it was Effie. But I was not ready to think about him now; not in the same way as I thought about Sensei. I needed time — time to heal my spirit.

As a spy, I was trained to always expect the unexpected. However, I never anticipated that my life would change as dramatically as it did in such a short period of time. I went from being a proud relative of the most powerful dictator in the Middle

East, to being an international spy, to now, serving as an Israeli agent cooperating with the Zionists to topple the very dictator, the very uncle, who turned me into an assassin. Now I wait for the day to exact revenge for taking my family and loved ones away from me.